CROW CALLING

BY SHERRY ROBERTS

Crow Calling
Warrior's Revenge
Down Dog Diary
Book of Mercy
Maud's House
WriteTips

CROW CALLING

A Novel by

SHERRY ROBERTS

Sherry Roberts

Osmyrrah Publishing | Apple Valley, Minnesota

Osmyrrah Publishing
Apple Valley, Minnesota 55124
www.osmyrrahpublishing.com
info@osmyrrahpublishing.com

ISBN: 978-1-7340113-0-2

Library of Congress Control Number: 2019913737

Printed in the United States of America
First Edition

Cover Digital Art by Kathey Amaral: designbykatt.deviantart.com
Cover Photograph by Cathleen Tarawhiti: www.facebook.com/pages/
Cathleen-Tarawhiti-Photographer/95878166172
Model: Monique Wanner

TO SABRINA LUZ AND IVY LUCIA,
MAY YOU ALWAYS BRING GOODNESS AND LIGHT.

TO THE MONARCHS,
MAY YOU ALWAYS HAVE A HOME HERE.

CHAPTER 1

A MURDER IN GABRIEL'S GARDEN

THEY KEPT COMING. CROWS. Sitting at my kitchen table, I could hear them overhead and outside the window—caws and clacks and rattles. Their presence pressed against the old fire station where I live and work, sliding a Hitchcockian finger down my spine one vertebrae at a time. The trees and air shivered with their agitation.

My neighbors, the people of Gabriel's Garden, wondered and worried: What do they want? Our town is not on any migratory flight path that would account for this phenomenon, and besides, it was early summer and not the time for immense bird migrations. Looking for answers, I turned to the journal in front of me, the Down Dog Diary.

The Down Dog Diary is not its official name, but I had to

call it something. And I think Book of Shaman Gibberish and Strange Smells is a bit much. All old books have a fragrance, but the shaman's diary keeps changing its mind. One day the odor of stinky shoes drifts from the pages; the next it smells of bubblegum. And here's the thing: only the keeper is privy to these bouquets, and I am its current keeper and protector.

As the keeper, I have learned it is wise to follow the diary's olfactory clues. They lead me to passages that give me strength just when I need it, provide direction when I am lost, or offer some fortune-cookie absurdity which later turns out to be not so crazy after all. While I do not grant these writings supernatural powers, as some people have done, I do see the diary as a resource and a responsibility. That's why I keep it locked in a safe most of the time.

Today, book in hand, I chased the scent of snowy air to an entry made by the man who left me the diary, James Tumblethorne. It said:

Once my tattoos were just about power: bringing it to me, warning others to walk lightly. Now the tattoo of the crow sits on my shoulder, whispering dreams of transcendence in my ear. The tattoo celebrates my first year at Whispering Spirit Farm. My first winter of peace. Only a year, and I am being transformed. I can feel the power of the crow.

Whispering Spirit Farm is the New Mexico commune founded by my parents and where I grew up. I had an artist mother, a geeky father, an older sister who prayed every night for a "normal" existence, and James "Tum" Tumblethorne, my nanny and mentor. There was also a whole community of adults who considered themselves family as well. Call "Mom" and five heads turned. It was why my sister and I referred to our parents as Evie and Larry. It was less confusing and more efficient.

James Tumblethorne, who died to protect the diary, was a reformed Hell's Angel turned shaman. I am not a shaman, but sometimes people treat me like one. Tum used to explain it like this, "Maya Skye, you are hardwired to help. You lead with your heart and follow with your fist." Not the best combination for a yoga teacher committed to raising the spiritual consciousness of this fragile place we call Mother Earth.

A peck at the window interrupted my reading. I glanced at the crow, then the clock, and realized the Monday afternoon yoga class would soon be arriving. "You're right," I said to the bird. "It's time."

I closed the diary, returned it to its home in the safe hidden behind the bookcase, and went downstairs. Standing outside Breathe, my yoga studio, I looked up and down Orchard Road, the main street in Gabriel's Garden. The trees in my yard were thick with crows, and more were lined up on the rooftops of the nearby buildings. With my appearance on the doorstep, the clamor of the birds grew as if they all wanted to speak to me at once.

Peter Jorn strolled over from Northern Lights, the coffee shop down the block, with a black yoga mat tucked under his arm and a cup of strong fair-trade roast in his hand. Jorn and I met more than a year ago when, under doctor's orders, he came to his first yoga class. At the time he told me he hated two things: yoga and being called Peter.

Jorn frowned at the crows. Then he looked me in the eye and took a deliberate sip of coffee, knowing full well that I disapproved of imbibing stimulants, especially before yoga.

Motioning toward the trees with his cup, he said, "Can't you do something about this?"

"Me?"

"Yeah, tell them to go away."

"I don't speak bird."

"They don't seem to know that."

He was right. The countless birds flitting from limb to branch, from maple to pine and back, appeared concentrated on my home. We were standing at Ground Zero.

With another glance at the crows, Jorn said in a disgruntled tone, "It's New Mexico all over again." Jorn was a reporter by trade, and he helped me investigate the murder of James Tumblethorne. When we went to Tum's home in New Mexico, the mountaintop property Tum had left me along with the diary, we found crows everywhere, guarding the house and ceremonial kiva that Tum had built with his own hands. The air was heavy with their voices and their sadness. I surmised that they were mourning Tum, an idea the fact-obsessed Jorn found preposterous. Jorn was many things: former war correspondent, truth-seeking small-town publisher, and the man who sometimes steals my bedcovers, but he was not a bird lover.

Our small Minnesota town sits on land once lovingly cultivated by Amish labor and now home to families who mostly earn their paychecks in offices an hour away in the Twin Cities. Every household has a computer, a sturdy snow shovel, and a working car. Wrapped around Lake Michael like a scarf, the town was a quiet place to live—until a murder of noisy, messy crows invaded.

Jorn had written articles about the crows for his online newspaper, *The Independent.* From the responses to the articles, the residents of Gabriel's Garden speculated this incursion could be caused by anything from climate change to pet owners leaving out too much food for their dogs. Neighbors dashed from door to car, wary eyes cast to the sky. Some of my students feared walking past the trees shimmering with *Corvids*. That's why I stood at the door, a reassuring presence, to greet them.

I smiled at Julia Lune, scurrying up the walk. Julia is our local celebrity; she writes steamy romances. As usual, there was a chocolate smudge on her round-framed glasses and her loose knot of hair was secured by a pen. She swept past us, head ducked into her shoulders like a startled turtle, and said, "Weird, huh? I am *definitely* using this in my next book."

Fifteen-year-old Olivia Chen and her friend, Tessa Miley, pulled up on their bikes. They fitted the bikes into the rack in front of the fire station, not bothering to lock them. As they entered the studio, Olivia, a jittery kleptomaniac with innocent-looking anime eyes, said to Tessa, "I think the crows are cool."

Calm Tessa, a minister's daughter, laughed. "Val says they're signs of evil." Her brother, Valmer Miley, was suspicious of both yoga and unexplained natural phenomena.

Alice Dunkirk approached, making the sign of the cross as she passed the birds but not altering her stalwart stride.

"Good afternoon, Alice," I said.

Alice rolled her eyes as if to say that was yet to be determined. She was in her sixties and filled her days walking and attending mass at St. Michael's Catholic Church. She was the town's relentless trekker, counting steps in all seasons. Jorn speculated that she came to yoga just to rest.

More students arrived, and finally, when the dozen or so

regulars were accounted for and inside, Jorn and I joined them. The fire station had been renovated to accommodate my home on the second floor and my yoga studio on the main floor. In the studio, I lit the candles on the long table behind my mat and turned on music, the soothing tones of violins, cellos, and trickling brooks. Jorn unrolled his mat in his usual position at the back of the room. I started the class moving between Cat and Cow, two poses to limber backs stiff with crow-created tension.

As I arched and flexed my spine, I thought about something my mother, Evie, told me while sitting on my back patio watching the birds come and go. She said that, other than the occasional rabid or sick animal, creatures in nature did not act without purpose. In other words, there were no crazies in the natural world. Unlike humans, crows did not abuse their children, seek revenge, or deliver unwarranted death. They were watchers and warners.

As I felt my spine loosening, another memory flitted into my head. This one of Tum discussing the complex language of the crow. "Crows carry messages, Maya," he'd said. "Listen to them."

Of the many messages of the crow, I knew the one creeping under the skin of Gabriel's Garden. And it scared me.

Trouble was coming.

CHAPTER 2

RESCUE MISSION

POUNDING ON THE DOOR pulled me from the recurring dream: I am racing toward some unknown destination. I careen around corners, plunge down halls, fling open doors—but I never arrive where I am desperate to be. I'm not afraid. I just want to reach my objective, my destiny, my *duty*. But I can't.

When I shared the dream with Evie, she said, "What you're looking for isn't something you can run to, Maya. It's inside." Sometimes my mother takes inscrutability to new heights.

More pounding.

I stumbled down the spiral staircase from my apartment and flung open the firehouse door. "What? It's three in the morning!"

On my doorstep, hand raised to hammer again, was a kid,

a teenager actually. The boy abruptly stopped in mid-motion, shoved his hands in the pockets of his baggy cargo shorts, and hunched his shoulders. When I recognized the tangle of blond corkscrews exploding from a backward-turned baseball cap, I nearly fell over, "Snowboard Boy?"

He pushed his way past me. "It's Mike. I need your help."

I first met Snowboard Boy more than a year ago on a frozen lake, where he and two friends were tormenting a kitten, which they had trapped in a bag and were dunking in an ice fishing hole. Some would have come upon that scene and said, "Boys will be boys," but I don't accept such excuses. I hold all humans to a higher standard. Snowboard Boy was the obvious leader, wearing a cocky attitude and an expensive ski jacket; thus my name for him. I saved the kitten, who was now grown and crouched at the top of the stairs, her unblinking Siamese blue eyes intent on our late-night visitor. Bella had a long memory.

"Why should I help you, *Michael*?" I stressed his full name. "Michael" wasn't as tough as Mike. It held the expectation of civility. "You almost killed my cat."

Michael seemed about to object, thought better of it, and instead looked at the feline on the stairs. Bella hissed.

"Hey, that was, like, a year ago. Carry a grudge much?"

I folded my arms in front of me and stared at him. He curled deeper into his vintage Prince T-shirt, but his voice was defiant, "The way I see it, I introduced you to each other."

After our encounter on the lake, Michael and his friends came into my life again, when they were hired to break into my home. That was another part of our history. "You also robbed my house," I reminded him.

"That was business."

"You put my cat in a bag—twice. Traumatized her for life. I can't get her into a pet carrier without bloodshed—mine."

"Look, I'm sorry. There. You happy?" He raised his voice and directed an apology to Bella. "Sorry!" He turned back to me. "Now, will you help me?"

Michael had changed since we last met. He was taller, and his features were sharper, the chubbiness of childhood melting away to reveal the carved cheekbones of a handsome young man. I couldn't imagine what he wanted from me. Still, the kid's distressed energy roiled around him like boiling water. I was good at reading energies in people and places. Something had truly scared him.

"What do you need?" I asked.

"I think I killed it."

My pulse leapt. "What?"

"A deer. I hit it with my car."

"A deer?"

"I need to find it and, like, take it to a vet or something."

I couldn't believe it. The boy who had shown no regard for the life of a tiny kitten was now worried about the health of a two-hundred-pound deer. Arrogant juvenile delinquent turned concerned nature lover—it was difficult to swallow. How I wanted to throw this kid out. I didn't have to help him. He was rich and spoiled and could pay someone else to go out in the middle of the night and help him ease his conscience.

I dropped down on the bottom step of the stairs. "It's crazy dark out there," I said with a yawn. "And I want to go back to bed. Wait until morning and tell your dad."

He shook his head. "No way. I just got my license. He'll take the car away."

I rubbed my face and mumbled, "Why me?"

It was rhetorical, but Michael answered it anyway. "Because you owe me."

My hands dropped into my lap, and I lifted my head. "How do you figure that?"

"You threatened my sister."

Actually, he was right. Our last meeting hadn't been one of my shining moments. I had wanted to know who had hired Michael to rob me. I followed him and his younger sister to a playground and threatened to tell the adoring sister about her brother's fun with helpless kittens—unless he gave me what I wanted. Of course, after one look at cute Lissa, swinging upside-down from the monkey bars, I knew I couldn't besmirch her idol, but Michael hadn't known that. So, I stood on that playground and lied to the boy who was now asking for my help.

"And what's with the birds?" he asked in a conversational leap that reminded me I was still dealing with an easily distractible child. "You're living smack in the middle of crow hell."

That was when I decided to help Michael.

Yes, I felt guilty about deceiving him to get my way, but that wasn't the only reason.

I have a need to help people. I take on trouble when others can't or won't. For days the crows had been forecasting trouble, and now it had arrived in the form of a scared teenage boy.

I started up the stairs. "I'll get dressed. You stay here. And don't touch my cat."

I insisted on driving his car, a demand Michael submitted

to with only token reluctance, a sign of just how shaken he was. In the dark, I couldn't tell how damaged the new SUV was, but it drove fine. He directed me out of town toward the Chapel of the Forgiving Heart. The narrow, empty road was as lonely as country gets. All the farmhouses were dark, the hum of the engine the only sound disturbing the quiet.

Just past the lane to the church, Michael said, "Here." I pulled over to the side of the road, which had no shoulder, and peered into the dark fields and woods all around us. Grabbing the flashlight I had brought, I stepped out of the car. Michael lit up the flashlight on his smartphone and followed me. We headed across the field and toward the trees, a likely shelter for a hurt animal.

Looking for signs of disturbed foliage, a trail of blood, anything to indicate that a wounded deer had come this way, I said, "You know, this animal can wander for miles injured."

"God, I hope not," Michael muttered.

"It's probably listening to every step we take. It'll flee as soon as we get close."

"I'm fast."

"And if we do find it, there's no way we can haul it back to the car."

"I can stay with it while you go for a vet or a park ranger or something."

"There's nothing like a well-thought-out plan," I said, tripping over a hidden rock.

We stayed together, at my insistence, walking in silence and ever-widening circles, searching the area where Michael had last seen the deer.

I was about to suggest that we give up and come back in the

daylight, when my beam illuminated a mound in the distance. I was surprised when it didn't bolt. Surely, it had heard us or smelled us. That meant only one thing: the deer had collapsed and died. Exchanging looks, Michael and I approached with caution. As we drew closer, my intuition warned that something was wrong.

Prepared to jump out of the way of flailing hooves and swinging antlers, I carefully reached out and touched . . .

Fabric.

Not fur.

I rolled the large object over. We both stepped back.

"Oh hell no," Michael cried out, "I did *not* do that."

CHAPTER 3

THE WRONG PLACE TO DIE

THE MAN WAS DEAD.

I have experience with this. I have seen the life force leave a body. There is an emptiness, a stillness, to the body, to the hovering air. As a reiki healer, I believe we are bathed by energy all the time and that energy can be channeled to help the injured. I can pass my hand over a person and feel where the person is hurt, where cells are screaming for help. And that's when I place my hand on the injured area and become a conduit for healing energy.

This man was beyond reiki.

With the light of my flashlight, I studied the vacant eyes, the bloodied and torn flannel shirt, the grungy jeans, the worn-down hiking boots. There was dirt under his fingernails and bruises on his face. Could he have been hit by a car and crawled this far from the road? I glanced in the direction of Michael's car across the field of trees, scrub, and tall grass; it was a quarter mile away.

I heard a noise behind me and turned to find Michael bent over, barfing. He'd dropped his phone when we found the man, and now it lit his terrified face. I plucked the phone from the grass, swiped a splatter of vomit off on my jeans, and handed it back to him. He wiped his mouth with his sleeve, took the phone, and shoved it in his pocket. Poor kid, he'd probably never seen death upclose. I placed a comforting hand on his shoulder, but he shrugged it away.

"C'mon," I said. "We're going back to the car and calling this in." Although we had cell phone reception in the field, I wanted to get Michael away from the scene. No kid, even one as cocky as this one, needed to stand around staring at a dead body.

He followed me without a word, our steps crushing the tall prairie grass the only sound. When we reached Michael's car, I called 911 and reported the body and our location. Then I called Jorn.

Sleepily, he answered, "Where are you? Are you hurt? Do you know what time it is?"

"Yeah, I do. Listen, I have a situation."

Jorn exhaled into the phone "Why am I not surprised?"

"There's a dead man in a field just past the Reverend Miley's place."

"What the hell are you doing out there?" he growled. There was a rustling in the background, and I pictured him, phone clamped between shoulder and jaw, pulling on pants and whatever unmatched socks were lying around. "That's Val's territory. Get out of there."

Suffering nightmares from his army experiences in the Middle East, Valmer Miley tended to shoot first and wake up later. It was a testament to the severity of our current situation that running into Val, armed and hunting imaginary enemies in the midst of a PTSD episode, barely registered a concern. I turned away so Michael, who was slumped against the bumper of the car, wouldn't hear.

I whispered, "I don't know what's going on, but it doesn't feel right, you know what I mean? Really bad vibes. I think this guy's been shot."

There was a pause on the other end of the line. "I'll be right there. Don't touch anything."

We hung up, and I walked over to Michael.

"You okay?"

He grunted.

The sky was beginning to lighten, and the morning birds were stirring. In the gray scene I saw a tired, scared child. Head down, he stared at his huge space-age sneakers. I crouched and examined the front bumper. It was crumpled on the right side, but there was no blood. He'd hit something all right, but the victim was long gone. I sent up a prayer that the animal had made it to safety and would recover.

Rising, I stepped next to Michael and leaned against the car. "Gonna need a new bumper," I said.

"Yeah."

"Did you call your dad?"

"Yeah."

We heard sirens in the distance. He looked up then and searched my face.

"I didn't do that."

I considered the boy who appeared both young and old at the same time and said, "I know."

Then we looked away, watching the flashing lights of law enforcement come closer and closer.

When Sheriff Watson Holmes arrived, I told Michael to stay by the car while I led Watt to the body. With a name like his, Watt took a lot of grief about his investigative abilities, but I had found him to be caring and fairly good at his job. He had answered the call when my house was burglarized by the boy waiting for us back on the road. We were definitely on a first-name basis.

It was hard not to like Watt Holmes, a cycling-obsessed sheriff who was raised on British mysteries. He was the only person I knew who actually wanted to watch every boring hour of the Tour de France. When Watt started coming to yoga shortly after the break-in at my house, my sister teased that he was interested in me. But I really couldn't see myself dating someone in law enforcement. My family had a long history of avoiding authority.

Watt circled the body, careful not to touch anything, then he crouched and looked more closely at the wound in the chest. The man's blue plaid shirt was red with blood. Watt shook his head. "Maya, you ever think about taking up knitting or something? Stumbling onto crime scenes is a lousy hobby."

I said, "The kid didn't do it, Watt."

Watt stood and dusted off his pants. "I know it. This guy's been beaten and shot. No bruising on the kid's knuckles, and I bet that nice pile of puke contaminating my crime scene is his."

I studied the man on the ground. His bruised face was haggard and shadowed with grizzled whiskers. Sunbaked crinkles radiated from the corners of his eyes and mapped his cheeks. The worn soles of his scuffed boots told the story of miles in wild places. I'd seen this kind of wear on the boots of thru-hikers on the Appalachian Trail. A 2,190-mile foot path can eat up footwear. I didn't think the man was as old as he appeared. A life of roughing it had roughened him. Still, he looked at home in the outdoors; he belonged here.

"Do you recognize him?" I asked.

Snapping on a pair of rubber gloves, Watt began patting the man's pockets, searching for identification. No wallet.

"What about his bag?" I pointed to a worn leather satchel lying beside the body.

Without moving the satchel's placement, Watt flipped open the top flap and stuck his hand inside. He pulled out a fistful of black dirt.

"Now, what could he want with dirt?" Watt wondered aloud. "Could he have been testing for something out here?"

Both Watt and I scanned the area. What was this man doing here? And why had someone killed him? Was it a hunting accident? A murder? Who was this guy?

Warning me to stick around for questioning, Watt replaced the dirt in the satchel then radioed for help: deputies, crime scene technicians at the Bureau of Criminal Apprehension, the coroner. I left him with the body.

As I neared the road, I saw Jorn standing by Michael's car, hands in his pockets, head down studying the ground. Then I heard raised voices.

"What the hell were you doing out here in the middle of the night?"

"Dad, will you just listen—"

"You're supposed to be at home, in bed, not joy riding."

"Dad—"

"Now you're mixed up with who knows what. Dead bodies . . . and look at your car." The man grabbed Michael and shook him. "What were you thinking?"

I sprinted toward Michael, but before I could reach him, Jorn spun the father away from his son. "Take a breath," Jorn ordered.

Michael's father flung off Jorn's grasp and shrugged the jacket of his silk suit coat in place. "Keep your fucking hands off me!"

Jorn didn't move. "Cool off, man."

"Who the hell are you?"

"Peter Jorn from *The Independent.*"

This enraged the man even more. "If I see my son's name in the newspaper, I'll sue. I will bury you."

"You can try."

Michael had drawn away and was watching the two men warily: the icy calm and implacability of Jorn against the barely suppressed anger of his father. From the tip of his glossy shoes, now covered with dust, to his professionally coiffed and tightly controlled blond curls, Michael's father dressed to convey power. He was the sort who did not appreciate surprises or disorder. I was beginning to understand Michael's need to act out occasionally and slip those suffocating reins.

The man turned to his son. "Have the police interviewed you?"

"No, sir."

Pointing a finger, not an inch from Michael's nose, he warned, "Don't say a word without me being present."

"Yes, sir," said Michael, eyes downcast.

I tapped Michael's arm. He jumped and looked at me. "Introduce me, Michael." I kept my tone friendly but uncompromising. He swallowed.

"Dad, this is a—" he hesitated. I saw the problem. I wouldn't call us friends, exactly, either.

"Maya Skye," I said, holding out my hand.

The man smoothed his hair before shaking my hand. "Chris Donovan, Mike's father. How are you involved in this mess?"

I smiled at Michael, which generated a look of concern. "Michael knows I'm a great nature lover. He thought he hit a deer and asked for my help. He wanted to make sure the deer was cared for." Michael shifted beside me. "Michael would never want an animal to suffer."

"A deer?" Chris Donovan frowned at his son then threw his hands up in exasperation. "Minnesota and its damn deer."

"Dad—"

"Shut up, Mike. This is all your mother's fault. This car was her idea."

Michael suddenly straightened. "Leave Mom out of this."

The Donovans lived down the street from Heart on Mulberry Lane. I knew the house: a brick colonial with the air of secrets, drapes drawn in the day, painfully neat gardens behind a white picket fence. While my orderly sister appreciated the fastidiousness of the Donovans' landscaping, she was not so approving of Mrs. Donovan. According to neighborhood gossip, Margot Donovan liked to curl up with a glass of bourbon behind that picket fence. What a house to live in—a little sister to care for, a weak mother to protect, and a domineering father to defy. I liked it better when I could just think of Michael as an irresponsible, snotty, rich kid.

"I'll pay for the car," Michael said.

"You bet you will," his father snapped.

And that's when something in me snapped. I shoved my way between father and son. "Michael has had a horrible experience tonight. He's seen a dead body. That's not something *anyone* can unsee. I'll talk to Sheriff Holmes about interviewing Michael later today. In your presence. But for now, take your son home and let him get some sleep."

Chris Donovan did not like to be told what to do. He looked ready to explode. It was Michael who defused the situation.

In a tired voice, he asked, "Dad, can we go home now?"

With a hard stare at me, Donovan abruptly turned around and headed for the Lexus parked behind Jorn's Jeep. "Michael, with me," he ordered, not looking back at his son.

Michael said to me, "What about my car?"

"I'll get it back to you," I whispered. I still had the keys in my pocket.

He looked from Donovan to me, then nodded and ran to catch up with his father.

Jorn stepped beside me and watched them leave. "Nice family."

As Jorn and I walked over the uneven ground toward the body, he held my hand. With a squeeze, he whispered, "Are you sure you're all right?"

I nodded and thanked Spirit once again for Jorn.

I knew Jorn still heard the call of stories waiting for him in the world's hot spots. But, for now, my intrepid reporter with the shaggy Robert Redford hair and the mismatched socks had chosen to stay in Gabriel's Garden and run a small-town newspaper. Despite our differences—with Jorn firmly planted in the logical and me always ready to give the magical the benefit of the doubt—he had chosen me. And that made me happy.

Jorn didn't release my hand until we reached the crime scene. A deputy was marking off the perimeter with yellow tape. It would be awhile before the BCA investigators arrived.

"Don't cross that," Watt ordered.

We stopped at the tape. Jorn pulled a reporter's notebook from his back pocket. The long and narrow notebook fit perfectly in the palm of his hand. "Fill me in, Watt."

The sheriff walked over. Glancing at the body, he reeled off a description, "White male, looks to be in his fifties, no ID. Could be a hiker. No backpack, though, just a satchel. Could be a hunter but that doesn't feel right either. We haven't found any firearms, either his or his attacker's. There was a fight. Old bruises and new. Shot once in the chest. Can't tell you when, but he hasn't been here long."

"What's in the satchel?"

"Dirt."

"Dirt?"

"Yup."

Watt placed his hands on his hips, searched the surrounding

countryside, and asked the dead man, "What were you doing out here, fella?"

I still couldn't shake the feeling that the man was both familiar with and at home in the natural world. Here—amid the patient turn of the seasons, the song of the bird, the warmth of the earth—he had found rightness and peace. Until this day.

Jorn circled the taped-off area, taking notes, then crouched. Peering under the tape, he studied the man's face for a long time then rose.

"I know this guy."

CHAPTER 4

THE TALE OF JACQUES PINE

I WAS RAISED ON TALES of do-gooders. What would you expect of bedtime stories in a nonviolent community of artists, gardeners, and bread makers? Bonnie and Clyde? Many nights in our cabin on Whispering Spirit Farm I drifted to sleep with my father's voice in my head, a whispering wind of activism and how one person can change the world. Larry told stories of people who *did* something about wrongs: Mother Jones, for instance, who was arrested at the age of eighty-two for organizing mine workers. And Crazy Horse, who the whites thought *was* crazy but who was revered by the Lakota because he fought to preserve their way of life. These were the stories I was told each night, not Dr. Seuss.

Now, as the rising sun lit the dead body, I listened to another story: the tale of Jacques Pine.

"He was an odd duck," Jorn recalled, "but I liked him. I interviewed him years ago."

Watt flipped open a small notebook of his own and patted his pockets, searching for a pen, "What's his name?"

Jorn handed Watt the spare pen he always carried. "Don't know his real name. He *called* himself Jacques Pine."

Watt looked up, pen paused in the air, a note of disbelief in his voice. "Jack pine. Like the tree?"

Jorn nodded. "I know. Hokey, but it fit, considering the business he was in."

"And what business was that?" Watt asked.

"Saving the planet. One tree at a time."

I caught the susurrus of a Whispering Spirit tale on the wind.

Jorn said, "He planted trees, anywhere and everywhere."

I grinned at him. "A modern-day Johnny Appleseed."

"Not quite," Jorn said. "When I compared Jacques to Appleseed, he set me straight. John Chapman, a.k.a. Johnny Appleseed, was not an early eco-warrior fighting the good fight with apple seeds. He was a businessman."

"How's that?" Watt asked.

"In the 1800s, according to frontier law, a man could lay claim to land by planting fifty apple trees. Johnny Appleseed was a land baron. He owned more than twelve hundred acres of Midwestern wilderness and prairie when he died at the age of seventy."

Watt shook his head. "No shit? A land baron. Man, I used to love that guy."

Me too. The story of Johnny Appleseed was a favorite in Larry's bedtime repertoire.

"And it gets worse," Jorn said. "They weren't even good eating apples. Chapman planted trees that produced small tart apples called 'spitters'—not good for eating but perfect for making hard cider and applejack." Jorn smiled at Watt. "During Prohibition in the twenties, FBI agents took axes to the Chapman orchards. They slaughtered thousands of trees in their attempt to kill demon hooch."

Watt slapped his notebook against his thigh. "Don't tell me our dead guy was some kind of folk hero too."

"Actually, he was, in some circles. Jacques Pine was a well-known environmentalist. Led pickets against development. Lived to protect the land. He stole saplings from nurseries and planted them on land that had been damaged by overuse, mining, or neglect."

Mulling over this information, Watt looked across the field to a small grove of trees. Several crows were perched there, watching the sheriff and deputies work. "Damn crows everywhere. They better not shit on my crime scene."

I laughed, which felt disrespectful to Jacques, but I couldn't help it.

Watt frowned at me.

"Sorry," I said.

He turned back to Jorn. "Anything else?"

"You won't find an address for him. He lived in his tent." Jorn motioned toward the nearby woods and fields. "If you look around, you'll find his camp."

Watt nodded. "We'll search the area. You make him sound crazy but harmless."

"I never had the feeling he was dangerous." Jorn thought for a moment. "Just steadfast in his beliefs. I don't know who would do *this* to him."

We heard a shout and turned to see two men striding toward us through the tall grass, their steps sure and comfortable on the uneven terrain. Both carried guns.

The crows scattered.

Well before the men reached the yellow crime-scene tape, a deputy stopped them. We walked over to them. The older man, Frank Hollister, pushed up the brim of his seed cap with the end of his rifle and demanded, "Sheriff, what the hell are you all doing on my property? This land is posted."

I had a nodding acquaintance with Frank. His son, Fritz, had taken a few yoga classes, and I often said hello to his wife, Louisa, who worked part-time behind the counter at Northern Lights.

As for the second man, I knew him quite well. It was Valmer Miley. Val and I did not have a cordial relationship. He didn't like his sister, Tessa, attending my yoga classes, and I didn't like her sleeping down the hall from her brother's arsenal. Both gun-crazy Val and independent Tessa lived with their father, the Reverend Harold Miley, in an old house behind the Chapel of the Forgiving Heart. Val worked for Frank.

"Now, Frank, this is official business," Watt put his hands up to calm the property owner. "A man died here, and we're going to be awhile."

"Died?" Frank dropped the barrel of his rifle toward the ground and slid it slightly behind his leg.

"Shot." Watt pulled up the heavy utility belt slipping off his thin cyclist's waist. "You men haven't been doing any out-of-season hunting, have you?"

"Course not, Watt," Frank said immediately.

The sheriff glanced in Val's direction.

Val looked bored. "Not me." Val had stepped out of high school and straight onto the sands of Afghanistan. He was young, unbalanced, and still carried the army in his straight stance and his buzz-cut hair. Jorn believed Val suffered from a serious case of post-traumatic stress disorder. I labeled him plain scary. He patrolled these woods at night, armed and edgy.

Watt stuck a hand out. "I'll need to look at your weapons."

Frank handed his over right away, an old hunting rifle. Val was more reluctant; he clutched his gun, a newer model than Frank's, and kept his eyes on me. I stared back, silently daring him to surrender his gun to the sheriff. With Val and me, it was always a battle for the psychological high ground. To show me he wasn't concerned, he gave his gun to the sheriff.

Watt examined both guns and handed them back.

He said to Val, "That's a lot of gun. Twelve-gauge shotgun, pump action."

I didn't tell Watt that if Val's shotgun wasn't the murder weapon, there were lots more to choose from in his bedroom, just down the road.

"Did either of you hear any shots last night?" Watt asked. "See or hear anything strange?"

Frank shook his head. "Slept like a baby."

Val simply said, "No."

Watt sighed. "Well, it looks like the deceased is a fella named Jacques Pine."

At the mention of Jacques's name, Val's head came up. The news drove a new tension through Val, making me wonder: Had their paths crossed in these lonely fields and woods?

"Some kind of tramp?" Frank did not like the sound of that.

"Environmentalist."

"Damn." That was just as bad in Frank's view.

"We believe he was planting trees . . ."

Frank angrily swept his cap off. "On *my* land? I'm not paying for that."

"Free trees," I said.

Frank looked at me for the first time. "If I want trees, I'll plant 'em. Aren't you that gal who runs that yoga place?"

"Yup," I said.

Frank shook his head in disgust. "I got it posted for no trespassin'. Do I gotta post 'No Yoga' too?"

CHAPTER 5

BEHIND THE CURTAINS

As THE DOWN DOG Diary says: *It is never right to let a spirit pass on alone.* It did not matter that I had not known Jacques Pine. His violent and unremarked demise weighed heavily on me; someone needed to say good-bye to Jacques. And so, I went home, lit candles, sat on my yoga mat, and wished Jacques Pine peace.

A few hours later, after he'd posted the first of what would be many articles on Jacques Pine (murder not being a common activity in Gabriel's Garden), Jorn followed me in his Jeep to Michael's house. I drove Michael's car past the crows in my yard, past the house where Larry tapped out the code for popular computer games and Evie painted, and past the strange dog waiting on Roselyn Barrie's porch. Roselyn was one of my yoga students. The middle school art teacher, known as the Blue Lady because of her affinity for the color, came out the door, patted the dog, and waved to us. Then she climbed into a powder puff blue Volkswagen and putted away. As far as I knew, Roselyn did not own a dog.

The Donovans lived in the house next to Roselyn's. The two structures were polar opposites: one stern and unapproachable, the other a wild clapboard child. Roselyn's teal porch was festooned with busy bird feeders and singing wind chimes. Music from the porch twisted like an otter through the air and over the proper fence into the Donovans' regimented flower beds and the big pots of geraniums guarding the door.

Jorn and I met at the gate of the picket fence and perused the yard. There was not a blade of grass out of place or a centimeter too long. No hose was hopelessly tangled under the faucet.

"This much neatness gives me the willies," said the guy who probably had a forgotten pizza box under his bed.

"Michael lives with Stepford Mom," I said.

Jorn pretended to shiver and teased, "Let's drop off the keys and get out of here." I elbowed him.

We went through the well-oiled gate and proceeded to the Donovans' front door. I pushed the doorbell. Inside, Westminster chimes reverberated through the house. Footsteps approached, hesitated, then stopped. Silence. Someone was standing on the other side of the door, probably eyeing us through the peephole. I said loudly, "It's Maya from the yoga studio. Is Michael home?"

A series of locks—more security than necessary in Gabriel's Garden—clicked, and a bird-boned woman edged the door open. Her stork-like legs were encased in black leggings, and her bony shoulders were obvious through a long, white silk tunic. A gold chain, heavy enough to keep her from blowing away in a strong gust, circled her neck. Her style—flawless makeup and excessively sprayed immobile hair—was the complete opposite of mine, which usually ran to rips in my jeans, moisturizer for makeup, and my long hair escaping from a ponytail.

The woman stared at us. "I'm Maya Skye, and this is Peter Jorn," I said, holding out a hand. When she didn't move to take it, I dangled a set of car keys in front of her. "We're returning Michael's car."

The woman looked from me to Jorn. She ignored the keys.

There was something fragile about Michael's mother, a china doll balanced on the edge of a shelf, ready to fall. I understood immediately why Michael was protective of her, and I searched for a way to put her at ease. The only switch that I could think to flip was Michael.

Giving her a friendly smile, I said, "You have quite a son, Mrs. Donovan."

The doll came to life. She let the door swing wider. "Michael?" she asked in a confused voice. "You know Michael?"

"Yes." I jingled the keys again. "His car?"

After a moment, the confusion cleared from Mrs. Donovan's face and she said, "Oh yes. I remember. He said you were coming by." She stepped back to let us in. We stood awkwardly in the quiet foyer. She fiddled with the chain at her neck.

"He's not here right now," she explained. "Last days of school."

She swallowed and glanced toward the back of the house,

obviously eager to escape us. Jorn nudged me to wrap things up, but I was curious about Michael's mother. So, I did not press the keys into her hand and run. I waited her out. And finally, reluctantly, good manners won out and she came through with an invitation.

"Would you like something to drink?"

"Thank you," I said.

Jorn gave me a strange look.

"And you, Mr. Jorn?"

Jorn recovered quickly and said, "That would be nice, Mrs. Donovan."

"Please call me Margot," she said, locking all the locks on the front door. "You own the newspaper, right?"

"Yes."

Abruptly, she turned and led us through the foyer, the soles of her ballet slippers slapping the travertine tile. Over her shoulder, she said, "Actually, I'd like to talk to you." Jorn and I exchanged puzzled looks.

The front hall opened into a large room reeking of masculinity with wood-paneled walls, overstuffed leather sofas and chairs, and paintings of bloody hunt scenes. And then there were the animals. Deer, elk, bighorn sheep, Cape buffalo, lion. Dead animals with eerie glass eyes stared down at us from the walls. The sense of death in the room took my breath away. I stopped, stunned, and Jorn bumped into the back of me.

"A lion," I said.

Margot looked back with a helpless smile. "My husband is a trophy hunter," she said. "Chris goes to Africa every year. I can't bear to go with him." She made a face. "Bugs and tents."

The soul-sucking energies here were overwhelming. It hurt

to think of Michael and Lissa walking through this room every day. I felt Jorn's hand on my back in reassurance.

Giving me time to recover, he said, "I understand certain animals are prized because they're the most dangerous to hunt. The more deadly, the more expensive."

"Yes." Margot pointed to the lion. "That animal cost Chris more than fifty thousand dollars. He's quite proud of it. But his dream is to take a rhino."

There are few rhinos left in the world. In my book, anyone who would hunt one of those endangered animals was capable of anything.

Margot turned and we continued through a dining room that was as feminine as the previous room was masculine: a large elegant table, drapes and upholstery in soft colors, floral prints on the walls. Next was the kitchen—roomy, state-of-the-art, and not a crumb in sight. On the granite-top island was an opened laptop beside a lowball glass half-filled with ice and clear liquid. As we passed, Margot shut the laptop with a click. We followed her out through a bright sun-room and into a large back garden, which looked as if it belonged on Roselyn's side of the fence. Flowers of all varieties kissed the stone paths in a riot of color. While the front yard adhered to a definite color scheme of red and white, the back landscaping was a wild Matisse palette.

Offering thickly cushioned seats at a wrought-iron patio table, Margot insisted we sit while she disappeared back into the house. Jorn and I each took a gulp of fresh, calming air.

"That room . . .," I said, unable to find the words.

Jorn nodded. "Yeah, it was weird, all right, and I don't even believe in vibes."

Margot returned with a tray. On it was a plate of scones, arranged in a neat pinwheel display, and three goblets of orange juice. Suddenly thirsty, I reached for a glass, but Margot beat me to it. "Allow me," she said, handing me one of the other glasses. After seeing to Jorn, she chose the glass I had originally selected. It was not yet ten in the morning, but I suspected the juice was spiked. After seeing Chris Donovan's trophy room, I thought about fighting her for it.

Seated, Margot said, "As you can imagine, Mike is quite upset about finding that poor man. I wanted to keep him home from school, but Chris insisted that Mike had to 'man up' and go." Margot considered her drink. "Sometimes, Chris can be . . . inflexible."

Silence fell on the table.

"I'm sorry a kid had to witness that," Jorn said in sympathy.

Margot took a sip from her glass. "I read your article in the paper, and I noticed you didn't mention my son."

Jorn said, "I wouldn't put the name of a minor in the paper."

Jorn's words reassured Margo. She released a sigh, "Good, thank you. I was worried . . . I don't want Mike's involvement to become an . . . issue."

"An issue?" I asked. "He didn't do anything wrong."

"I know, I know, but to have his name connected with a murder. It's not good for Mike. Or the family."

A couple of big crows flew into the yard with a squawk, settled on the path, and began poking around. Immediately, Margot flung up her arms and shooed them away. After they had gone, she said, "I hate those things. I wished they'd all go away."

Jorn looked at me and lifted a brow as if to say, "See, I'm not the only one. Those birds are freaky."

Margot picked up her drink, turned to me, and refocused the conversation. "How did you meet Mike?"

I paused. Meeting Michael's mother made me feel things I did not want to feel for the boy. He was a bully and a smartass. He did not respect life, as my nearly drowned Bella can attest. And yet, last night he was worried about a wild animal; last night he came to me, not his alcoholic mother or his domineering father.

Somehow, Michael Donovan had wormed his way under my protection.

Finally, I said, "He helped me find my cat."

She nodded, relaxing. "That sounds like Mike. Always taking care of things. He's my angel."

"He's an angel, all right," I said.

Jorn choked on his orange juice.

Margot said, "I don't know what Lissa or I would do without him. Chris, too, of course."

"Of course."

"Mike's a great brother. Lissa adores him. She's in preschool today. I thought she didn't really need to go to this session; she'll be in kindergarten next year. And she already knows her numbers and alphabet. But Chris insisted. Socialization, you know."

"Learning to get along," I said, "is a lesson some of us never learn."

Nodding, Margot fussed with her helmet hair. The long sleeve of her blouse slipped down, revealing a bruise circling her skinny wrist. When she saw me staring at the bruise, Margot quickly adjusted her blouse.

I looked away and out at the lush garden. "Gardens are such sanctuaries," I said. "Both your front and back gardens are lovely."

Margot said, "I don't touch the front. That's Chris's domain." She cradled the glass of juice against her chest, her gaze caressing the expanse of exuberant blooms, lush shrubs, and tall decorative grasses waving in the breeze. "This is my work. . . . This is mine."

CHAPTER 6

A NIGHT SUMMONS

A VISITOR EMERGES FROM A cloud of crows in a long black duster, dragging a cello behind him. He stops at my door and taps with his bow. The taps are light and musical and send sparks into the night. The sparks catch the wood frame of the door, and with a whoosh, flame crescendos to life. The visitor, now wearing a coat of crows, steps back and watches. The irony is not lost on me: a firehouse burning down. My home is burning, and yet the tapping continues, growing louder. It turns into banging.

Suddenly, I lunged awake. Leaping out of bed, I dashed down the spiral staircase before the fiery cellist could turn Bella and me into cinders. Halfway down the stairs, I stopped. What was I doing? There was no musical arsonist. As the confusion from the dream cleared, my next thought was that someone needed help. Ordinarily, this would have me flinging the door open wide, but I had recently discovered a dead body and there could be a murderer walking the streets of our quiet town. With echoes of the dream still singing through my body, I drew a shivering breath and tip-toed to the door.

Through the windowpane of the door, I saw a shape. My gut told me to ignore this visitor, go back to bed. I'd be stupid not to . . .

I clicked on the light and opened the door.

It was Valmer Miley, dressed in his usual: a black T-shirt and camo pants tucked into heavy black boots. Without a word, he pushed past me into the softly lit foyer. He gave the room a swift inspection, his glance searching out the dark corners. This was a guy who always looked under his bed before settling in for the night.

I shut the door. "What's happened? Is it Tessa?" I couldn't think of any other reason for Val to dare enter the den of his enemy. He and I agreed on only one thing: the safety of his sister. We approached it in vastly different ways, however—he with enough guns to arm a coup and I with a view that we kept people safe by nurturing a kinder world.

Satisfied no bogeymen were waiting in the yoga studio, Val came to parade rest, legs solid and apart, arms behind his back, chin up. He looked me in the eye. "Tess is fine."

"Then why are you here?"

"I found something."

While Val appeared calm and all business, his energy screamed a different language: suppressed secrets and reluctance laced with anger. He didn't want to be here, but something—a guilty conscience? a sense of duty?—had brought him to me. He was as uncomfortable with this alliance as I was.

"Why come to me?" I asked, as curious Bella made an appearance. Giving Val a wide berth, my cat circled me, twitching her champagne and brown-tipped tail against my legs.

Val watched the cat's hypnotic dance and frowned. "Tess, Tess says I need to be . . . friendlier."

I laughed. "This is your idea of being a good neighbor? Dragging me out of bed in the middle of the night?"

Val dropped his arms to his sides. "Look, I didn't have to come here. Tess said I should talk to you. She said you'd know what to do, since you found him."

"Who?"

"The dead guy."

"Jacques Pine? If you know something, you should take it to Sheriff Holmes, not me."

"I'm not going to the cops."

I knuckled my tired eyes, tossed back my long hair, and shifted my weight to one hip. "Okay, okay. What exactly did you find?"

As if talking to an idiot, Val said slowly, "The dead guy's nest."

I straightened, my eyes and head suddenly clear. "His camp?"

Val stepped around me and reached for the doorknob. "Didn't I just say that? Come on, I'll take you to it."

"Wait." He turned back to look at me. "I'll change clothes and call Jorn."

"I'm just taking you. No reporter. Or the deal's off."

I didn't want to go anywhere with Val, not alone and

especially not to a patch of dark woods in the middle of the night. I knew what Val did prowling the countryside when nightmares wouldn't let him sleep. Jorn and I had paid a visit to the Miley home one night to check on Tessa and witnessed Val in a PTSD episode so deep that he didn't know where he was. We watched him "kill" a swath of menacing trees, bushes, and foliage, laying down more firepower than I ever wanted to experience again. It was Tessa, who finally calmed him down and led him back to bed.

But Jacques Pine's camp could tell us a lot—perhaps who killed him. I had found poor Jacques and felt some responsibility to see he rested in peace, with his murderer brought to justice.

I signaled Val to wait. "Okay. Just let me change."

I ran up the stairs, stripped off my pajama bottoms and tank, and pulled on jeans, a T-shirt, and hiking boots. Bella had followed me upstairs, and I gave her a quick caress. "If I don't come back, Bella, you can have all my stuff."

I texted a quick message to Jorn: *Val found Jacques's camp. He's taking me there.* Then I grabbed my satchel, dropped my cell phone in it, and left with Val.

On my doorstep in the dark, locking my door, I wondered again if this was a good idea. Val was taller than I, well-muscled from combat and farmwork, and entirely too jumpy. When I paused, Val said, "We ain't got all night." I climbed into his car, which was old but ran with a well-cared-for smoothness. Hugging the door, I kept an eye on Val, his profile edged in the yellow glow of the dashboard. He was not a talker and never glanced my way the whole trip. We passed the turn-off to the Chapel of the Forgiving Heart and pulled to the side of the road near where Michael and I had parked. We got out of the car.

I stood with my door open, scanning the area, remembering the night Michael and I found Jacques Pine. My phone vibrated and I jumped. As Val strode toward the back of the car, I slid the phone out of my satchel. It was a text from Jorn: *ARE YOU NUTS? DO NOT GO WITH HIM.*

Before I could reply, Val popped the trunk with a slap of his hand and hauled out a rifle.

"Whoa," I said, gripping the passenger door. "No guns."

"I'm not going anywhere unarmed," Val said, loading the rifle.

"Then I'm not coming with you."

Val stopped, a look of disbelief on his face. "You're already here."

I waved my cell phone at him. "I'll call Jorn to pick me up. I'm not going into the woods with you and a gun."

"But the killer could be out there," he said, the grip on his gun tightening.

I folded my arms and remained steadfast. For all I knew, Val had killed Jacques Pine. He owns guns and knows how to use them. He reconnoiters this land night and day. It's as familiar to him as his bedroom. Maybe Jacques surprised Val one night, and Val shot him accidentally. Or maybe Val took umbrage at a stranger in "his" woods and got into an argument with Jacques.

My mind raced. Why hadn't I thought of these possibilities before taking this ill-conceived ride? My eyes swept the area, looking for options. Running was out; I was not faster than a bullet. I peered inside the car and noticed Val had left the keys in the ignition. I could dive in, start the car, and make a quick getaway.

"No guns," I said, readying my legs to make the jump back inside the car.

Val glared at me, and I glared back. Suddenly, he whirled away in disgust and muttered, "Women!"

His back was turned—this was my chance. Scramble over the gear shift and turn the key, Maya. But I didn't go for it.

Val kicked at the ground, stomped back to the car, and tossed the gun into the trunk. I started to relax, but then he reached in for something else. I estimated again the distance between me and the key in the ignition. I could make it.

Val slammed the trunk closed. In his hands were two powerful flashlights. He circled the car, slapped one into my palm, and turned away. "Come on."

I closed the door, and we entered the darkness.

We walked for about a half hour, scattering night creatures hidden in the scrub and tall grass, rounding a copse of oak and aspen, crossing a field of mostly rocks and cow patties, climbing a stile into another field, this one planted with corn. We followed the edge of the cornfield, Frank Hollister's probably, and cut back into the woods, and I realized we were on a rudimentary path.

"This is how I tracked him," Val said. "He's made some trails, going back and forth, from his nest to," he paused, "whatever he was doing."

And then we reached it. Jacques Pine's home.

The tent under the spreading boughs of a big oak was old and patched. A tarp, stretched from the top of one tent pole to the nearby trees, formed a lean-to. A neat circle of rocks defined a fire pit. Next to the pit, lying on its side, was a pan with a burnt bottom. There was a rumpled sleeping bag under the tarp.

The flaps of the tent were folded back, perhaps to air it out while he was gone. I swept my light inside the tent. Propped in one corner was a big frame backpack. Like everything else, it was well used. Strewn on the floor of the tent were clothes and books. Lined up against one wall were bags of seeds and a flat of seedlings.

"Have you touched anything?" I asked.

"What do you think?" Val said, pushing past me and crawling into the tent.

"Don't," I said, "this is all evidence in a murder investigation."

"You don't think I'm going to leave a setup like this without checking it out, do you?" Val rolled his shoulders. "What if there was some bad shit here, a bomb or something, and Tessa stumbled on it?"

I squatted at the entrance of the tent, still unwilling to contaminate the scene further. "Look. We need to call the sheriff."

"First, I want to show you something." Val grabbed the backpack and dumped out the contents. Out fell money, bundled money, a lot of it.

I crept into the tent and knelt by the pile of cash. "What in the world—"

"Newspaper said this guy was some famous environmentalist, fought for the land, never sold out to big money interests." Val's eyes met mine. "This looks like big money to me."

CHAPTER 7

TROUBLE WITH RAISINS IN IT

THE DAY AFTER WE found Jacques's camp, I received an ominous text from Evie: *Your grandmother is back.*

My grandmother, Sylvia Skye, is a multimillionaire matriarch with an endless supply of Chanel suits, matching handbags, and bank accounts. She has the confidence of a woman who has multiplied her dead husband's fortune many times over and the granite-like determination to keep what was hers. And that included the son she had single-handedly raised. Unfortunately for Gran, her overbearing approach resulted in her spending decades estranged from her son and his family, years when I didn't even know she existed.

Grandmother had fought hard against what she called Evie and Larry's "unsuitable" love. Evie disrupted all of Gran's plans for her son: law school, a partnership in his father's old firm, a place in society at Sylvia's side. Gran threatened my father with disinheritance and tried to buy off my mother, who as Gran put it was "just a waitress" when the couple met. Neither worked. In fact, it drove my parents underground. Fearing that my forceful and relentless grandmother would tear the family apart to get her son back, they cut her from their lives—until a year ago. That's when Gran showed up on our doorstep, shoving her way into our lives with her old bony elbows and stubborn beliefs.

Gran could set my mother on edge with, "Hello," and turn my father into a silent child with a glance, but I liked her. I maintained that our outspoken grandmother was lonely for family. Heart didn't believe it, "Don't fall for it, Maya. Grandmother is crafty."

Heart was suspicious of most people until she got to know them, and she had grown even more paranoid with motherhood. I, on the other hand, couldn't turn down those who came to my door, no matter how much trouble they brought me. In my sister's opinion, it was a personality flaw I should work on, but as James Tumblethorne, the biker, used to tell me, "Sitting on the sidelines of life is like riding two days straight. All it gets you is a numb ass."

At my proper grandmother's insistence, a proper family dinner with proper place settings and a proper grace said by Gran was in order to launch her visit. It was a command performance. Evie sat on one end of the table; Gran at the other end, facing off over formal china and fresh flowers in crystal vases. Seated between the two were Larry; Heart, her husband David, and their daughter, Sadie; Jorn; and me.

My grandmother fired the first salvo. "What a lovely table, Evangeline. Reminds me of the first dinner at my house when Lawrence introduced us."

Evie had a strange look on her face. She couldn't find the memory. My mother was shot in the head a year ago. Although she had survived, she still battled with the sudden blankness that came out of the blue. It was painful to watch her struggle, as she was now, with scattered images that fogged and teased. I leaned forward to rescue her, to say anything to save Evie this digging at memory, but then my mother relaxed and said, "I don't remember, Sylvia. Why don't you tell us about it?"

My religious grandmother had been here during the days when we sat by Evie's side in the hospital. If this conversation had occurred before the shooting, I would have thought it done out of spite; bringing up an old feud to disarm the enemy was not beyond my grandmother. But in the past year, the relationship between Evie and Gran had shifted. Although it would always be rocky, today I believed my grandmother was actually trying to be nice. It was totally out of character.

"I didn't know anyone who wore penny loafers," Gran began. "And I wondered how you were ever going to fit into our lifestyle." Penny loafers have been Evie's shoe of choice for as long as I can remember. Gran paused. "But I guess I didn't need to worry about that, did I?" It was on that visit that Larry informed Gran that he had quit college and was moving with Evie to a piece of land he'd purchased in New Mexico with his trust fund money. Larry had been twenty and Evie twenty-one at the time. They were going off the grid, trading a mansion for a tent, electricity for a candle. In Sylvia's mind, Evie had stolen her son and led him into lunacy, and it still irked.

Evie took a sip of wine and said, "I remember . . . knocking on the front door. Lion-head knockers. A servant answered in traditional butler livery. Just like a gothic novel."

"Gothic." Sylvia laughed, and I saw something one didn't often see in my grandmother's eyes—embarrassment. "I wanted to make a good impression."

From the look on Evie's face, she had never attributed this motive to her mother-in-law.

"I worried so much about that meal," Gran admitted, "nearly drove Chef Henri insane over the lobster thermidor."

"And I'd never had lobster before," Evie said, with a wink at Larry, "or ever again."

Larry reached along the table, touching the tip of his finger to Evie's, a gesture of connection I had seen a million times. If Eskimos kiss by rubbing noses, my parents show affection with the bump of a finger. Evie's strength replenished my father's and vice versa. At the touch, both of my parents' shoulders relaxed and Larry said, "Well, the lobsters are safe tonight, Mother. We're having lasagna, my specialty."

Gran stared at her plate. "You made this, Lawrence? I'm sure it will be delicious." But her expression said she doubted it. Gran preferred her meat, pasta, and vegetables in neat, discernible positions on her plate, not in one oozing block.

Sadie said, "Grandpa makes the best lasagna. Really packs those layers."

Gran poked at the slab with her fork. "I can see."

After Gran said grace, we began to eat.

"As the limo entered town," Gran said, "I noticed an

uncommon number of crows, especially around your fire station, Maya." As if it was my fault.

"Neat, huh," said Sadie.

"Trouble," muttered Jorn, "trouble with raisins in it."

I elbowed him and nodded toward Sadie, who had stopped eating and was staring at Jorn. I had invited Jorn for the excitement and to draw some of Gran's fire from Evie and Larry. Except for *The Wall Street Journal,* Gran considered the press to be a shabby, ambulance-chasing realm. Jorn knew he was fodder and took her disdain for journalists with good humor.

"Raisins?" Sadie asked, her forehead wrinkling up to her blonde curls. "Are the crows eating our raisins?"

"No, there's nothing to worry about," I reassured my nine-year-old niece.

To Gran, I said, "I'm taking the crows as a sign that something in our world is simply out of balance."

Gran nodded. "Balance. Ah, yes, I remember, your dogma."

My grandmother considered any belief not originating from the Bible, preferably the Old Testament, as suspect.

Changing the topic of conversation, Larry said, "Mother, Sadie and I have a summer project."

Talking around a hunk of garlic bread, Sadie said, "Yeah, we're going to save the monarchs."

"Didn't know royalty was in dire straits," said Gran.

Sadie giggled. "Butterflies, Great-Gran, butterflies."

David smiled at his daughter. "Yup, they've been hard at it, growing milkweed seedlings in a corner of the greenhouse." David Simpson owned the local landscaping company.

"Now we're ready to transplant the plugs into the field,"

Larry said, reaching across the table and giving Sadie a fist bump. They grinned at each other.

"Field? Where?" Gran was always interested in real estate. Who knew what all she owned around the world?

"I bought a few acres out of town, a nice sunny spot. The milkweed will love it."

"And the butterflies too," said Sadie.

Jorn turned to Larry. "Where is this property?"

With a bit of hesitation and a sudden interest in his dinner, Larry said, "Out north of town."

Larry's tone and evasion brought me up short. That was the direction of the Reverend Miley's place and the location where Michael and I had found Jacques Pine. "Where you know what happened?" I whispered.

"Maybe," Larry mumbled. He dipped his head, suddenly intent on chasing a cherry tomato around in his salad.

"I thought that was Frank Hollister's land," Jorn said.

The Hollister farm had been in Frank's family for generations, but times were hard. Louisa Hollister had to take a job at Northern Lights, much to Frank's shame, and one of the reasons Frank had to hire Val Miley to help on the family farm was because the Hollisters' only child, Fritz, had dropped out of agriculture college "to lick envelopes for Greenpeace," as Louisa put it. When Fritz left home, telling his parents he just couldn't support the agri-polluters, Frank's blood pressure skyrocketed and the doctor ordered him on bed rest for two days.

Larry explained, "Frank and I have been negotiating for months. Given current events, he was eager to unload the property."

Heart threw down her linen napkin. “Larry, tell me you are not taking my daughter to a crime scene *and* turning her into an activist.”

“Heart, they’re just planting a few seedlings,” said David, the instinctive peacemaker. Then, after giving it a thought, he admitted, “Well, maybe a little more than a few. But it’s all good. Pollinator habitat *is* disappearing.”

“Crime scene?” asked Sadie, then, “What’s an activist?”

Larry sent his oldest daughter a beseeching look. “Heart. C’mon.”

Clutching her knife, Heart gave him a look that could melt crayons.

Larry quickly said, “Heart, we’ve stayed away from all that stuff. We’re just learning about taking care of the environment.”

“Yeah, we’re environmental warriors sticking it to the Man,” Sadie told us. Jorn muffled a laugh in his napkin, Gran lifted an eyebrow, and Evie and I exchanged grins.

“You’re what?” Heart’s voice rose a register. “Larry . . .”

“It’s just a saying, Heart,” Larry sighed.

Sadie tapped her mother’s arm to get her attention. “We’re going to save baby butterflies. Isn’t that cool?”

Heart finally tore her gaze away from Larry and smiled down at Sadie. “Yes, that’s cool.”

Evie said, “I’ll help you plant.”

“Me too,” I piped in.

“Sounds like a story,” Jorn said.

Heart immediately turned on him. “No pictures of my daughter in the newspaper.” Heart was strict about family images in the press and social media. No one in our family dared to even post a picture of our latest breakfast on Facebook or

Instagram. That was company policy. Skyes the Limit was the family software company, creator of the extremely successful *Spirit Snatchers* and *Peace Hero* games. Evie designed the graphics, Larry wrote the code, and Heart managed the business. I was a silent stockholder. As Heart always said, when you run a family business worth millions, you don't give potential kidnappers and extortionists your address wrapped with a bow.

Jorn held up his hands in surrender. "I promise. Only photos of cute little seedlings."

But Heart wasn't finished with Larry. While serving dessert, Evie's ever-popular Viennese chocolate torte, Heart leaned over Larry and hissed in his ear, "Leave my child out of your causes!"

Heart had had her fill of "causes" during our years on Whispering Spirit Farm, which still existed. It remained a small community for the like-minded who believed in living a simple, nonviolent life in tune with nature. After growing up there, Heart couldn't leave Whispering Spirit fast enough. The day she embarked on a new life at college, she told me, "I'm going to be a normal person, at last." But even Heart couldn't shake her alternative roots. As the excellent manager of the family business and investments, she adamantly refused to support companies that wrecked the environment, enslaved children in sweatshops, or lacked a moral compass. My sister was a strange mix of *Good Housekeeping* and *The New Yorker.*

We were scraping the last bit of torte from our plates and Sadie was begging for another slice when Gran tapped a spoon against her water glass. "I have an announcement," she said.

We all turned toward her. The satisfied look on my grandmother's wrinkled but well-moisturized face made me nervous.

"I'm moving to Gabriel's Garden."

The silence was broken by the clatter of Evie's fork hitting her china plate.

CHAPTER 8 

FIELD OF FLUTTERING DREAMS

AROUND GABRIEL'S GARDEN THE plains rolled gently and pleasantly. The dark and fertile soil was a souvenir of glaciers from the Ice Age, and in May it beckoned to growers. On this gorgeous day, farmers across the state were following the agricultural blueprint drawn by generations before them. They were planting corn and soybeans mainly, but also some hay, sugar beets, and wheat.

And my father was growing wildflowers.

The wildflower field was a small part of the fifty acres Larry had purchased from Frank Hollister. It was edged on two sides by the asphalt country road, which made a sharp right angle at this point. There were woods, a brook, a giant boulder punching up through the soil like a fist, and a column of tall pines along the road. The brook continued through a culvert and under the road onto the rest of Frank's land, more than a thousand acres of corn and soybeans.

Standing on the edge of the field, Larry turned to me and asked, "Do you feel it, Maya? I walked across this land, and it gave me chills. Man, the vibrations."

When my parents left Whispering Spirit Farm more than fifteen years ago, they trusted the winds of fate and their intuition to lead them, and they ended up in Gabriel's Garden. Neither had been to Minnesota before; they had no connections to the state, no reason to stop here, except here they had felt something that was beyond explanation. They called it a vortex. Whether it was the pull of inexplicable energy or the allure of family, my sister followed them, and eventually so did I.

Of course, my grandmother thought we were all nuts.

"There are no such things as vortexes," says Gran. "That is simply hogwash. And to link these places with anything spiritual is . . . heathen."

Jorn agreed with her about vortexes and vibes. He did not believe in spiritual magnets, places on this Earth where energy amassed and eddied like a whirlpool. He refused to accept that energy hot spots existed, much less that they could help us balance our spirit and find harmony. But I was a creature of energy. I worked with it all the time, and I came from people who gave energy its due.

I glanced at Evie and Sadie. Mirroring Larry's stance, Sadie had hands on her hips, feet planted firmly in the soil, and a smile on her face. Evie watched Larry with a smitten expression. This was the man she had fallen in love with, the man who approached everything he did—from wooing her to writing computer code—with single-minded passion and child-like glee. This fierce focus was the quality Grandmother Sylvia and her rigid lifestyle had been unable to conquer.

I closed my eyes and opened my senses: the warmth of the sun-filled day on my cheek, the scent of pines, the chirping voices of the insects rising and falling in a lazy-day aria. And then I felt it. A tingle. A good energy rising from the clods of freshly turned soil. A rightness. I opened my eyes and found Evie watching me now. I nodded. She wrapped an arm around my shoulders and squeezed.

This was a pretty place with a good feel, despite recent events involving Jacques Pine. Noticing me staring across the field, at the spot where Michael and I had found Jacques, Evie said in a low voice, "It is good to cleanse this place."

I nodded. "Who plowed the field for you?"

"I hired Val Miley to do it," said Evie.

I didn't like that. "It's not good to get too friendly with Val," I warned her.

Evie simply smiled at me, plunked a sunhat on her head, and said, "Let's plant."

There were the four of us and two wheelbarrows crammed with flats of milkweed plugs, an assortment of seeds in bags, gloves, hats, hoes, shovels, and water bottles. Unable to contain himself, Larry lifted Sadie into the air and shouted, "This is it. I christen this land Sadie's Papillon Farm." The name was appropriate given that *papillon* was French for butterfly and that my niece adored all things French. She often wore a beret, her room was a shrine to Paris, and her preferred food was croissants.

Sadie giggled, her skinny arms hugging his neck. "Ooh-la-la. Our sanctuary!"

Still not sure of the scope of this project, I said, "Explain."

Larry set Sadie down. "We're gonna plant milkweed for the adult butterflies to lay their eggs on and for the baby caterpillars to eat," said Sadie. "They only eat milkweed, you know. That's *all* they eat in the whole wide world."

"Is this entire field going to be milkweed?" It looked immense to me.

"We'll also be planting native wildflowers," Larry said. I checked out the bags of seeds.

Sadie said, "Food for the adult monarchs." She counted off on her fingers. "Thistle, goldenrod, bergamot, blazing star. All their favorites."

"Imagine, Maya," Larry said, "monarchs migrating to Mexico from up north will spot this sea of goldenrod from the sky and stop."

Evie said, "Spots like this along the migration route give pollinators a place to rest, refuel, reproduce."

"Butterflies, bees," Larry said. "The vibrations will be outstanding." He and Sadie shared a high-five, then Larry let out a battle cry. "Protect the pollinators!"

"Protect the pollinators!" Sadie echoed, a fist raised to the sky, then leaned toward me and said in a tone that sounded suspiciously like Larry, "You only get one world, you know."

While Evie and Sadie took a wheelbarrow and headed to one end of the field, Larry and I wrestled the second wheelbarrow over the rough clods of dirt to the opposite end. Donning work gloves and baseball caps, we got to work. We planted the plugs about a foot apart and scattered flower seeds as we went, pushing the seeds into the soil with a tap of our shoe.

For a while we worked in silence: squatting, poking a hole big enough for the seedling's roots, inserting the seedling until just the leaves showed, and patting the earth securely around it.

"This must feel like old times," I said, stopping for a moment to take a sip of water.

Larry rose and looked out on the field. "Yeah, we did a lot of planting at Whispering Spirit."

"Feels good?"

He smiled at me. "Real good."

I picked up another plug and was about to resume planting, when Larry cleared his throat. "Maya, there's something I want to talk to you about."

I waited, standing by the wheelbarrow, a seedling in my gloved hand. Larry's graying ponytail lifted off his back in the light wind. His eyes searched the field as if considering what to say. Finally, he turned to me, "I have to find out what happened to Jacques, Maya. Will you help me?"

I set the seedling carefully back in the flat. There was no question that I would help my father, but I was slightly confused. "What do you have to do with Jacques Pine?" I asked.

Larry ducked his head and kicked at a clod of dirt with the toe of his tennis shoe. "Well, we sort of knew him."

"We?"

"Evie and I. He lived at Whispering Spirit for a time."

I stared at him, not sure what to say. From the corner of my eye, I counted the crows gathering in silence in the nearby pines. *One for sorrow, two for joy . . .*

"I'm sorry, Larry. I didn't know he was your friend."

Larry looked out over the field. "You were a baby when Jacques lived at the farm, and Heart was a tot. He was with us for about a year, then he left to do his own thing."

People passing through Whispering Spirit Farm often left to do their own thing. Some returned and some didn't.

More crows arrived and the old nursery rhyme continued in my head. *Three for a girl, four for a boy . . .*

"Is Jacques Pine his real name?" I asked.

"I doubt it."

"What *can* you tell me about him?"

"He was younger than Evie and me, maybe in his fifties. Never said where he was from, but he had a trace of an accent, especially when he was excited or angry. I'm not good with accents." Larry crouched, gently planted a seedling, then rose. "He had more energy than three people. At first, I thought he was hopped up on drugs, something we didn't encourage. But then I realized Jacques's mind and metabolism always ran at twice the speed of anyone else's."

That was saying something since my father could be a dynamo once he zeroed in on an idea, like creating a wildlife sanctuary. Larry continued, "Man, I never knew anybody who loved the outdoors as much as Jacques. He loved his tent, feeling the ground beneath him. He dug being alone, except when he was at Whispering Spirit. There he made camp beside our cabin. I tripped over his lines and stakes at night.

"He didn't say much, unless you started him on his favorite subject: the damage man was doing to nature. Then you couldn't shut him up." Larry paused. "He was so damn passionate, and a little nuts."

"He wanted to save the world," I said. This was not surprising. Everyone at Whispering Spirit took planetary responsibility seriously.

Larry scattered some seeds. "We all railed against global pollution and environmental destruction. We all protested. But Evie always suspected that Jacques did more than walk the protest line."

"Why?"

"He would disappear for days at a time and never tell us where he'd been. Sometimes, he'd come back . . . well, worse for wear."

"What do you mean?"

"The occasional black eye, bruises, a limp. He could have been simply protesting a new dam in a peaceful sit-in turned ugly. Or some lumber guys could have caught him hammering spikes into trees."

"Monkey wrenching."

"Yeah. He never admitted to that, knew we didn't approve of that approach. He especially didn't want Evie to know what he was doing."

Jacques had never married, according to Jorn. Was this why? Had Jacques Pine been in love with my mother?

Five, six, seven crows. *Five for silver, six for gold. Seven for a secret never to be told.*

I asked Larry if he had kept in contact with Jacques.

"Sure," he said, "Sent him money every once in a while. Bailed him out of jail a time or two."

"He was your friend."

Larry looked down again, kicked another clod. "It's more than that."

"What?"

My father turned to me, guilt written on his face. "Maya, I brought Jacques here."

CHAPTER 9

SAINT MICHAEL ON SPEED-DIAL

IN THE "LAND OF 10,000 Lakes," trying to think creatively about geography must have grown tiresome. Sadie claimed there were more than two hundred Mud Lakes in Minnesota, a fact she learned from her father who grew up fishing and skating on one of them. Some lakes have native names such as Lake Winnibigoshish, whose name comes from the Ojibwe language and means "filthy water." Locals and the tongue-tied just call it the affectionate Lake Winnie.

No one knew where Lake Michael in Gabriel's Garden got its name. Perhaps one of the town's Amish settlers was named Michael. Or maybe when the Catholics moved in and built St. Michael's Church, they got carried away with all the naming. Archangel Michael was the patron saint of warriors and was best known for hurling Lucifer from Heaven for his treachery.

Although Saint Michael was supposed to be a protector, this lake brought out the protector in me. Shaped like a shoe, as if that famous lumberjack Paul Bunyan had passed through one day and left a giant footprint, it held both sweet and terrible memories. Here was where I found solitude and answers on countless walks; it was also where I rescued Bella the cat from Michael Donovan and his friends one wintry afternoon and where Evie was almost taken from me. She was shot here. Evie doesn't remember that day on this trail, but I will never forget it. I had grown watchful here, even on a mild morning like this one as I walked with my mother and sister.

Evie, Heart, and I circled Lake Michael at a sturdy clip. Heart, who has always been athletic, set the pace. If it had just been Evie and me, we would have spent more time communing with nature and less time plowing through it. But Heart was determined to show the fitness app on her phone who was boss.

Finally, I called a rest stop.

I steered Evie to a bench on the side of the path. Heart walked back and said, "What's wrong? Was I going too fast?"

"No," said Evie.

"Yes," I said.

In her sixties, my mother doesn't bounce back from injury as quickly as she once did. She favors one leg, especially when she's tired, and then there is the whole memory issue. Evie has never had the nervous energy of Larry; my mother is the still one, the one who tackles adversity with a calm resilience. Strangely enough, the shooting has not upset that serenity; in fact, it has expanded it, made her wiser, more patient with others and herself.

Heart flopped down beside us on the bench and studied her phone, her fingers tapping. My multitasking sister was probably counting miles and steps, or organizing her business calendar, or setting up Sadie's next play date. In Heart's mind, play dates were wonderfully regular. At Whispering Spirit no one had arranged play dates. Why would they? We lived, ate, learned, and played together all the time.

Evie watched her older daughter, an understanding expression on her face. I stretched out my legs, closed my eyes, and surrendered to the songs of the summer air—the twittering of the birds, the murmur of the leaves.

Eyes still closed, I said, "There's an entry in the Down Dog Diary that says, 'Nature knows all. It is never lost. No two trees are the same to the bird or the squirrel.' I like the idea of that."

Heart, who disliked the diary and didn't trust its insights, said, "I know one piece of nature I'd like to lose—all those damn crows. They're pooping all over town, Maya. They're a health hazard. We should hire some crow trappers or do something before the Centers for Disease Control declares the whole town toxic."

I opened my eyes and looked at my sister. "Crow trappers."

"We could buy plastic owls and install them all over town," Heart suggested. "Owls are the natural predators of crows, aren't they? They attack crow roosts at night."

"Crows are smart. They would figure out fake owls," I said.

Evie said, "I've heard of some towns using noise—fireworks and recordings of crow distress calls—to convince crows to relocate."

"I'll light the firecrackers," volunteered Heart.

"That's just cruel," I said. "They'll leave when they're ready to leave."

Heart caught my eye. "You think they're here to give you some big cosmic message, don't you? Like their little gifts of buttons and paper clips. I swear, Maya, they're just birds. Noisy, dirty birds."

The crows, or maybe it was just the same crow over and over, had started leaving me gifts. The items appeared on my step or on the patio, and I had begun collecting them and tossing them into a small basket on the patio table. A basket of shinys. Crows were attracted to objects that glisten in the light, that sparkle in the woods, but they were not discriminating scavengers. My basket contained paperclips, a crumpled wad of foil, buttons, a gum wrapper, a green shard from a broken beer bottle, a blue Lego, and an antique key.

I frowned at Heart, and she glared back. I was not on board with the harassment or eradication of the crows. Whether Heart believed it or not, the crows were here for a reason. We just had to wait and listen.

Evie lifted her face to the sun and commanded, "Girls."

Slowly, never breaking eye contact, Heart and I sat back, our arms crossed over our chests, a pose we had fallen into when we were fighting as kids. It meant we would agree to disagree—but only for Evie's sake.

Evie changed the subject. "Maya, Sheriff Holmes dropped by to see us last night."

Suspicious Heart straightened and turned to Evie. "Why?"

"Evie and Larry knew the man who was killed," I told my sister.

Heart threw up her hands. "Of course they did."

I looked at Evie. "Should I tell her?" My mother nodded. "Actually, Heart, Larry brought Jacques here to help start Sadie's Papillon Farm."

"Why did nobody tell me that our family is connected to the murdered man?" Heart asked, exasperated.

I explained that it was only yesterday that I had learned of the relationship. After we finished planting, I followed Larry and Evie home and they told me the whole story about Jacques Pine. Although Evie hadn't wanted me within a mile of any murder investigation, she also knew I could not ignore someone in need, especially not when it was my own family.

Heart frowned. "What are *you* doing? Investigating?"

"Not in an official capacity," I said.

"Maya, I know you feel like you have to help every ant that crosses your path, but can't you just sit this one out?"

I knew Heart was thinking of what happened a year ago, when Jorn and I inadvertently brought a deranged mind into our midst and Evie suffered the consequences.

Evie said, "Jacques was a friend and a good man, Heart."

"And the world needs good men," I said. "We can't just sit and do nothing."

My rational sister sighed. She has never understood my faith in myself, how I can know things and accept them without proof. I am the one who will chase fireflies in the dark, while she won't enter the night without a flashlight.

With a plea in my voice, I said, "I can help, Heart. The Universe always lays a trail. I just have to follow it."

Heart looked away. "Don't bring trouble to our doorstep again, Maya."

I reached out and touched her hand in reassurance, a promise I hoped I could keep.

Clearing my throat, I turned to Evie and asked, "What did Watt want?"

"He found Larry's number in Jacques's cell phone." Evie shifted in her seat. "We admitted that we knew him and that Jacques had lived at Whispering Spirit Farm for a brief time."

Heart began typing furiously on her phone; I peeked over her shoulder. She was writing an email—to herself. "It is a good thing I have our lawyers on speed-dial," she said.

We all seek protection from somewhere.

I hid a smile.

But Heart caught me, "It does a lot more good than who you have on your speed-dial. How's Guru Bobolink these days?"

His name was Guru Bobistani or Guru Bob, and he was my go-to sage, the guy who took me in when I was broken and gave me time to heal at his ashram in India. I had always tried to live by *ahimsa*, to do no harm to any living being. But then I'd taken a life, by accident and while trying to protect another, but still a life. It devastated me. So, I ran away to Guru Bob's, looking for some way to live with myself again. Your karma suffers when you kill another human, even if that human is a no-good drug dealer beating the crap out of a helpless woman in an alley.

I had been hiding at the ashram for about a year when James Tumblethorne showed up at the ashram's door to drag me home. In words that might have come from plainspoken Guru Bob himself, Tum said to me, "If you're gonna kick ass, Maya, you gotta accept the consequences."

I turned to Heart and, in a snooty accent, said, "Guru *Bobistani* does not have a cell phone."

Still a little mad, Heart tried not to smile. I nudged her. "Who do you think Gran has on speed-dial?"

Heart nodded toward the water. "Saint Michael maybe?"

Evie and I laughed, and Heart joined in. Now was a good time to inform Heart it was her turn to drive our religious grandmother to Sunday service at the Chapel of the Forgiving Heart. My sister and I agreed on one thing: the evangelical message of the Reverend Harold Miley was not for us. Still, every Sunday one of us had to chauffeur Grandmother to the small country church. Heart yielded with grace. "Okay, okay. Now, you might as well tell me everything about this Jacques character."

After hearing that Jacques had for years been part of the environmental activist movement along with our parents, and that Larry had brought Jacques here to help with the butterfly farm, Heart sank back onto the hard bench. "We're definitely going to need a lawyer."

I said to Evie, "How much did Larry tell Watt?"

"You know your father." My mother watched the ducks in the lake for a moment. "The less time spent with law enforcement the better."

As activists, my parents naturally didn't trust authority, and they'd passed that bias on to Heart and me. Too often they had seen peaceful demonstrations turn violent, and it was always the unarmed activists who were at the mercy of the clubs and water cannons.

I asked Evie. "How much did Larry pay Jacques to come here?"

Evie made a so-so gesture with her hand. "A few thousand, enough to buy supplies and food, enough for a bus ticket here. I don't know the exact amount. He mainly came just to help us."

Val and I had found more than a few thousand in Jacques's backpack.

I was about to mention that to Evie when Heart, looking over my shoulder, muttered, "What in the world is she wearing?"

We all turned to see Roselyn Barrie plodding up the trail. She had squeezed her pudgy shape into a pair of tight leggings and matching top. The pattern of the ensemble was a mosaic of blue stained-glass shapes. Running up one leg was Picasso's *The Old Guitarist* from the artist's Blue Period, of course. Roselyn collapsed onto the bench. We shuffled to make room. The man following her was dressed in monochromatic fashion—black jeans and T-shirt. Unlike Roselyn, he was not the least bit out of breath. Good thing because there was no more room on the bench.

"Glad I spotted you. I needed a rest stop." Roselyn fanned her face.

Evie asked, "What are you walking off today?"

"Baked Alaska," Roselyn sighed. "Nate didn't believe I could make one."

"You showed him," Heart said.

"She sure did," the man said.

"Except he can eat a thousand baked Alaskas and not gain a pound. He has the metabolism of a third grader." Roselyn massaged a calf muscle, giving us a nice view of Picasso's poor, nearly skeletal musician.

Roselyn's friend gave a boyish grin and stuck his hands into his back pockets.

Roselyn introduced us. "This is Nate Nelson. He's from Florida. He's scavenged and found treasure all over the world."

Roselyn was a fifty-two-year-old schoolteacher and a self-described "unclaimed treasure." Now it appeared that someone had claimed her—a real treasure hunter.

Nate carried the relaxed manner and air of an aging yet ageless beach bum. The sun had worked its way into the dashing lines of his face, and age had streaked his dark curls. A gold hoop twinkled from one ear. When his gaze touched upon Roselyn, his expression softened.

"Roselyn's giving me and my metal detector too much credit," he said with a grin.

I asked, "Have you ever found any sunken treasure?"

"Not in Gabriel's Garden." Nate's idea of a joke.

Roselyn giggled; I simply looked at Nate.

"I don't dive anymore," he said. "Too many damn regulations now. Takes all the fun out of it. Now it's just me, my metal detector, and dry land."

"Regulations?" Heart asked.

"To protect the ecosystem. You can't just scavenge anywhere you want anymore. The environmentalists have spoiled it for all of us."

I studied Nate. "Sounds like you don't think it's important to protect the environment."

Nate didn't say anything.

Roselyn looked up at him. "Now, Nate just hunts in the fields around here with Angus."

Nate said, "And speaking of Angus, where is that dog?" He scanned the area, whistled.

After a few moments, a dog bounded out of the woods on the east side of the lake. The black and brown sheepherding mix dashed down the path, halted at Nate's side, and immediately sat, tongue hanging out of the side of its mouth. Nate reached down and scratched behind the dog's ears. It was the dog Jorn and I had seen sitting on Roselyn's porch.

Delighted at anything to do with Nate and Angus, Roselyn laughed and Evie joined her. I had to admit the dog's blue eyes were strangely attractive.

All Heart said was, "You know Gabriel's Garden has a leash law, right?"

With another appealing yet mischievous grin, Nate the scofflaw pulled Roselyn from the bench and nudged her toward the trail.

After Roselyn and Nate left, Angus herding them down the path, Heart punched a button on her cell phone and jumped up. "Ready to go?"

I rose and offered a hand to Evie. She took it with a pensive smile. "What is it, Evie?" I asked.

She shook her head in puzzlement. "This silly old brain of mine. For a moment there, I could have sworn that I knew Nate from somewhere."

"Really? Where?"

"I don't know." She watched the couple disappear down the trail. "But that face is familiar."

CHAPTER 10

BETTER THAN BETTY CROCKER

WE SAT IN JORN'S jeep, spying on Michael Donovan and his sister, Lissa, as they reached for the sky. Their legs pumped, and they laughed with each kick. His legs were twice as long as hers, but her sneakers, with sparkles and flashing lights, were cuter than his. She had pulled her pink baseball cap around backwards to mimic her big brother's. They had identical clouds of soft blond curls, the same dimples. She leaned back into the air and trusted her swing, just as she trusted her brother.

This playground was a brief walk from the Donovan home. School was out for the summer, and the Donovan siblings came here nearly every afternoon, Lissa skipping and Michael sauntering down the sidewalk under the canopy of shade trees. I knew because I sometimes made a point of driving by. Ever since I met the precariously balanced Margot Donovan and witnessed her husband's idea of wholesome decorating, I couldn't stop thinking of the Donovan children.

Michael knew I was there, but he pretended to ignore me.

Jorn shifted uncomfortably in his seat. "Why do we have to do this?"

"I'm just checking on them."

"It feels like we're stalking them."

Michael and Lissa leapt from the swings and scrambled up a lattice of thick ropes, Michael stopping to give his sister a boost when she needed it. "Does Michael seem distracted today?" I asked Jorn. "Worried about something?"

Jorn studied the brother and sister. "I don't know him well enough to tell. Why?"

"Just a feeling."

Jorn blew out his breath. He hated when I said that. "You and your feelings."

I'd asked Jorn to investigate Chris Donovan. Something about the guy seemed off. Not taking my eyes off the Donovan children, I said, "Okay, Mr. Facts, what did you find out about their father?"

"Guess where Chris Donovan works," Jorn said with relish.

"Haven't a clue. He's a suit in the city."

"Donovan is a vice president of Mary Ella's, a manufacturer of consumer foods—cereal, popcorn, cake mixes, potato chips."

I knew the brand. There was a bag of Mary Ella's sweet potato chips in my cupboard. "Really," I said, thoughtfully, but didn't see why this was significant.

Staring out the windshield at the playground, Jorn continued, "Mary Ella is a shrewd businesswoman who, after her husband died, turned a failing Minnesota farm into a multinational corporation. She knows how tough it is to make a living from a few acres, even with good luck. She is famous for saying, 'If the weather doesn't do you in, the government will.' She isn't a fan of regulations, especially ones that keep farmers from using whatever they want on their land, including their pesticide of choice. She started the company in the 1950s."

"I doubt she was welcomed in many boardrooms back then."

"Didn't matter. The *wives* of board members loved Mary Ella's packaged foods. She made their lives easier and happier, if not always healthier. She was more beloved than Betty Crocker."

"What kind of company is Mary Ella's today?"

"Mary Ella's children run it now, although their mother keeps a tight hold on the reins. The youngest daughter is the rebel; she keeps the board meetings lively by introducing 'new and ridiculous ideas' like using social media to sell more breakfast cereal."

"What does Donovan do exactly?"

Jorn turned to me. From the look on his face, I'd just pitched one into his wheelhouse. "He's in charge of sustainability."

The irony hit me like a cast iron skillet. "Let me get this straight. A guy who dreams of shooting endangered species is the environmental corporate conscience of Mary Ella's?"

"Interesting, isn't it?" said Jorn. "In the past year, the company has donated millions of dollars to help save pollinators. Another one of the youngest daughter's projects."

I whistled. "That's a lot of goodwill."

"So far, Mary Ella has let her daughter run with it because she knows the current climate demands that her company be viewed as the sustainable choice in agriculture. But you can bet if it starts straining the company's bottom line . . ."

"What does this pollinator program involve?"

"The company is working with the US Department of Agriculture to establish pollinator habitats on its supplier farms."

"Encouraging farmers to give up valuable farmland for bees and butterflies. That's a hard sell."

"But it makes sense. Pollinators are key to protecting our food supply."

I knew that. Larry had already regaled me with the statistics: Between 75 and 95 percent of flowering plants need the help of pollinators. A world without pollinators is a world without apples, oranges, berries, and many vegetables.

"Does Mary Ella's plan do anything about pesticides?" I asked.

Jorn shifted again, and the springs in his seat squeaked. He shook his head. "It's a work in progress."

"Organic" is practically my family's middle name so there was no doubt where we stood on the pesticide issue. But I also knew many farmers depended on the use of pesticides to increase their yields. Still, reestablishing pollinator habitat was a start.

"This all sounds like a good thing," I said. "What's bothering you?"

Jorn drummed his fingers on the steering wheel. "Something isn't connecting."

"You have a feeling there's more to this project or to Chris Donovan?"

"I don't do feelings. I'm saying I need more facts—" He stopped and nodded toward the playground. Michael, hands in his pockets, was wandering over to our car. Lissa had moved from the rope wall to the slide, whooshing down it, climbing back up to the top, and doing it all over again. Michael leaned into my window.

"What's up?" I asked.

"You tell me," he said. "You two make lousy spies."

"We're not trying to be covert."

"It's a little stalker-like," Michael said.

"I told you," Jorn said.

I ignored him and focused on Michael. "You doing okay?"

Michael turned away, leaned against the car, his back to us in his tough guy stance. He watched his sister. After a few moments, he said, "Dad wants to take me on safari this summer."

Oh no, I thought. "Exciting," I said.

"Yeah. See the world. Make friends. Kill things," he said sarcastically.

"If you don't want to go, tell him no," I said.

Michael pushed off from the car and waved for Lissa. It was time to go home. "Nobody tells the great white hunter no."

CHAPTER 11

TREASURE AMONG THE WILDFLOWERS

HEART AND I STOOD together watching Larry and Sadie pick their way across Sadie's Papillon Farm. Every once in a while, they stopped and crouched, their heads nearly touching, as they examined a sprout or discussed the name of a flower. It was June. Summer flowers that pollinators crave—poppies, forget-me-nots, coneflowers, bergamot—were in bloom or thinking about it. The milkweed was pushing toward the sky.

While Sadie and Larry made regular pilgrimages to check on the development of their sanctuary, it was Heart's first visit. Jorn was there, taking photos for the story he'd promised to write for *The Independent*. Heart raised her voice. "You make sure my kid's face is out of focus," she warned Jorn.

"I got the memo," Jorn said, heading for Larry and Sadie.

"And you can't quote her either," Heart yelled.

As if an interview was even needed. Larry had already flooded Jorn's in-box with reports, studies, and links to more reports and studies on the decline of pollinators.

I nudged my sister. "You're being a worry-wart."

"Somebody has to look out for this family."

I personally never worried about publicity and the family business. But my sister mixed her mother heart with her business brain—and ended up not trusting anyone. Sometimes not even her own father.

Not taking her eyes from her daughter, Heart said, "You know Larry is filling her head with stories of Mother Jones and Crazy Horse."

"I loved those stories," I said.

"We grew up in an activist training ground." Heart secured her ball cap more firmly on her head and stood straighter. "I don't want that for Sadie."

"Sadie loves being out here with Larry," I argued.

"I want her to be a regular kid, not jumping on every crusade that comes along."

I teased, "Well, she's young. She has plenty of time to harden her heart."

"Make fun, Maya, wait until you're a mother and the world is lurking outside your child's door with sharp teeth."

Before I could comment, the meadow filled with barking and a dog sprinted past us, low to the ground, heading straight for Sadie.

With the speed only a fearful mother can generate, Heart took off after the dog. "Hey!"

Nate Nelson came up behind me, slightly out of breath, clutching a metal detector. He shouted, "Angus, come back here!" Then to Heart, he called out, "Don't worry; he won't bite." Like Heart was going to believe that.

Ignoring Nate and his assurances, the dog knocked Sadie flat. She giggled as Angus slathered her face with kisses. Heart screamed, "Get off her!" Larry leaped forward, took hold of Angus's collar, and dragged the dog away from his granddaughter.

Heart dropped to her knees beside Sadie and snatched her to her chest. "Are you all right?"

Sadie struggled to free herself from her mother's protective embrace. "Of course I am. Angus wouldn't hurt me. He and Nate come here all the time."

As Nate, Jorn, and I reached the group, I saw Heart slowly release her daughter, rise, and tighten the ponytail waving from the back of her cap. Tension swept across the grass like a wind. She turned on Larry. "Is this true?"

My father could stand up to an oil company intent on running pipelines through environmentally fragile land, but he is lousy in confrontations with his daughters. And in this case, he didn't understand why Heart was upset. "Sure. What's the big deal?"

Wrong approach. My sister's chest expanded with wronged-mother indignation. "Big deal? Big deal! Nobody informed me, that's the big deal."

Larry still didn't see the problem. "Nate and Angus just like to walk around the property. I gave them permission."

Heart started to sputter.

I stepped forward. In a soothing tone, I said, "Larry, she's just worried. It's her job to protect Sadie from strange dogs and strange men. No offense, Nate."

Nate lifted a shoulder. "Angus *is* a little strange." I glanced down at the dog with the unsettling blue eyes, sitting at our feet, then back at Larry.

For a moment, the expression on Larry's face reminded me of the day we lost Heart.

I was five and Heart was seven. We were at a protest march in Albuquerque, and we were supposed to walk together, but one moment Heart was beside me, holding my hand, and the next she was gone. I immediately pulled on Larry's hand for him to stop. When he leaned down toward me, I shouted over the crowd, "Heart's gone! Heart's gone!" Larry jerked to standing and scanned the crowd. Gripping my hand tightly, he leaned toward Evie and said something to her. Then he tossed down his sign and whisked me into his arms. He pushed through the crowd like a snowplow to reach a bus stop bench and leapt up on it. And then he began yelling Heart's name.

Evie, who had followed us, was yelling, too, and standing on tiptoe on the curb to see over the marchers flowing past her. Larry clutched me in his arms. I could feel his heart hammering against my hand. When I looked out at all the people, they didn't seem as friendly as they had before. That morning the protestors had welcomed us and our signs screaming, "Save Our Sacred Lands." But now the faces were serious, the bodies stiff with defiance, and their chanting mouths yawned before me like dark caves.

I wrapped my arms around Larry's neck and looked away, and that's when I saw her. Heart was huddled against a storefront, her arms wrapped around her legs, her head hidden in her arms. I rapped on Larry's shoulder and shouted, "There! There!" He whirled around in the direction I was pointing, and I felt him give a shudder of relief. He quickly passed me to Evie, hurdled over the back of the bench, and ran to my sister. When Evie and I reached them, he was sitting on the sidewalk with Heart in his lap, rocking my crying sister. He looked up at Evie.

"It's all right. Everything's all right," he'd said over and over.

Just as he was telling Heart now. It would never occur to him that he might be thought of as an inadequate protector for his granddaughter. He looked hurt and confused. "Heart?"

Heart looked away, made a big deal of dusting off her pants. "I just want to know who you guys are hanging with when you're out here communing with nature. Keep me in the loop. Okay?"

Larry nodded, then touched Heart's hand, part apology, part reassurance.

With the excitement over, Sadie, now standing beside her mother, turned to Nate. "Did you find anything today?"

I saw Nate stick his hand in his jeans pocket, pull out a small object, and slyly drop it beside his leg. He handed the metal detector and headphones to Sadie and said, "Lean pickings today. Why don't you give it a try?"

Sadie's face lit up. She held the metal detector like a pro, hovering it close to the ground and slowly swinging the detector's searchcoil over the area around us. Obviously, this was not her first time with the detector. Although the headphones kept slipping off her small head and the detector's stem was nearly as long as she was, she managed.

"Good hunting," Nate called. Without looking up, Sadie nodded and began searching, swinging the detector side to side as she tiptoed around a patch of low ground-covering sweet alyssum. Angus walked slowly beside her until a couple of crows landing on the ground distracted him. He chased them away, but they just moved to another part of the field. Angus returned to Sadie's side.

Heart watched her daughter for a moment, then turned to Nate. "What kind of treasure could you possibly expect to find around here?"

"Any place where there is a chance of human activity, there is a chance for treasure," Nate said.

Heart frowned. "I don't understand."

Nate swept an arm encompassing the meadow of wildflowers. "Maybe once there was a farmhouse here and the farmer buried his money to keep his spendthrift brother from getting it. Maybe there was a battle here and soldiers dropped coins, lost copper buttons from their uniforms, or threw aside broken sabers. Maybe kids once played under those trees and left a toy that was buried by time. The possibilities are endless. You just have to imagine where humans have walked, lived, breathed—and go hunting."

I found myself inspecting the landscape and wondering what could be underneath us. I loved this place, and every time I came here, I loved it more. It felt right—healing nature that had been psychically damaged not only by Jacques's murder but by the general disappearance of the bees and butterflies. Sensing the energy all around us, I could believe that this piece of land once had a life of its own.

"Relics often work their way to the surface," Nate was

telling Heart. "Just because something is buried a foot deep doesn't mean it's going to stay there. The earth is always moving, shifting, reorganizing itself."

Heart looked at the ground. My sister the control freak did not like the idea of constant change. I caught a grin on Nate's face. He winked at me then turned to follow Sadie. I fell into step beside him.

"Why have you been looking for stuff in these woods?" I asked.

"Once a treasure hunter always a treasure hunter."

"Ever run into Jacques Pine out here?"

Nate thought for a moment. "The man who died?"

I nodded.

"I might have. But I'm pretty much in my own world when I have my headphones on. Just me and the next discovery." He grinned at me, the same grin that I imagined had thawed Roselyn's spinster heart and left it a gooey mess of blue.

Before I could question Nate more, Sadie shouted, "Nate! Nate! I've found something."

We all came running. Sadie's headphones, now a chunky necklace lying on her chest, sounded a beep, beep, beep, as she passed the detector over an indentation in the ground. It was not the spot where Nate had planted a treasure for Sadie to find. This discovery was near the large boulder.

"Is it treasure? Is it?" Sadie's eyes were alight with excitement, and so were Nate's.

"You know the rule."

Sadie immediately recited, "When in doubt, dig it out."

"Let's see," he said, kneeling where the detector was emitting the loudest response. "Sadie, lift the detector straight up over the spot." When she did, the beeping changed tone.

"It's big," Nate said.

"Really?" Sadie's eyes grew round.

Nate slid off his backpack, rummaged around in it, and pulled out a small gardening spade and an object about the size of a long skinny flashlight. Jorn nudged me and tilted his head toward the pack. Nate quickly zipped the pack closed, but just for a moment I caught a glimpse of . . . my eyes met Jorn's in surprise. Nate was carrying a gun.

"This pointer will pinpoint the object for us," he said. He poked the pointer into the ground several times, searching for a strong signal. "Hear that squeak, Sadie?"

Nate dug, and we all crowded closer. Finally, he pulled a dirt-encrusted, flat object from the ground. He dusted it off.

"That's it? A crushed pop can?" Sadie was disappointed. We all were.

Nate sat back on his heels. "Yup. Pop cans, pull tabs. Gotta dig those up 'cause you never know. Next time that signal might be a gold wedding ring."

"Seems like a lot of work for nothing," said Heart.

Nate smiled at her. "Where's your sense of adventure?"

Heart's idea of adventure was balancing the books at Skyes the Limit.

With a dreamy expression in his eyes, Nate went on, "There's a bit of Robert Louis Stevenson in all of us. Everybody loves hidden treasure."

"I love treasure," piped up Sadie.

Nate got up and handed the can to Larry. Shouldering his

backpack, he motioned to Sadie, "C'mon. I think we'll have better luck over where we started."

And he led us back to the spot where he had dropped the mysterious object he'd pulled from his pocket, but it was nowhere to be found.

CHAPTER 12

WHAT A MAN CARRIED

MY GRANDMOTHER WANTED HER portrait done. This was a bad idea.

In Gran's perception of art, the women were elegant, haughty, swimming in silk and dignity. She preferred realism to abstraction and avoided modern art as if Kandinsky's geometrics could leap off the canvas and stab her in the eye. All my grandmother wanted was an accurate and artistic representation of a respectable woman in tasteful pearls and a lilac Chanel suit with matching handbag.

When I entered Evie's studio and saw the painting, I knew we were in for trouble.

I would call Evie an instinctual artist. My mother doesn't exactly paint a subject; she paints what she sees as the inner self and is often as surprised by the result as others are. In short, she renders the person's spirit. Usually in animal form.

In this case, an old fox eyed us from the canvas, tufts of hair growing out of its ears, a secretive look in its eyes, pince-nez spectacles perched on its long, narrow nose. Wearing an expensive purple suit, pointy high heels, and pink anklet socks with lace, it lounged at a Parisian bistro table, one knobby-kneed, skinny leg crossed over the other. In its paw dangled an antique chatelaine with a set of keys and a large cross.

"Well, that's one way to go," I said, studying Evie's work.

Evie pushed up the paint-spattered sleeves of one of Larry's old shirts and tilted her head in assessment. "Maybe I could do something with the background."

"I don't think that's the problem," I said.

My grandmother, sitting in an armchair by the window, strained to see the painting. "What is it?" She began struggling to get out of the chair. "Let me see." I walked over and offered her a hand.

Old bones creaking, she circled the easel and silently appraised the painting.

"That's not me at all," said Gran, "and where's my purse?" She shook the boxy, lilac handbag in front of Evie's face.

I don't know what Gran keeps in that purse, but she clings to it like a life preserver. I bet she even sleeps with it.

"I tried to tell you," Evie said, "I don't paint portraits. I paint images of the soul."

"That's my soul?" Gran's voice rose. "I bet God would have a thing or two to say about that."

I stepped in. "Actually, Gran, I was betting you'd come out as a toad. This is really . . . an improvement."

"Not helping," muttered Evie.

Gran leaned closer, her eyes squinting. "And what am I wearing on my feet?"

"Lacy ankle socks," I said. "*Tres* cute, as Sadie would say."

My grandmother was not the lace or cute type. Straightening to her full dignified height, she said, "I am a single mother with a head for business and, apparently," she nodded toward the painting, "a heart of gold."

Evie and I leaned toward the painting. Sure enough, painted on Gran Fox's Chanel chest was a tiny gold heart. I turned to Evie in puzzlement, but she just shrugged. She couldn't explain it any better than I could.

Clearing her throat, Evie began to take down the canvas. "Sylvia, I obviously can't paint what you want."

Gran placed a hand on Evie's arm to stop her. "Who says this isn't what I wanted? I always get what I want." She pointed to the painting. "Except I don't know why I had to sit for hours in the hardest chair in the house for *that*. You could have done *that* using a *National Geographic* for reference."

Gran turned to leave, stopped, and looked back at the painting. "Don't touch that. I'll get it when it dries."

Dumbstruck, Evie and I watched Grandmother walk out of the studio.

With that precious, rather absurd painting still on my mind, I climbed the stairs to Larry's cave/office. Dark as Evie's studio was bright, it was lit by wall-to-wall monitors powered by a nest of cables and computer towers under the U-shaped desk. Larry rolled in his office chair over the hardwood floor in this circle of technology, conducting code and coaxing information from one keyboard to the next, while the music of Queen crashed from the speakers.

"Hello!" I shouted over the pounding beat of Queen's "Under Pressure." Larry jumped up from his chair, took me into his arms, and whirled me about. He sang in my ear about last dances and love's chances and people in the streets. At the end of the song, he spun me with a final twirl, and I landed right in his spare chair. When I looked up, he was back in his office chair, tennis shoes propped on his desk. He turned down the music.

"How's the portrait going?" he laughed.

I nodded. "It's different . . . but Gran seems to like it."

"Nobody does different like Evie," he said with pride in his voice.

After catching me up on a game he was developing, I asked if he had any new information on Jacques Pine.

"I've been trying to track Jacques's movements for the last few years. Figure out who he'd been talking to. Create a timeline."

"You think Jacques was killed by someone he knew?"

I could tell Larry didn't want to go down that road. "Maybe, maybe not. It's easy to trace where our paths crossed. I have records of when I sent him money and where; when I bought him bus tickets or cars."

"Cars?"

He ignored me. "In recent years, I have made bail or paid fines for him in Washington, New York, Florida, and Georgia. Trespassing charges near oil refineries; resisting arrest in rallies about climate change. So far, I've found two outstanding warrants."

"What about his friends?"

"I've asked people when they last saw Jacques and where. Still, there are gaps."

Jacques had lived under the radar.

"What about credit cards?"

"Too traceable. If he used any, they were prepaid."

"What does that leave you?"

My father glowed with accomplishment. "Telephone records."

"You hacked the phone company?" I could hear Heart speed-dialing lawyers.

Avoiding my question, Larry said, "Jacques always called me from burners. He carried a couple of them on him. Usually he used a phone once, then destroyed it. By examining my records, I realized that in the last year or so, he had called me several times from the *same* phone."

"Why would he do that?"

"I don't know. Maybe he simply forgot or was in locations where he couldn't conveniently replace it. He did spend a lot of time in hard-to-get-to places."

"How were you able to trace Jacques's last phone?"

Larry gave me a carefully worded reply. "The location of a burner and its usage can be determined . . . with a little work."

I sat back. Oh boy, this was something Heart must never know.

Larry continued, "In the past months, Jacques made frequent calls to Canada."

"Friends? Family?"

"I don't know. I've tried calling the number in Canada. It's been disconnected."

I said, "You mentioned a timeline. What have you surmised about his movements?"

"Talking to people who've seen him in recent years . . ." Larry typed on a keyboard, calling up an image of the United States on one of the monitors. It resembled a flight map in the back of an airline magazine, red lines arcing across the country.

I stood and leaned over his shoulder. "It looks like he's been everywhere."

"Except here." Larry tapped the upper Midwest.

That seemed strange given the obvious friendship between Jacques and my parents. "I wonder why," I said.

"When I talked to Jacques and invited him to help plant the pollinator way station, he was excited. But he said the strangest thing at the end of one of our conversations. He said, 'He won't be happy.'"

"He who?"

Larry lifted his shoulders.

"Do you think he knew someone here, other than you and Evie?"

"It's possible."

"Someone from his past?"

"Jacques was never forthcoming with personal history. He was all about the movement. He was impulsive and daring and secretive. Jacques often complained that I was too patient, that I moved too slowly. 'You only get one world, Larry,' he would say."

"So I've heard," I said, recalling those were the very words Sadie uttered when we were planting milkweed for the monarchs. The spirit of Jacques was here, even after he was gone.

Thinking, Larry tapped a beat on the desk with a pencil.

"It took me awhile to finalize the deal with Frank and buy the land, and I should have known Jacques would get bored, just hanging out in his tent. I have a feeling he was planting milkweed and wildflowers that he got from somebody else to create pollinator patches along many farms in the area."

"Without the farmers' permission," I guessed.

Larry waved his hand in a helpless gesture. "That was Jacques."

"Do you think he ran afoul of one of the farmers, like Frank Hollister?"

"I don't see Frank harming anyone," Larry said, tapping, thinking. "He's a guy in a tight spot, but he's not a killer."

In my experience, people in tight spots were capable of many things.

Larry's investigations started me wondering about all the stuff Val and I had found in Jacques's tent. I called Jorn. "Hey, have you seen an inventory of Jacques's belongings?"

"No, but I want to."

"Meet you at the sheriff's office?"

"Give me an hour. I just finished interviewing the Troll Lady. I need time to recover."

"Who's the Troll Lady?"

"An eighty-five-year-old collector of troll dolls. She has a million of them. Even looks like them. Big round bug eyes and orange hair sticking straight up like she just did five rounds with a light socket."

I laughed. When Heart and I were growing up, we played with good luck trolls. Mine was named Ork the Dragon Slayer and resembled a wizard. Heart's troll, June, wore an apron, baked cookies for the other trolls, and nagged them to brush their teeth. Ork did not get along with June.

"Al says the paper needs more human-interest stories." The hardened foreign correspondent sulked, "I hate human interest."

Retired Al Jorn faithfully read *The Independent* while enjoying the view from the pool of his Florida condominium, and even though he had handed over all operations and ownership of the newspaper to his nephew, he was not shy about calling with advice.

Jorn and I met at the office of Sheriff Watt Holmes. Watt's taste in office décor was far different from that of his predecessor who had favored posters of trucks with wheels capable of crushing houses. The walls of Watt's office were plastered with peaceful scenes from France: fields of French lavender, a Paris street romantically lit at night, pelotons of Tour de France cyclists peddling twisting roads through the Pyrenees. Our family Francophile, Sadie, would have approved.

When we asked to see Jacques's belongings, Watt leaned his whippet body back in his chair and said, "Leave the investigating to us."

Like any good lawman, Watt was patient and steady, but he also was willing to occasionally color outside the boundaries. When the city council refused to fund bike lanes for Gabriel's Garden, Watt bought the paint himself and walked the streets marking off the lanes with a high-powered spray gun. No one dared question how legal this was.

"C'mon, Watt," I said, sitting in one of the visitor chairs across from him. "I led you to Jacques's campsite." Val had insisted that I do the honors and take all the credit.

"That doesn't earn you special privileges, Maya."

"What about the public's right to know?" Jorn said. "I have a newspaper to put out, Watt. According to Al, you haven't had a murder in this town in, well, ever. People are worried. Scared. They're wondering if they're living next door to a murderer."

"You think I don't know that?" Watt said, frustration in his voice. "That's all people ask me about—when am I gonna catch that killer. It's right up there with—when am I gonna get rid of those crows."

We remained silent. Minutes passed.

Finally, with a shake of his head, Watt stood. We followed him into another room, where long tables were filled with various items. "This is everything from the crime scene. Do not remove anything from the crime scene bags." He looked at Jorn. "And for the record, my official statement is that we are pursuing all avenues in this investigation."

"Got it," Jorn said.

After Watt left us, Jorn and I approached the tables. Each bag was clear so we could see the item in it and labeled with a bar code that meant nothing to us. I skipped over the dented coffee pot, food-crusted pan, tin bowl and mug, bent silverware, Nalgene bottles of water (of which there were two). The bags of raggedy clothes were uninteresting and looked as if even Goodwill would reject them. One contained Jacques's bloody shirts: a black T-shirt and a plaid flannel shirt that reminded me of Larry. I picked up the T-shirt bag and tried to read the white lettering that was partially obscured by blood stains.

Jorn stepped beside me. "Can you make out what it says?"

I shook my head. It looked like a concert souvenir shirt, similar to the ones Larry always wore. For all I knew, it could be one of Larry's.

Jorn moved on to the books, which were individually bagged. There were more books than clothes, all paperbacks. Jacques's reading material was what I would expect from the man Larry described. There was a nearly disintegrating, and obviously much loved, copy of Rachel Carson's *Silent Spring.* Edward Abbey's *The Monkey Wrench Gang* appeared to have been another favorite as was Henry David Thoreau's *Walden.* Only one really stood out: *Dr. Zhivago,* Boris Pasternak's novel of love and loss during the Russian Revolution of 1905.

After some thought, I realized it wasn't difficult to imagine Jacques bent over the book by the campfire, reading it over and over. When *Dr. Zhivago* was rejected for publication in the USSR, it was smuggled out of the country by a Pasternak supporter and then distributed by US government agents to the rest of Europe. Pasternak's story—the romance of defiance—would strike a chord with Jacques.

Jorn lifted one book after another. "The man was a reader, I'll give him that," he said, a note of admiration in his voice. When on assignment, Jorn had always carried a book in his pack, reading it over and over during quiet and not-so-quiet times. He bought and discarded books in his wake: in airports, hotel rooms, restaurants—a habit he couldn't break. There were books piled under tables at Jorn's house, left on chairs and beds, stacked in towers on the floors. "When I interviewed Jacques, he said everyone should have to carry their homes on their backs. Then you'd really find out what is important. You'd feel it in your spine and your knees."

We glanced at the tables, at the collection of what Jacques Pine carried. There was his burner phone and flashlight but no wallet. There was, however, an expired driver's license issued in New Mexico and a Canadian passport. I wrestled open the passport in the see-through bag, trying to make out the name. It was issued to Jacques Pine, Vancouver, Canada.

"Do you think this passport is legit?" I asked.

"I doubt it." Jorn took the passport from me and examined it more closely. "I still don't believe that's his real name. Jacques was far too cagey when I questioned him about his identity. You'll notice there are no ticket stubs—airline, train, bus. He religiously destroyed anything that could track where he was and where he'd been."

My eyes went to the phone in the plastic bag. So, Jacques, why did you keep the burner? And why was there only one phone here? Larry said Jacques usually kept a couple of them at a time.

"Our Jacques was not a trusting person," Jorn said. "You'll also note there's no computer."

"He thought the authorities could find him through his computer?"

Jorn nodded.

Also conspicuously missing were the bundles of cash that Val and I had stuffed back into Jacques's backpack. "No money," I said.

Jorn scanned the collection. "Probably in the sheriff's safe."

He walked over to a corner of the room where there were

bags of seeds and a plastic tray of seedlings confiscated from Jacques's tent. "Do you recognize any of these?"

"No. I asked Larry. He said he hadn't given seedlings and seeds to Jacques yet. Jacques was supposed to plant with us that day at Sadie's Papillon Farm. I don't know where he got these."

I turned back to the table and picked up two small bags. Each contained a photograph. One was of two boys and a girl, obviously siblings, from the similar shape of their noses and the matching gaps between their front teeth. They were laughing, squatting over a bucket, holding out frogs for the cameraperson to see. It was an old photo, colors fading, corners chipped.

The second photo was newer but in similar well-loved, much-traveled condition: three people, arms around each other, two men and a woman snug between them. The woman had long hair, wore jeans and penny loafers, and smiled directly into the camera. Both men were focused on the woman. There was a shadow over their faces, making it hard to distinguish their features, but I knew that place and I knew those penny loafers.

"Jorn, that's the lodge at Whispering Spirit Farm. And I think that woman is Evie."

CHAPTER 13

A SHINY DELIVERY

FIVE YEARS AGO, MY father built me a garden. As always Evie admonished him to "Keep it simple," but Larry's mind travels mazes of complexity and dreams big. It was one of the reasons they left Whispering Spirit Farm. The power needs for all his technology had simply outgrown the community of simple cabins and gardens, spotty communications, and sporadic outages (many caused by his electrical demands). So, it was no surprise that when I casually mentioned that I wanted to someday turn the slab of concrete behind the fire station into a decent patio, Larry showed up shortly thereafter with blueprints. When I examined them, I nearly fell out of my aluminum lawn chair. At the time, I only had the one, sitting squarely in the middle of the empty slab.

Larry's idea of restraint was a patio with multiple stone

terraces, a fire pit *and* a fireplace, an arched pergola crafted of fine Douglas fir and bedecked with fairy lights, a fountain flowing into a tiered creek, several trees and pots of flowers, and a Buddha statue. I agreed to the pergola, trees, flowers, Buddha, and fairy lights.

And each year since, in early June, a few weeks before my birthday, Larry and David have filled the pots on my patio while Evie and I sat and directed. It was my birthday gift. They knew what I liked: dahlias, verbena, petunias, geraniums. This year, because David had to work, Jorn volunteered to be Larry's assistant. Since Jorn's garden consisted of one zebra cactus sitting on his kitchen windowsill, I doubted his expertise in horticulture. But he said, "Give me that flat of petunias. When I was a kid, I planted vegetable gardens that brought *Better Homes & Gardens* knocking."

"Really?"

"Not exactly, but my grandmother did measure the straightness of the rows with a yardstick."

Thinking of the constant messy state of Jorn's house, I asked, "Did you ever pass the yardstick test?"

"Of course I did. Crooked rows meant no fried bologna sandwich for lunch, and I loved fried bologna."

I wrinkled my nose at just the thought of smelly cold cuts. I was willing to venture only so far into the world of meat.

As Jorn and Larry planted, Evie and I supervised from comfortable wicker patio chairs. Sadie was on the love seat, her body and attention curled around a Harry Potter book. A crow was perched on the pergola, silent and gleaming in the sun.

"What do you think about Roselyn's new boyfriend?" I asked Evie.

"She's quite excited about him," Evie said with a smile. "He's color blind."

That would make a difference to Roselyn, who had been dressing in blue since she was two. In her kitchen, puffs of soft white clouds drifted across sky blue painted walls. She ate off of cobalt dishes and purchased cerulean towels. But her obsession had cost her in the romance department. One lover had warned, "If you drag one more piece of blue furniture into this house, I'm gone." Roselyn fondly remembered him as the sapphire sofa guy.

As Jorn and Larry disagreed on whether to group the petunias by color or just throw the whole mess in pots and be done with it, Evie said, "Whoever thought Roselyn would fall for a treasure hunter?"

Sadie, her multitasking ears pricked, peeked around her book. "Nate said once he found a gold chalice from a *real* Spanish galleon."

A shiny artifact with a mysterious history was all the credential Sadie required, but I was not so trusting of Nate Nelson and his golden tales of digs and dives. Something about the guy didn't add up. Under his surfer languidness burned a drive I couldn't name. Maybe it was just as Nate said, "Everybody loves hidden treasure." So, why did it feel like, with Nate, it was so much more?

From the petunia flats, Jorn called, "Maya, will you settle this? Mixed or separate?"

"Mix 'em," I directed. I subscribed to the potpourri approach to gardening and life.

As the men went back to work, Evie said, "According to Roselyn, the reward for finding the chalice set up Nate for life."

"A gold chalice," Sadie sighed.

Brushing her hand through her pixie cut hair, which had grown back after brain surgery even softer and more silver-streaked than before, Evie said, "Ever since we met Nate and Roselyn by the lake, I've been trying to place him."

Larry looked up. "What do you mean?"

"I swear, Larry, he reminds me of Amelie Reece."

Jorn stopped, a petunia dangling in his gloved hand. "The Troll Lady?"

Evie nodded. "Strange. Every time I look at him, I think of her."

Suddenly, the crow from the pergola swooped down, dropped something on the wooden table beside my chair, then lifted up into the air and away. Sadie was out of the love seat in a shot and kneeling by the table. She and I exchanged looks.

"What did he bring this time?" she whispered.

It was a coin.

I held the silver coin up to the light, squinting to make out the design, and read, "Canada. Twenty-five cents. 1900. It has a hole in it. It's from a necklace or bracelet."

Larry stopped digging in the pot at his feet and rose. Stuffing his work gloves into the back pocket of his jeans, he walked over. "May I see?"

I handed him the coin. He studied it, frowned, and passed it to Evie. She too looked it over closely and gasped. "It's his," she said softly.

"Whose?" Sadie leaned against her grandmother's knees, trying to see the coin better.

Larry and Evie traded thoughtful looks. "Jacques's," Larry said.

That lured Jorn away from his pot of petunias and over to the group. "Are you sure?"

"Yes, he always wore this on a leather cord around his neck," Larry explained. "Never saw him without it."

"Why was it so important to him? Do you think it was a family heirloom?" Jorn asked.

"We never thought to ask," Evie said. "We always felt people at Whispering Spirit were entitled to their secrets."

Evie handed the coin to Sadie, who turned it over and read, stumbling over the words, "*Victoria Dei Gratia Regina.* What does that mean?"

Larry translated, "Victoria, by the grace of God, the Queen."

"A queen," Sadie whispered again, awe in her voice. "This must be valuable."

"Not now that someone's drilled a hole in it, but once . . . it's very old," Jorn said.

Silence. We were all thinking of the tragedy that had separated Jacques from his beloved coin. For some unknown reason, environmentalist Jacques Pine had sidestepped the upper Midwest until his friend Larry Skye invited him to Gabriel's Garden to help establish a pollinator way station. Who had he known here that he wanted to avoid? He'd carried bundles of cash in his backpack and a Canadian passport. From the dirt found in his satchel, we can assume he was planting milkweed plugs on land where he had no business being. And someone had shot him. Was it an accident or murder? Was it because of his illicit planting? Or had someone from his activist past caught up with him?

Jorn did not believe in the accident theory. "I'm sorry," he said to Larry and Evie, "I know he was a friend of yours, but Jacques made a lot of enemies."

Evie nodded. "Yes." She sighed. "Dear Jacques. If he was in trouble, I wish he had come to us."

As Jorn and Larry finished planting, I thought of a recent entry in the Down Dog Diary, the pages redolent with the smell of rusty pipes. It said: *Beware of that which shines. It is either magical or radioactive.*

CHAPTER 14

ANOTHER PRETTY FOR MAYA

WE SAT TOGETHER ON my red sofa, the one Jorn called a ridiculous color for a piece of furniture. Both of us had our laptops open. I'd swung my feet up in his lap, and he'd propped his laptop against them. His fingers flew across the keyboard as Bella wedged herself between my outstretched legs and the back of the sofa. I was reading Jorn's article in *The Independent.* The article started:

Saving Pollinators in Gabriel's Garden

Video game developers Larry and Evie Skye have established Sadie's Papillon Farm on 50 acres north of Gabriel's Garden to create a habitat for pollinators.

"We all need to take the plight of the pollinators

> seriously," said Larry Skye. "Humans are destroying the places where pollinators live and breed. When bees, butterflies and other insects disappear, so will our food supply. We only get one world. For the sake of our children and grandchildren, we can't afford to mess this up."

As per Heart's edict, there were no photos of Sadie accompanying the article, just an earnest-looking Larry standing in a field beginning to bloom, his hands on his hips, his serene face lifted to the sun. He looked happy, and once again, I was reminded that my father loved a mission. In some ways, he and Jacques Pine were much alike, men who never gave up when social change was on the agenda.

Jacques had wandered the countryside, from one protest march to another, planting trees or unrest, depending on the situation. While Jacques's expertise had been in revolution, in firing up people for the environmental cause, Larry's had been in delivering the message of accountability through technology. With Evie at his side, Larry had built a company founded on social responsibility. None of the video games marketed by Skyes the Limit catered to gamers who desired gratuitous violence or enjoyed cyber degradation of human beings. Heart had written that imperative into the company's mission statement, a document Evie thought was entirely unnecessary but didn't object to, for her older daughter's sake. Every Skyes the Limit game had to have Heart's stamp of motherly approval before release. After all, Sadie had been playing the company's games since she was three.

I picked up Jacques's coin from the coffee table and rubbed it between my fingers. Eventually, I would have to turn it over to Watt Holmes as evidence, but for now I kept it. Maybe

Heart was right. I did feel the crows were here for a purpose, and somehow that purpose was connected to me—and apparently, the late Jacques Pine. But what did they want me to do?

Stroking Bella's head, I said to Jorn, "Thanks for not making Larry look like a complete crazy in the article."

Continuing to type, Jorn mumbled, "It's tough, making your family sound sane."

He was sending another email to his endless supply of sources. He kept up with an inordinate number of them, in the States and beyond, in newsrooms, government offices, and law enforcement. He generously hooked up other journalists with sources of information he'd spent years developing, and they often returned the favor. He still kept his hand in affairs beyond the requirements of a small-town newspaperman. If I thought about this too much, as I lay in bed at night beside him, it worried me. Was it really possible for a globe-trotting reporter to stay put?

I nudged Jorn with my foot. He finished a sentence, punctuated with a flourish, then lifted his hands from the keyboard. "What?"

I said, "Remember the day at the butterfly farm? We both saw a gun in Nate Nelson's backpack. I can't stop thinking about that. What does that mean? Why would he have one?"

Jorn absently rubbed my ankles as he stared off into space. "Protection? Treasure hunting has always been a dangerous business. I'm sure there are competitors, thieves. People ready to swoop in on your big find."

I nodded. "I was thinking the same thing. Still, I don't like the idea of a guy with a gun hanging out with Sadie and Larry."

Jorn looked at me. "Should we tell Larry?"

I thought for a moment. There was no need to upset my father. "No," I said. "I'll take care of Nate."

"Not alone."

"I'm just going to tell him that firearms are not welcome at the butterfly farm. If Nate wants to continue to hunt there, he'll have to leave his gun at home."

"Not alone," Jorn repeated.

I rubbed Bella's head, and she began to purr. "You're as curious about him as I am."

"I would like to know what he's looking for," Jorn admitted.

"You don't think he's just taking the old metal detector out for pleasure?"

Jorn shook his head. "He definitely has a plan."

Jorn had not met Nate Nelson before seeing him at the farm, but he apparently already had an opinion of the man. "You know his type," I said.

"I know that look. He's after something, something specific, something that brought him to town. He's not your retired beachcomber happy to waste his days digging in Minnesota black dirt."

"He seems good with Sadie. And Roselyn. And his dog likes him."

Jorn's lips quirked. He didn't think much of the canine recommendation.

Jorn's laptop pinged with the arrival of an email. He punched a few keys and read the message. "Watt Holmes says there is no gun permit issued in the state of Minnesota to Nate Nelson." So Jorn was already investigating Nate and the firearm. "Watt wants to know why I'm interested."

Jorn typed a reply and showed it to me: *Just doing a feature on our local treasure hunter.*

Watt's response pinged moments later: *You'll tell me eventually, and it better be before someone gets hurt.*

"No permit here, but that doesn't preclude one elsewhere," I said. "Maybe Florida. That's where Roselyn says he's from."

Outside, the crows were quiet, for once. It was a Sunday morning, maybe they were sleeping in or reading the newspaper, like the rest of us. Quiet except for an insistent tap on the window. I looked over and saw a crow, fluttering, shiny black eyes on me. Bella's head popped up. She spotted the bird and made an acrobatic departure from the sofa, her body spread through the air in a leap for the window and the crow. She fell short.

"You'll never catch it," I told her.

I pulled my legs off Jorn's lap, disrupting his computer. "Hey—" he said.

Getting up, I went downstairs and out the back door to the patio. Jorn followed. As soon as I appeared, a black bird cawed and bopped its head. I looked down at the wooden table. Beside the basket of crow treasures was a new delivery. I picked it up. Smaller than my palm, filthy, wide-eyed and ugly. A troll keychain.

Hands in his pockets, Jorn said, "Crows bearing gifts. Creepy."

CHAPTER 15

PEBBLES IN THE POND

THAT EVENING, I SAT on the patio, legs in lotus, meditating. In my hand was the gift from this morning: the troll keychain. It was encrusted with dirt, and something had been chewing on the doll's head. I should clean it up and give it to Amelie, I thought, but instead I placed it in the basket of shinys.

Upstairs, in my apartment, Jorn was writing the Troll Lady story, a project he had been avoiding until his uncle Al called to remind him that he was looking forward to Jorn's "human-interest" piece on Amelie Reece and her troll doll collection. To which, Jorn responded: "You know how they say dog owners grow to look like their dogs? This woman looks like her dolls."

Taking a breath, I gently pushed to the back of my consciousness the sounds of the evening breeze ruffling the trees, the dusk conversations of the birds, Jorn's mutterings drifting from the open window (he talked a lot to himself when he wrote). I slowed racing thoughts, sat in the "pond of serene nothingness," as Guru Bob used to call it, and waited for the fish of direction to nibble my toes. Eventually, a sense of purpose would find me. It might not be today; it might be in a week. But I had to put in the work now. Turn over the soil of the mind for something to grow.

And into this calm horticulture, I felt a presence arrive. I opened my eyes and found Michael and Lissa Donovan watching me. They apparently had come in the front entrance, walked through the yoga studio and out the back to the patio.

"Don't you ever lock your doors?" Michael grumbled. Four-year-old Lissa took a step closer to him. Shy, she considered me.

I slowly surfaced from meditation, unwrapping my legs from lotus and standing. "I have an open-door policy."

Lissa continued to watch me as I walked toward them. I smiled at her. She did not smile back.

For a few moments, we stood in the doorway between my studio and the patio, eyeing each other. Then, Lissa said, "You have a lot of birds."

I lifted my shoulders and said with absolute assurance, "They won't hurt you." The crows were stones tossed into the lake of my life, creating ripples. And now before me were two more pebbles about to change my life. I felt the nibble of direction.

I motioned them to follow me. "C'mon. I'm hungry."

I led them through the yoga studio, up the spiral staircase, to the kitchen table where Jorn was working. He looked up and raised an eyebrow as, without a hello, the two kids slipped into chairs at the table and stared at him. I rummaged through the cabinet for cookies. "Chocolate chip or chocolate chip?"

Lissa voted, "Chocolate chip." Michael's expression said I was *so* not funny.

I placed a plate of cookies in the middle of the table. "Milk or lemonade?"

Lissa said, "Lemonade."

Michael said, "She'll have milk."

I poured milk for all of us. Jorn grimaced at his glass but didn't say anything. He watched the two siblings reach for cookies. I joined them, took a bite, and said casually, "What's up?"

Michael and Lissa exchanged looks. Lissa shook her head at him, but Michael had already decided, by their very presence here, on a course of action. "Can you keep Lissa for a while?"

"No, Mikey." Lissa scooted her chair closer to his.

Michael told her, "I have to take care of Mom, Liss."

"But . . ."

"Michael," I said, "what's happened?"

Lissa shook her head at her brother again. Leaving her second cookie half-eaten, she slid off her chair and was at his side, leaning against him. Michael rubbed her back, and she leaned closer. "It's okay," he whispered to her. "It'll be okay."

I waited and, finally, Michael lifted his head. Our eyes met. He said, "It's Dad. He's–he's mad . . ."

Lissa turned to me. "Madder than ever."

I took a deep calming breath, thinking about the bruise I'd

once seen on Margot Donovan's wrist, about the guns in that house. "Why is he mad, Lissa?"

She leaned slightly toward me and whispered, "Daddy yelled at me. He never yells at me."

"I should be so lucky," muttered Michael.

I kept my attention on Lissa. "Yelled at you, Lissa? About what?"

"I did a bad thing." Lissa ducked her head. "It's my fault."

"No," Michael reassured her. Michael looked at me over the top of Lissa's head, and I knew this was one secret he was not going to share. Watching the siblings huddled together, I didn't press for more information.

"I don't like this scary daddy," said Lissa.

"Look, I gotta get back there," Michael said. Whatever had happened had disturbed the Donovan children enough that they had fled their home. Jorn shut his laptop with a click. There was no way Jorn and I were letting Michael face this situation alone.

Michael started to rise, but Jorn placed a hand on his shoulder. "Tell us what you know, Michael," Jorn said. Part rebellion, part scared, Michael stood there for a moment, then shook off Jorn's hand. His shoulders drooping, he sat back down with a sigh. Between the immense responsibility he felt for his sister and mother and keeping the family secrets, he carried a heavy burden for a kid.

Jorn, accustomed to sneaking into pockets of information like a thief, came at the subject in a different direction. "Is this something that just blew up suddenly or has it been brewing?"

Michael thought for a long time, still unsure about trusting us with the whole story. Finally, he said, "Dad's been acting weird for a while. It started about the time that guy was killed."

"Jacques Pine?" I asked. "Is your dad still angry about you finding him?"

Michael cast a glance toward Lissa, who had returned to her chair and was sipping her milk. "Yeah, but this is something more."

Lissa piped up, obviously mimicking her father, "He's mad about those damn—" Michael cleared his throat. "Darn seeds."

"Seeds?" Jorn and I looked at each other, puzzled.

"It's business." Michael scrunched up his face in thought. "Something to do with the seeds in some project. It's a work thing."

Smelling a story, Jorn asked, "What about them?"

"I don't understand it. And that's not what's important now." Once again, Michael started to stand, and once again Jorn stopped him. "I need to take care of Mom. I can't leave her alone. With him."

I said, "Let me check on your mom."

Michael hesitated.

"Your sister needs you here, Michael. We'll help your mother," I promised.

"It's not your job," Michael objected, but it was half-hearted. Deep inside, he was still just a kid who would much rather let adults handle adult messes.

Jorn said, "Stay here with Lissa. Have some more cookies. We'll check out the situation, make sure everything's okay."

"But Mom—"

Bella leapt up on the table. "Kitty!" Lissa cried and reached for the cat.

Taking advantage of Bella's diversion, Jorn and I rose. As we started for the stairs, I issued instructions to Michael, "Don't let Bella drink the milk. It'll make her barf. She's lactose intolerant."

Michael said, "Weird cat."

When I looked back, Lissa was cuddling Bella, but Michael's eyes were intent on us. I nodded in reassurance.

On the ride to Michael's house, Jorn said, "Should we call Watt? Domestic situations can escalate fast."

How could we do that? Michael had come to us, not the police. I said, "Not yet."

We pulled up in front of the Donovan house. The drapes were closed, as usual. Walking up the sidewalk, we had just reached the steps when a sound sent us diving for the perfect flower beds.

The bark of a gun rang out from inside the Donovan house.

CHAPTER 16

SHOOTING WATER BUFFALO IN A BARREL

"NOW DO WE CALL?" Jorn whispered, but I had grabbed his hand and already was leading him toward the back of the house. Although some would consider it a fatal flaw, I have always instinctively run toward trouble rather than away from it. Somewhere in my heart, even when I'm scared to death like now, a drum beats: *Something has to be done, and you're here, Maya, so it has to be you.*

Staying low, we crept below the windows and rounded the corner of the house. We stepped into Margot's rebellious back garden and edged toward the French doors. On the patio table was an open book and a glass, overturned and branded with lipstick. I tried the door and found it unlocked. We stepped into the mudroom and navigated through the kitchen and into the dining room. As we tiptoed toward the living room, we heard angry voices.

"My God, Margot, do you know how much that water buffalo cost me?"

"Is that all you're worried about? A hole in your precious water buffalo? It could have been our daughter!"

Jorn and I halted and peeked around the corner of the dining room doorway into the living room. Margot stood, arms crossed, chin lifted, facing off with her husband. The room was much as I remembered it: the animals with vacant eyes, the depressing energy of death, the dark wood paneling, more dead animals in the form of the plush leather furniture shining in the light of the overhead chandelier (itself crafted of elk antlers). On a desk by the window were a small brass lamp, strewn papers, a whiskey decanter, a half-full cut glass tumbler with no edging of lipstick, and a handgun.

Chris Donovan lifted his arms in frustration and dropped them. "So I stepped away for a phone call. It was work."

"It's always work."

"I was only gone a second, Margot. Lissa shouldn't have been playing with the gun in the first place. She knows that."

"You left it right on the desk." Margot's voice rose, incredulous. "Loaded."

"I was about to *clean* it."

"Oh Chris—" Margot's voice trembled, and suddenly she clutched her chest as if the thought of her child with a gun had stopped her heart.

With an impatient tone, Donovan said, "You're making a big deal out of nothing. As usual. She's okay. I took it away from her."

"You asshole, my baby had one of your goddamn guns!"

Raking his hands through his hair in frustration, Donovan shouted, "Nothing happened!"

"Guns. Everywhere!" She swept her arm out. "These animals—"

"Hey, I worked hard for every one of these trophies."

"Dead. They're all dead!" Margot shook her head again and again.

Donovan tried to put his arms around his wife. "Get control of yourself, Margot."

Margot pushed him away. "That's your answer to everything. 'Control yourself, Margot.' I don't want to get control."

"It's over, Margot. Mike and Lissa know the rules. It won't happen again. Look, I'm sorry, okay? I have a lot on my mind. I never thought—"

"No, you didn't." She nodded at the water buffalo on the wall, a note of satisfaction in her voice. "Well, now you know how easily accidents can happen."

Donovan stabbed the air with his finger, inches from Margot's face. "This was no accident. You shot that buffalo on purpose."

"Right between the eyes," she said with pride.

That stopped Donovan.

After a moment, he asked, incredulous, "Did you imagine that was me?"

Margot leaned in, face to face, daring. "What if I did?"

Donovan looked stunned.

Then suddenly, her voice filled with weary defeat, Margot cried, "You care more about these stupid trophies than your own family!"

"Don't be ridiculous."

"It's true!"

Donovan lunged for his wife, and she squeaked. It was time for our entrance. When we walked in, Chris Donovan had his wife's upper arms in a white-knuckled grip, and she was leaning away. Jorn cleared his throat loudly. Both Donovans froze then turned toward us. I saw a flash of relief, quickly covered by wariness, in Margot's eyes.

"We heard a shot," Jorn said. "Is everything okay?"

Donovan dropped his hands, stepped back, and said, "What the hell are you doing here?"

There was so much wrong with the energy in this room I could barely endure it. Still, I tiptoed around a zebra skin on the hardwood floor and approached Margot. The smell of her amply applied perfume hit me before I reached her.

"Margot, it's Maya from the yoga studio."

"I-I—" Something clicked in Margot's brain. She said, "You're–you're Mike's friends. You brought his car back."

Jorn joined me, also stepping around the zebra on the floor and placing himself between us and Chris Donovan. "Mrs. Donovan, are you all right?"

"Of course, she's all right," Donovan said in disgust. He was a fit man, the type who worked out in a gym near his office at lunch or before he came home at night. His hair was slicked back and made Jorn's shaggy mess appear even more unkempt than usual.

Jorn persisted. "Mrs. Donovan—"

Margot quickly glanced at her husband. "Yes, yes, everything's fine." She smoothed her unmovable hair.

Donovan stared hard at his wife, then turned to us. "I was cleaning my gun, and it went off. By *accident*."

Jorn looked at the gun laying on the desk. "By accident?" Jorn said, disbelief in his voice.

The Donovans remained silent, she not meeting our eyes, he daring us to question him further.

I said, "Margot, your children are at my house."

Her gaze flew to mine; she stiffened.

She and Donovan said at the same time, "What?"

"They were scared," Jorn said.

I kept my attention on Margot. "They're safe, Margot."

Margot searched my eyes for the truth. Then her shoulders relaxed. As if it was suddenly all too much, she spun away, walked straight across the room to the desk, and downed the rest of the drink in the glass. She carefully placed the empty glass beside the gun on the polished desk and wiped the edge of her lip with her little finger.

I looked at Donovan. He was watching his wife, and I saw the muscles in his jaw tense.

Suddenly, he focused on Jorn and me. "I sent them to their rooms. What the hell are they doing at your house?"

I felt Jorn edge closer to me. Neither of us knew what Chris Donovan was capable of. I sent out calming vibes.

Jorn said, "They said you're upset, Donovan. Yelling."

There was the clink of glass. Margot was pouring herself another drink. She took a swig, turned, leaned against the desk, and noticed us all staring at her. She saluted her husband with the drink.

"You've had enough," Donovan snapped.

"How would you know? One glass is your limit, not mine." Margot sipped again. Then she tipped her head toward Jorn and me and said in a confiding tone, "It's his work. Work is so stressful." Cradling the glass in her hands, she smiled at Donovan. "Isn't it, darling?"

"Margot." A warning in his voice.

"Kids notice stress." With each sip, Margot grew calmer, more philosophical. She asked me, "Maya, yoga's good for stress, isn't it?"

"Yes," I said.

Donovan neatened his polo shirt, tucking it into his slim waist, smoothing his creased chinos. He saw me staring at the necklace he was wearing and hurriedly gathered up the silver chain and tucked it back inside his shirt.

Margot carried on. "Maybe you should try yoga, Chris. As a stress reliever."

Donovan stopped organizing his clothes and gave Margot a stern look. "Enough."

"I mean it's got to be easier than shooting something."

"Margot!"

Donovan strode across the room. He snatched the glass from Margot's hand and placed it on the desk with a snap. Then he rounded on Jorn and me. "Well, this family therapy session has been fun, but it's now time for you two to get the fuck out."

Margot tsked-tsked Donovan's language. With his back turned, she reclaimed the glass.

Donovan ignored her. He speared us with a stare. "And send my kids home."

After a pause, I nodded. "Your son's smart. Protective. But he's still just a kid." Before Donovan could reply, I continued, "Do you really think you should be taking him on a safari this summer?"

"What?" Margot's glass dropped to the thick Aubusson rug with a thud.

Donovan threw me a look that could kill.

"Are you insane?" Margot swung her husband around and clutched his shirt. "No! I won't allow it."

"We'll discuss this later, Margot."

"We'll discuss this now."

"Margot, get a grip."

"You promised."

"Not now." He pulled at her arms to release his shirt, but she held on.

"He's a child. A child!"

"Hunting will make a man of him," Donovan replied.

"I don't think killing makes someone a man," I said.

Donovan glared at me. "Get out. Now."

Jorn tapped my arm and motioned toward the door. After a long moment, I nodded. I'd seen Margot Donovan stand up to her husband. She might not be able to do it for herself yet, but she was willing to take him on for her children. And that was a start. We headed for the front door with its column of dead-bolt locks. I paused at the door and looked back at Donovan. "By the way, did you know the man who was killed? Jacques Pine?"

Silence.

Donovan studied us for several long moments then finally said, "No."

Outside, in the twilight, Jorn held the gate open for me. "He's lying."

Jorn the reporter had a nose for this kind of thing. I agreed with him, and not just because of the dark vibe pouring off Chris Donovan.

"Yes," I said. "Did you notice his necklace? It has a coin on it, just like the one Jacques wore."

CHAPTER 17

ON A MISSION FROM GOD

GRANDMOTHER SYLVIA HAD PLANNED a trip to the Minnesota Zoo. This was a "granddaughters-only" outing, much to Larry's disappointment. She instructed Heart, Sadie, and me to pick her up at eight o'clock sharp because, as Gran pointed out, "Much later than that and half the day's gone." Then she ordered me to drive, assigning lead-foot Heart to sit in the back with Sadie.

Leaving Larry standing on the porch looking like someone had pulled the plug on his computers, Gran walked toward the car, ready for an adventure in one of her usual summer Chanel suits, the ever-present handbag, a dignified but useful sunhat, and designer sneakers. She parked herself in the passenger seat. I complimented her on her comfortable yet stylish footwear, a plaid design made of tweed and calfskin and stamped with the Chanel logo.

"This is not my first zoo," she said.

"Really," said Sadie from the backseat. "What's your favorite animal?"

As I pulled away from the curb, Gran buckled her shoulder harness and squared the handbag on her lap. Settled, she answered, "I prefer the grizzlies, but if you don't have any of those, I'll take sharks."

My gaze met Heart's in the rearview mirror. "Why does that not surprise me?" Heart muttered.

Sadie didn't hear her. She was rattling on about how she likes different animals for different reasons, "Sea otters because they're cute and cuddly . . ."

"You cannot cuddle a sea otter," Gran said in that tone of voice that probably had been insisting on precise language since Larry could put two words together.

"Yes, you can," Sadie shot back. "Otters cuddle all the time."

Gran turned and, peering over the top of her glasses, said, "They eat fish, you know. They have fish breath."

In the rearview mirror, I saw a stubborn look pass over Sadie's face, but Heart shook her head at her daughter. After a moment, Sadie continued as if Gran had never cut in, "I like the jellyfish because they're graceful; pronghorn because they're fast; the leopard because it has spots . . ."

While the litany went on in the backseat, I sneaked a peek at my grandmother. "Grizzlies, huh?"

"Your grandfather once hunted grizzlies in Alaska with his father—a family tradition apparently," said Gran, her eyes back on the road with an occasional glance at the speedometer. "He was determined to get one, but when he saw it, he couldn't shoot it. Couldn't go for the kill. He called me that night, so apologetic, and said, 'Sylvia, like you, it was just too damn beautiful.' That was the night I decided I was going to marry him."

We rode for several miles in silence.

Finally, I said, "I think I would have liked Grandfather."

Gran huffed. "Of course you would have."

The Minnesota Zoo covers nearly five hundred acres in a corner of Apple Valley, a southern suburb of the Twin Cities. There are no elephants or giraffes, which Sadie thinks is "a tragic mistake in planning," but there are hundreds of other animals, many of them endangered. Saving those who were about to disappear was part of the zoo's mission.

Under solid blue skies and a constant breeze that softened the heat reflecting off the concrete paths, Sadie and Heart vanished into the crowds, leaving me on Gran patrol. I stood at the back of the Russian grizzly exhibit, a cave-like structure with walls of glass overlooking the bears' habitat, and watched Gran watch the bears. She stood, her posture straight, her handbag dangling from her arm, her demeanor calm as all around chaos swirled. Parents rocked strollers; kids of all sizes chased each other and kissed the thick glass of the habitat. When the chaperones and stroller-driving parents shepherded their charges along to the next exhibit, we were alone with the grizzlies. I walked up beside Gran and breathed in a moment of quiet.

Before us, in the dirt, a bear napped in the sun, curled in a shaggy ball, while another tore into a stump with lethal claws.

A third bear was cooling off in the pool at the front of the habitat. He swam back and forth, occasionally stopping to surface and gnaw on a toy—a big, hard plastic donut that looked like it should have been indestructible. The bear was demolishing it.

Without taking her eyes from the giant furry beast sitting in water up to its chest, Gran began to talk. "Young Lawrence is much like his father. He wouldn't be able to kill a grizzly either."

My grandmother had spent much of her life living at a distance from her only relatives: us. But now she was thrusting her way into our world with her inflexible opinions and haute couture expectations. While Evie might feel as if a cloud of locusts had descended, I didn't sense that Grandmother was here to cause trouble. She did, however, have a reason for being here; I just didn't know what it was.

I asked, "Why do you like zoos, Gran?"

A smile slipped across my grandmother's face. "Your grandfather and I spent our honeymoon visiting zoos. My mother-in-law was apoplectic. She could understand a grand tour of the continent or a cruise around the world. That was something a Skye would do. But zoos—that was beyond the pale."

I laughed. "You must have gotten along great."

"She was an old bat," Gran snapped.

"Really," I said, not daring to draw parallels with Evie and Gran's tumultuous relationship.

Gran looked at me with suspicion. "But Lawrence and I didn't care. Tigers in London. Pandas in China. Elephants in India. What a trip. Of course, we didn't know anything about conservation back then. We never even considered how unhappy some of those poor creatures must have been, living in captivity, often in abominable conditions."

It was hard to imagine my imposing grandmother agreeing to such a wild and unconventional honeymoon. My grandfather must have been quite a persuasive character, and she must have been very much in love.

The bear that had been sharpening its long claws on the tree trunk loped over to the sleeping bear and took a swipe at its head. An affectionate invitation to play. The sleeping bear rolled away. Another swipe. This one generated a reaction, a roar and the baring of teeth that sent the bothersome roomie galloping up the hill and back to the mauled tree trunk.

Gran said, "After young Lawrence was born, my husband became quite interested in conservation. He had a great sense of responsibility for future generations. He was obsessed with the National Geographic Society and its work. I am still a supporter. As a child, young Lawrence spent hours paging through his father's huge library of *National Geographic* magazines."

That explained Larry's love of nature and his own dedication to preserving it. I said, "Then, you must have taken Larry to zoos too."

My grandmother didn't respond immediately. I turned to her, but she was facing the grizzly. Her forehead was wrinkled as if in pain. "I loved those trips, just the three of us. Of course, my mother-in-law was sure young Lawrence would fall into a lion's den or be swallowed by a boa constrictor. Then Lawrence passed and . . ." Her voice faded. My grandfather, a successful California corporate lawyer, died of a heart attack when Larry was ten.

After a few moments, she swept her hand down her jacket, as if tidying up the memories, and said, "Anyway, there was always a nanny to take young Lawrence to the zoo."

Remembering Larry's downcast expression when he learned he was not coming with us, I said, "But I think he would have rather gone to the zoo with you, Gran."

"That was long ago, Maya."

I could feel my grandmother looking at me, but I kept my focus on the bears. I said, "There seems to be an unspoken cease-fire between you and Evie, and I haven't seen you bullying Larry as much. Are you mellowing, Gran?"

She gave a start, then tried to hide it with a lift of her head. I called this her Queen pose. It was supposed to put me in my place. "I don't know what you're talking about," she said.

"What is the real purpose of this surprise visit?"

Silence.

"You know," I said, "Evie forgave you a long time ago."

"Really. Then why did she keep my family from me?"

"She forgave you, but she didn't trust you."

Grandmother turned away. "Is it a crime to want to be near my only family?"

The last time my grandmother visited she claimed she was called here by God, that God had told her our family would need her in some mysterious way. That was the time Evie was shot.

Suddenly, I figured it out. "You're on another mission from God."

Gran faced me. "Yes." She looked me in the eye, daring me to laugh. "I know my son has you mixed up in this Jacques tree business."

"His name was Pine. Jacques Pine."

"A ridiculous alias," Gran sniffed.

I laughed. Gran's voice hardened with conviction. "I'm here because the Almighty says there's going to be trouble. This family needs me. He also said you shouldn't be chasing murderers."

"She did not."

"*He* did too. Leave the investigating to the police."

I reassured her. "Don't worry, Gran."

"I'll worry if I want to, and I came prepared." She patted the handbag she never let out of her sight.

"I hope you don't have a gun in there," I said. "Evie wouldn't like it."

My religious grandmother pulled out a tiny bottle from her handbag. Holy oil. The same oil she had given me to press to Evie's chest when she was in a coma. Gran believed the blessed oil had healing powers.

She showed me the bottle then slipped it back into her handbag.

"It's better than a gun."

CHAPTER 18

SHOOTING CROW

MUCH HAD CHANGED SINCE we'd planted Sadie's butterfly sanctuary. As I sat in meditation on a knoll, I felt the warmth of the ground beneath me. The July milkweed was as high as my nose. Wildflowers brushed my arms. Insect voices alternately flared and hummed. My eyes were closed, and it felt like the entire world was trying to crawl inside me. I did nothing. I waited—for the insects' discourse to fade away, for the wildflowers to still in the wind, for calm and clarity to visit me. I waited for the vortex to swallow me.

And then I heard it. A gunshot.

It startled the woods into a moment of silence. Then came another shot and the skies screamed.

I told myself it was just someone blasting the heck out of a target pinned to bales of hay in the backyard. But my intuition—and the crows—told me otherwise. Chaos blistered the skies, birds swooping, warning. Flee, they cried. Flee.

I leapt up and ran for my car. Sliding into the driver's seat, I fired up the engine and rolled down the window. Where was it coming from? I had a general idea of direction, but still asked Spirit to guide me.

I sped down the county road, leaving Larry's land, and quickly coming upon Frank Hollister's farm. The shots had come from there. I wheeled into the dusty gravel drive and raced up to the Hollister farmhouse. As I was getting out of the car, Louisa Hollister burst out of the house. We ran toward each other. Meeting in the middle, I reached for her. "Louisa, are you okay?"

Another shot. Closer.

"It's Frank." She whirled and took off toward the red barn. I followed her.

As we rounded the corner of the barn, I saw Frank, rifle to shoulder, eye squinting down the barrel, shooting into the air. The skies over the fields were a swirling mass of black wings and confusion.

Frank was killing crows.

"Frank, goldarned it. Stop!" Louisa shouted. "Stop it!"

Frank ignored her.

I saw him miss, once, twice. Then I watched a bird tumble to the Earth.

"No!" I shouted and started for Frank.

"Maya!" Louisa's hand shot out to stop me, but I sidestepped her.

Frank got off more shots.

I tackled him. Instinctively, I grabbed the hot barrel of the rifle, to protect us both. Frank and I wrestled and rolled on the ground.

Then suddenly, hard jets of cold water hit us.

We froze and both looked up at Louisa, standing over us with a dripping garden hose. "Now, stop this nonsense, both of you. Frank Hollister, you're acting crazy. And Maya, what were you thinking? You coulda been killed tackling an idiot with a gun."

Frank and I awkwardly untangled from each other and sat for a moment in the grass, catching our breath. Water from my braid trickled down my drenched tank, and my jeans felt wet and clingy. Frank looked like a soaked owl; the eyes behind his old half-frame glasses blinked and tufts of gray hair sprouted from under his feed cap. Slowly we rose, Frank offering me a hand.

"What are you doing, Frank?" I swiped the cold water from my face. My hand hurt from its interaction with the hot rifle barrel.

He glared at me. "I'm doing whatever I want on *my* property." Turning to his wife, he said, "Goldarned it, Louisa, now I gotta change my shirt."

"The crows, Frank, why are you shooting at the crows?" I persisted.

"I've had it. This is the worst I've ever seen 'em. All over town. All over my fields. Eating my corn. Laughing at me. They just ignore my scarecrow." Furious, he stabbed a shaking finger in the direction of a straw man in faded overalls and raggedy sleeves; instead of a head, there was a Halloween mask of the Grinch tucked under a worn cap. "My crops are goin' to hell. And the prices are already lower than a snake's belly. I got taxes to pay. I gotta put food on the table."

"It's not right, Frank," I said.

Frank looked ready to explode. "Right? I'll tell you what's not right—"

Louisa reached out to him, but he evaded her touch.

He pointed a chunky, crooked finger at me. "Look, I appreciate Larry taking that land off my hands. Helped pay some bills. But that don't give *you people* the right to dictate to the rest of us. Just because you got money, you come in here and try to change everything."

I was shocked. "You people—"

Frank carried on, ignoring me. "You can play with your land. Fart around with your weeds. Let it go to hell. Good Minnesota soil. Well, I ain't got that luxury."

Then he turned and stomped into the cornfield, feed cap pulled low, rifle cradled in his arm.

I looked at Louisa, whose worried gaze followed her husband. Then, she sighed and said, "Come on in. I'll get you a towel."

I followed Louisa to the house, a dingy white homestead standing forlorn amid the fields. Close up, I saw the peeling paint and the missing shingles on the roof. The listing screen door groaned as we entered a porch crowded with boxes, two rickety chairs, an old card table, and an assortment of boots, shoes, and coats. Christmas lights escaped from one box; another was overflowing with beer bottles and crushed pop cans.

Louisa saw me eyeing the collection of cans and bottles. "When we visit his sister in Iowa, we take them for the deposit. Every bit helps."

This had been the home of Hollisters for generations. Through a doorway to the living room, I saw mismatched chairs and a sun-faded sofa. Old sheers hung at the windows, and water-stained wallpaper curled in the corners. On the walls were aging photos of serious people standing stiffly in housedresses and work clothes.

Pulling a towel from a closet, Louisa handed it to me, then crossed to the old refrigerator. She poured two glasses of lemonade, added ice, and set one in front of me. I wiped my face and arms with the towel and wrung out my braid. We both sat, picked up our lemonade, and sipped. The big, scarred kitchen table dominated a room that, like the living room, probably hadn't been updated since before Louisa was married. She cooked in the shadow of Frank's ancestors but had found small ways to make her mark. A regular at the local yard sales, Louisa the reader had stuffed kitchen shelves meant for cookbooks with used paperback novels, mysteries and romances mostly.

Relaxing into her chair, her shoulders slumped, she said, "What a day."

Wiry but deceptively strong, Louisa Hollister could twist the head off a chicken, wrestle baskets of berries from thorny bushes, and can more tomatoes than anyone would ever want to eat. There was a wave to her faded auburn hair, liberally streaked with gray. Once a beauty, Louisa now carried a well-earned grace in her demeanor and a lifetime of struggle in her bones.

I remained silent.

"It's Fritz's birthday today. My baby's twenty-five." She summoned up a grin. "Celebrating out on the big blue sea." There was a yearning in her voice, the tone of a woman who had never seen the ocean.

The Hollisters had lost three babies before Fritz surprised

them in their forties. He was the miracle child. Frank had taught Fritz how to shoot and throw a baseball. Louisa had taught him to always carry a book. In a photo on the wall next to a child's clay handprint, Fritz's long red hair was wild, wavier than his mother's. Although I had never seen Frank smile, Fritz must have inherited that grin from him. There was a stubbornness to it.

"He called this morning. Fritz did. Phone reception was lousy. Out on some Greenpeace boat. He sounded so happy. Said he was doing good work, which only irked the dickens out of Frank."

"Why?"

"It was the same old argument. When you coming home? When you gonna look after our land instead of other people's? When you gonna stop saving some damn fish nobody's ever heard of?" I could hear Frank's voice in Louisa's words. She looked around the tidy yet haggard kitchen, suddenly embarrassed for airing the family linen.

I nodded. "I did some crazy stuff in my twenties too." *Like accidentally kill a man who was beating a woman in an alley, then hiding in India for a year.*

"Every family has its secrets," Louisa agreed. She raised the perspiring glass and rested it against her cheek. She closed her eyes, her weariness filling the room.

I imagined it was hard for Louisa to find balance in her life, juggling her husband's anger and her son's determination to walk his own path. When she opened her eyes, they pleaded for some understanding. "Frank gets lost sometimes. He misses Fritz. And now I'm working at Northern Lights. He hates that. Hates that Val is working by his side and not

Fritz and me made. Well, I been readin' on the internet, and they say crows are scared of dead crows."

"You're going to hang them up?" I was shocked. "Display them?"

"Oh, Frank," Louisa whispered.

"Frank," I said, "Don't do this. It's cruel."

"Cruel! They're just birds, not good for nothin'. Trash birds. If you ever stepped foot on a farm long enough to know where all the food you eat comes from, you would know that life is hard. Death happens."

"In this case, Frank, murder happened," I retorted.

The old farmer stared at me, his expression hard. "My farm. My sky," he said stubbornly.

Louisa stepped toward her husband, a hand out in supplication. "Frank, please. Not on this day."

Her softly spoken words struck Frank, and he flinched. The couple looked at each other, something private passing between them. Frank whispered, "He coulda come home, Louisa. For his birthday, he coulda come home."

She was close now, near enough to touch his arm. "Maybe for Thanksgiving. We'll send him money for a ticket."

She took the knife from his hand and let it drop to the ground. "Today we'll bake a cake. I took off work." Frank dropped the rope. She threaded her arm through his and guided him toward the house. As they walked away, leaning into each other, I heard Louisa say, "Remember the day he was born?"

When the porch door closed behind them, I gathered up the

dead crows in a blanket from my car and drove to the butterfly sanctuary. There I gently moved the crows to a spot on the knoll and placed them on the ground, beaks toward each other, bodies pointing in the four directions of the compass. When I was finished, I backed away several yards and lowered myself to the ground in Kneeling Pose. Also called Thunderbolt, this pose helped calm and stabilize the mind.

I whispered a prayer to Spirit.

Then I waited.

Eventually, a single crow fluttered in and sent out a call. Soon it was joined by dozens of its comrades. They filled the trees and covered the ground around the dead. The air became a shroud heavy with their cries of mourning. They were grieving friends, perhaps a brother or sister. I'd read that crows remember family members. A couple of birds dropped twigs on the dead.

I don't know how long I sat with the crows. After a while, I closed my eyes and emptied my mind, all feeling swept into the vortex of this place. Slowly thoughts drifted in. I thought of Frank's fury and fear. I recalled the uneasy glances in Northern Lights, the whispers I pretended not to hear. No one had been arrested for the murder of Jacques Pine, and the people in a town that seldom locked its doors were now throwing their dead bolts.

As Louisa said, fear always looked for the easiest target.

I opened my eyes.

Evening was nearing and the crows had finished paying their respects.

With a feeling of helplessness in my chest, I stiffly rose and buried the crows that Frank had killed.

CHAPTER 19

AU REVOIR, JACQUES PINE

LARRY AND EVIE WANTED to plant a tree—a blue spruce in honor of Jacques Pine—on Sadie's Papillon Farm. They sent email invitations to a handful of old friends, activists who had stood beside them and Jacques in times of resistance. It was supposed to be a simple memorial, a small affair, a fond farewell. But somehow word spread along protest lines and cyber and telephonic trails. Much like the crows had done, strangers descended on Gabriel's Garden. They booked up the Strawberry B&B and set up tents and campers in the sanctuary fields that had yet to be planted. The Reverend Harold Miley offered his parking lot beside the Chapel of the Forgiving Heart for the overflow.

The memorial began at two in the afternoon on a Saturday

in July. Less than two months earlier Jacques had lain in this very field dying. Now the spirit of the place was clean and bright. About two dozen people milled around the butterfly farm, every one of them stopping to have a word with Larry and Evie. My mother looked at ease among these people. She waved away mentions of her own dance with death a year ago. Occasionally, Larry, who kept his arm draped around Evie's waist, leaned close and whispered a name in her ear, and she smiled and apologized for not remembering the face of an old friend.

I remembered many of the women—kind, pragmatic maternal figures who wore organic cotton and baked their own bread. They'd held the hand of a much younger me in protest marches or played checkers with me on the porch at Whispering Spirit.

The men were a hodgepodge, ranging from hippies to politicians. I remembered some, like Ran, the bony old man whom Sadie claimed "smelled funny" and who wandered past us, tired but unbending, in a fog of weed. In limp clothes and a straggly ponytail, Ran was the polar opposite of the California state representative, whom I did not know. Depending on who you talked to, the man in the short-sleeved plaid shirt and ironed chinos had either sold out or was working from within to change the system.

Others were strangers to me—younger females and males who clutched cups of expensive coffee and wore quick-drying, high-tech outdoor clothes. They carried resistance like a banner, and the air around them hummed with impatience and entitlement. "Let's get on with it," their strong, tanned bodies said. "This is our world. We're here to change it. Now."

A pod of kids buzzed by, Sadie among them, the wildflowers brushing her sun-kissed legs. These, I thought, were the future resisters.

The party geared up. A bear-like man wearing a native-style shirt and headband swung his long braid behind his back and launched a beat on a drum. A young willowy woman with a guitar joined in, her bare feet tapping the ground. Heads began to bob and bodies sway.

I spotted Sheriff Watt Holmes, standing apart from the crowd, watching the action. He was not in uniform. I walked over to him.

"What are you doing here?" I asked. "Think the killer will show up at the funeral?"

"They always do on TV," Watt joked, tucking his thumbs into his jeans pockets. "This is quite a reunion." He was studying the group with cop eyes. People were greeting old friends, talking, slapping backs.

Watching the California legislator embrace Ran, the smelly hippie, I said, "Comrades in arms."

"Yeah, I didn't know about this side of Larry and Evie," he said.

Since I really didn't want Watt looking too closely at any of these people, perhaps finding an outstanding warrant or two, I tried to distract him. I asked, "Has anyone claimed Jacques's body yet?"

He turned to me with a stony expression. "No comment."

"Then someone has."

"No comment."

"Do you know where he got all that money?"

"No comment."

"Any suspects?"

He didn't even grace that with an answer. Good thing Jorn walked up because I was running out of ways to embarrass myself.

"Watt," Jorn said, "what a surprise. Expecting to catch the killer here?"

The sheriff sighed. "You all watch too much crime drama."

Jorn laughed. "Actually, I'm glad you're here. I wanted to ask you something."

"Here we go again," said Watt.

Jorn continued, "I heard your office received an anonymous donation to pay for the cremation of Jacques Pine."

Watt stiffened. "Who told you that?"

"Then it's true," Jorn said.

Watt's brow furrowed. He lowered his voice. "Yeah, but that's off the record."

"You have no idea who the donor is?"

Watt's eyes went to Evie and Larry. "They were my first guess, but they deny it. No fingerprints on the envelope. Just cash left on the doorstep."

I asked, "Someone with a guilty conscience?"

"I don't know," snapped Watt, letting his frustration slip through. "The case is getting colder by the day. If it was someone who followed Jacques here and did the job, they are long gone. We'll never catch them. And that's not for publication, Jorn."

"Could be a local," Jorn mused.

"That's even scarier," I said.

"Yeah." Watt rubbed his neck. "The donation saves the county burial expenses, but it doesn't help solve the case."

We stood in silence, each of us considering the implications of never finding Jacques Pine's killer, what it might do to the town's psyche.

As people walked by, we heard snippets of conversation.

"I haven't seen you since . . . Selma. Bloody Sunday."

"Remember, when they turned the water cannons on us . . ."

"That shit hurts, man . . ."

"Where you been lately?"

"Buggin' the loggers up in Canada. You?"

"Demonstrating in New York. The People's Climate March."

Watt shook his head. "I really hope I don't have to arrest any of these people."

Jorn and I left Watt, the lone law enforcement presence, to his silent observations. As we walked across the field, someone grabbed me from behind and whirled me in the air. I screamed and laughed at the same time.

A voice said, "Maya Girl, how the heck are you?"

When I was set down, I found myself smiling up into a handsome dark face with one front tooth missing. A cascade of long braids spread like a cape over his shoulders, and there was a silver earring in one lobe. Soft eyes laughed at me through rimless glasses. Angelo. When I was a child, he broke my heart with stories of growing up in segregated southern classrooms with dirt floors and woodstoves, using schoolbooks the white schools had discarded. He'd marched against racism with the disciples of Martin Luther King Jr. in the South and to save ancient forests with Larry and Evie in the Northwest. In his sixties now, Angelo was still strong and big, an unflappable and old spirit.

"You never got those fixed," I said, nodding at the teeth that met with a nightstick during one protest and lost.

He laughed. "Nah, they'd just get knocked out again."

I introduced Angelo to Jorn. "Jorn, Angelo is my guardian angel."

"Pleased to meet you." Jorn held out his hand to Angelo.

Angelo shook it then slid an arm around my shoulders. "Somebody has to keep her out of trouble."

"Don't I know it," Jorn said.

Angelo laughed, a joyful sound that always made heads turn. Leaning into him, I smiled.

"How did he become your guardian angel?" Jorn asked me.

"I was maybe seven or eight. A logging company was destroying forests of redwoods, and we were going to have a sit-in. I begged Larry and Evie to take me along."

Jorn looked from Angelo to me. "You were going to climb the redwoods and sit in them?"

"Yup," I said, "although Larry had ordered me to stay on the ground with Evie."

Angelo said, "But things got rough, even before we got up in the trees."

"There were big trucks and people yelling and pushing," I recalled. "The whine of chainsaws hurt my ears."

Angelo nodded. "Lotta confusion."

"It was scary. I wandered smack into the path of a bulldozer. At the last minute, Angelo whisked me to safety."

"I'm faster than I look," said Angelo.

"Larry nearly had a fit."

Angelo laughed again. "Never seen a white guy go so pale."

After a while, Angelo sobered, grew thoughtful. "Can't believe Jacques bit it. Man, a bullet." He shook his head. "So not cool." Then he asked the question on many people's minds: "Who do you think did it?"

"I don't know," I said. "What's the word among the resisters?"

"Oil company sniper," he said, then lowering his voice. "Or the government."

"Of course." Conspiracy theories ran like wildfire in this crowd.

He stepped away and looked at me. "Sorry you were the one to find him, Maya Girl."

I tucked my arm into Jorn's. "I'm okay."

Angelo eyed Jorn and me, nodded, then planted a kiss on my forehead. "You stay away from bulldozers, you hear," he said, then lumbered into the crowd.

Finally, the memorial started, an hour late. Someone whistled and the group quieted, drawing into a circle around Larry and Evie. They stood next to a hole in the ground. It was big enough to comfortably fit the spruce's tree ball wrapped in burlap lying on the ground at their feet.

"Welcome, everyone." Larry cleared his throat. "When Jacques showed up at Whispering Spirit Farm looking for a home, Evie and I didn't know what to make of him."

Several people chuckled.

Larry continued, "But we recognized a kindred spirit. Through good times and bad, Jacques's commitment to Mother Earth never wavered. He dedicated his life to the cause," Larry looked at the faces around him, "to our cause. He told me once, 'You only get one world, Larry, so don't screw it up.'"

Angelo said, "That sounds like Jacques." Several people in the group nodded their heads.

Larry paused, looked down at his tennis shoes. Evie stepped closer; her hand slid into his. Softly, he said, "Jacques liked to quote Martin Luther King Jr.: 'The time is always right to do what is right.'"

"Hear, hear," said someone in the crowd.

"Jacques's path was a lonely one, sometimes, but he didn't mind. He never said he was too busy, or he couldn't get there. When you called, he came. He was always ready to do the right thing, no matter what it cost him. Jacques always believed that we could do better, that we could transform. We will miss him, but saying good-bye brings a measure of peace. So good-bye, my friend."

Larry bowed his head. There was a long moment of silence when the only sounds were the wind and the birds and the insects. Then the mourners began to speak. One voice after another spilled memories of Jacques like seeds on the ground. Some were sad; some were funny; some were bittersweet. And a picture of a man emerged, grew toward the light.

No one really knew anything about Jacques Pine's past, not even his real name. He never married and had no kids, that anyone knew of. He chose a tent over his head rather than a roof. He didn't vote or pay taxes. As one woman said, you wouldn't catch Jacques supporting a government that couldn't get its shit together about climate change. People gave him food; whatever cash they had in their pockets; old cars, which he used for a while and then abandoned, like paperbacks in an airport lounge. He was constantly on the move, even when sitting quietly by a campfire; his energy and dedication took him from one protest, one march, one cause to another. And when he wasn't protesting, he was planting. He stole seedlings from nurseries. He repopulated and brought new life to land that humankind had disrespected. He returned to Mother Earth what had been stolen; he healed her. How could that get a guy killed?

Finally, it was time for us to do the planting. Some men came forward to help Larry lift Jacques's tree, a twelve-foot spruce. They fitted its heavy root ball into place. Others picked up shovels, began filling the hole and covering the ball with dirt. When that was done, several people fetched plastic gallon containers of water from the back of one of the trucks to water the newly planted tree.

The music started again. Standing beside Jorn, I looked upon the crowd with fondness. I understood these people. Even though I didn't know some of them, I felt among family. My gaze stopped on two men who did not fit in with this crowd. I nudged Jorn and nodded in their direction.

"Why do you think Nate Nelson and Frank Hollister are here?" he wondered.

Nate said he'd never run into Jacques while metal detecting, and Frank certainly hadn't been a fan since Jacques had the nerve to die on his property.

"And what are they arguing about?" I asked.

Jorn pointed out another lone figure, standing away from it all, leaning against a tree, watching the spectacle: Valmer Miley. Of course, Val would want to keep an eye on these unwanted visitors inhabiting his neck of the woods, especially the resisters camped nearby.

But the strangest spectator of interest was tucked back in the shadows of the pine trees, hands in the pockets of his pressed pants. Watching intently as the men planted the spruce was Chris Donovan, the man who claimed he didn't know Jacques Pine.

CHAPTER 20

DEAL WITH THE DEVIL?

THE FINAL GOOD-BYE FOR Jacques Pine lasted three days. The music and drinking and visiting lit Sadie's Papillon Farm into the wee hours, but no one complained. A bonfire in the middle of the tents and campers was kept burning, day and night, and there were always groups of people gathered around it, sharing food, beer, wine, weed, stories. One night, I saw Val Miley again tucked away in the dark shadows, standing guard, protecting whatever his strange mind thought ought to be protected from these "hippies." I just prayed to Spirit that he didn't have another PTSD episode and shoot someone.

And then the environmentalists and activists and resisters folded their tents, packed up their cars, and went home, careful to clean up after themselves before they left.

On that morning of the mass leave-taking, I was in Northern Lights having a last cup of tea with Angelo. He had flirted shamelessly with Hallie, the owner, earning a hot-from-the-oven, extra-large cinnamon roll, and now his gap-toothed laughter filled the coffee shop. I sat across from him, inhaling the mint of my tea, the cinnamon of the pastry, the bonhomie of Angelo, and ignored the looks we were getting from the other customers. The resisters who came to send off Jacques seemed as strange to the townspeople as the crows—and were just as welcomed.

"This is a nice town," Angelo said, scooting the plate with the steaming cinnamon roll between us, handing me a fork, and taking a swipe at the oozing icing with his finger, "except for all the crows."

I took a bite, and my taste buds melted into bliss. "People keep asking me when they're going to leave. Like I would know."

He nodded, his braids brushing the shoulders of his T-shirt. "Ahh. They have a mission."

"Seems that way to me."

"Well, we all do, don't we?"

I told Angelo how good it had been to see him and invited him to stay longer. But he turned down the offer. "My girlfriend is an artist. Makes sculptures of claimed things. And some of the things she claims are mine. If I don't get back to Taos soon, who knows what will be left?" There was that laugh again, quick as a rabbit. Heads in the café turned.

Some people have an unquenchable spirit, no matter what they have to endure, and that was Angelo. I'd seen Angelo at a rally, face bloodied, and still cheerfully defiant as four cops hauled him away in handcuffs.

"I'm happy that you're happy," I said.

"No other way to be, Maya Girl," he said.

We sipped our drinks, fought over the last bite of cinnamon roll, and scraped the excess frosting from the plate with our fingers. Hallie sure knew how to make them, and Angelo told her so, shouting accolades all the way across the café with its domed ceiling painted to depict the wonder of the aurora borealis. Smiling Hallie's response was to turn up the jazz station from the Twin Cities and begin a weaving dance to Herbie Hancock behind the counter.

As "Cantaloupe Island" poured from the café's speakers, Angelo's head began to bob, and his eyes closed. I sat back and did the same, dissolving into the moment. At the end of the song, I opened my eyes and found Angelo watching me. The pensive look on his face was such an unusual occurrence for my friend that I felt the stirring of worry.

"Maya Girl, I think there's something you ought to know about Jacques," he said, then paused. "He was sick."

That took me by surprise. No one had mentioned it at the memorial or in any discussions about Jacques. This information surely would have been revealed in the autopsy, which was performed, but I didn't have access to that report.

"Sick?"

"He was dying." He looked at me with those beautiful, now sad, eyes. "Cancer."

Shocked, I shook my head.

"Was this common knowledge?"

"No, but I'm sure Evie and Larry knew; they were always closer to Jacques than the rest of us," Angelo said. And yet, they hadn't shared that information with me, the daughter

Larry had asked to find Jacques's killer. It was what Jorn the reporter would call "a vital omission."

"Wait a minute." I held up a hand. "If my parents knew Jacques was ill, they would have taken him to a hospital."

Angelo shook his head. "He wouldn't go. Said he wasn't going out that way. And besides, he couldn't afford it. No insurance. Hell, not even an address."

I didn't believe it. "Larry would have paid," I insisted.

Angelo played with his teacup, rolling the fragile china in his big hands. "Jacques wouldn't take it, said Larry had done enough over the years. I told him we could have one of those crowd fundraisers. Look at all the people who showed up at the memorial. Everybody loved Jacques."

"What did he say?"

"He wanted to keep it a secret. Said he was working some deal. To get money. If he needed special care in the end, he'd pay for it."

I thought of the bundles of cash in Jacques's backpack. Was that Jacques's hospice stash? And where did he get the money, if it didn't come from Larry?

"Even if he didn't want to involve Larry in his care, indigent people can get health services," I said. Angelo gave me a patient look, and I sighed, "But Jacques didn't trust government." Few of the people in my life did.

"He was pretty secretive about his final plan," Angelo said, "but he did have one. And it did not involve ending up in some public institution under the watchful eye of the government."

Jacques must have been in pain. I thought back to the inventory of his belongings but didn't recall any bottles of pills, anything that could be pain medication for the cancer.

"Did Jacques smoke marijuana to ease the pain?" I asked.

Angelo lifted his big shoulders. "Hell, I would."

And yet there were no bags of marijuana in Jacques's possessions or at least none listed in the sheriff's inventory.

"Poor Jacques," I said.

"Yeah," said Angelo.

As we were finishing our tea, the bell over the door jingled. Margot Donovan or, rather, an alternative universe version of Margot—blonde hair mashed into a serious case of bed head, a shaking hand clutching the shoulder strap of her purse close to her body, her lipstick chewed—hurried in. She marched straight to the counter and ordered. "Coffee. The strongest you have. And a scone." Pointing to the display case, she said, "I'll take that big one, Hallie."

When she carried her coffee and pastry to a table across the room, Angelo leaned toward me and whispered, "That's a woman who needs a friend."

He didn't know the half of it.

The breakfast crowd had thinned, and it was time for Angelo to say good-bye. He stood and smothered me in a hug that reminded me of James Tumblethorne, another giant who had changed the course of my life. From the window of Northern Lights, I watched Angelo haul himself into an old truck with mud-splattered New Mexico license plates. Then with a wave and a grin, he was off.

I turned away and walked over to say hello to Margot. At the sound of my voice, her mug rattled against the table, the coffee splashing on a napkin.

"Are you okay?" I asked.

"Oh, Maya. I didn't expect to see you here." Taking a sip

of coffee, she grimaced. "This place is usually slow this time of day." It was the mid-morning lull.

"I met a friend," I said.

Margot tensed and looked around the café at the smattering of customers. Apparently, she hadn't noticed me with a big, black guy whose personality could shrink a room. I stood beside the table, until Margot begrudgingly offered me a seat. Manners are such a useful tool.

"How are Michael and Lissa?" I asked.

"Good, good," she said, her grin stiff. "You know, kids and summer." Her gaze flicked to the untouched scone in front of her.

"Please," I said, "don't let me keep you. Hallie makes the best scones."

Margot didn't wait for another invitation. She picked up the scone and took a bite, letting her eyes drift partially closed in pleasure. "I don't usually eat these. Chris hates when I get fat, but . . ." Suddenly, her eyes popped wide with shock, guilty for confiding such private thoughts.

With a reassuring smile, I said, "Your secret is safe."

Margot carefully put down the scone and eyed me. "Is it? What do you want, Maya?"

Sometimes, because I felt sorry for her, I forgot that Margot was a smart woman, not a doormat. Just because she let her husband push her around didn't mean she would let a stranger do the same. There were lines in her life—her children and her garden—that no one, not even her husband, was allowed to cross.

"I don't mean to nose into your business, Margot."

"And yet you do. Quite often."

I lifted my hands in appeal. "It's just that I have this weird relationship with Michael. I want to help him and strangle him at the same time, you know?" Margot gave me a peculiar look. "But I'd never hurt him or let anyone else hurt him."

Margot relaxed the grip on her coffee mug. She looked down at the table. With a finger, she dabbed at the sugar dusting the plate, sucking the granules off her fingertips. When she looked up at me, she said softly, "Chris and I made a deal."

I waited. Patience is another useful tool.

"I get help with the, you know, and he won't take Michael on safari." Glancing around the coffee shop, Margot leaned across the table. "It helps to get out of the house. Away from . . . stuff."

It was so typical of Chris Donovan to think he could negotiate sobriety. Even though Margot was well-intentioned, I didn't put much faith in the scones-and-coffee plan for rehab. She needed professional help, not a business deal. Willpower alone won't do it.

As Guru Bob once said, "You cannot will yourself to escape suffering; you have to let go of it."

CHAPTER 21

FRIENDSHIP IN THE STORM

AFTER I TOLD JORN of Margot and Chris Donovan's deal, he decided to drive into the Cities and talk to a friend who worked at the *Minneapolis Star Tribune.* He wanted to find out more about Donovan and his job at Mary Ella's. I watched him drive away in his not-long-for-this-life Jeep and hoped he'd make it there and back. He stuck a hand through the tear in the canvas roof and waved good-bye. Storm clouds were stacking up in the sky. I felt the first raindrop and went to bring in the cushions from the patio.

Still mystified as to why Evie and Larry had not told me about Jacques's illness, I called Larry and complained.

"It sort of didn't seem to matter, I mean, after he was shot," Larry said.

"Did you know he had a hospice stash?" I asked.

"A what?" I could hear the creak of Larry's office chair. He was rocking and thinking. "I told him I'd take care of everything, anything he needed. Evie's going to flip when she hears this."

"Angelo said Jacques wanted to pay his own way at the end. He was getting money from somewhere. I saw bundles of cash in his backpack."

"That doesn't make any sense. Where did he get the money and why wouldn't he let us help?"

I thought of the photographs Jacques had kept, carried with him, no matter what. Three happy children and three grown-up friends. I didn't know who the children were, but I knew the others: Jacques, Larry, and Evie. Two men in love with the same woman. I'm sure Jacques hadn't wanted Evie to see him in his final days, to be a burden to her. He wanted to live on in her memory as the gallant, brave, dedicated—if slightly fanatic—environmentalist quick to scale an old forest redwood or face down a water cannon for a righteous cause.

I ended the call with Larry, plucked my satchel from the sofa, and ran between raindrops to my car. The issue of the marijuana bothered me. If Jacques had some, where did it go? Had the killer taken it? Or had someone else happened upon Jacques's campsite and helped himself to the environmentalist's only pain relief?

I drove to the Chapel of the Forgiving Heart and followed the narrow gravel road behind it to the old house that Valmer Miley shared with his sister, Tessa, and their father, the Reverend Harold Miley. As I turned into the yard, Val was waiting on the front porch. When the rain started, huge drops plopping on the windshield, I dashed for the steps.

"What do you want?" Val said, blocking the door to the house.

Figuring my chances of being invited in were not good, I plunked down on the porch step just under the overhang and said, "We need to talk."

At that moment, the skies unzipped and emptied walls of punishing water. Rain tap danced on my car, drummed the dirt yard, and sluiced off the roof. Thunder rumbled the air. I patted the wooden step beside me and lifted an eyebrow that said I wasn't going anywhere. Finally, Val unfolded his arms and took a load off.

We sat for a moment, just feeling the power of the storm. Then, since Val and I didn't tango well together, I got right to the point. "Did you take Jacques Pine's dope?"

Val's body tensed, and he turned to me. "What the hell . . . no."

I stared him down. "Somebody did because I know he had some."

Val looked away. "One of the deputies probably. Evidence disappears all the time. Everybody knows that."

Returning my gaze to the storm, I said, "I don't care if you took it. I just want to know when. Was it after he died or before—when he really needed it to cut the pain? Did you rob a dying man of his last relief just to get high in your bedroom like some teenager?"

Often Val's and my conversations deteriorated into barbs of provocation. It was a race to see who could get under whose skin first. He looked at me. If a stare could reach out and strangle, I would have been gasping for air. His fists, propped on his knees, were clenched so tight I could see the outlines of his bones. Anger poured off him like the water gushing from the eaves. Fear tightened my throat, but I didn't back down. Val and I had gone head to head at other times, and there was always something that pulled him back from the brink. I trusted that thin vein of self-restraint now.

"Well?" I nudged.

"You bitch! I didn't hurt that crazy old man."

"Then tell me what happened."

I waited. His eyes burned with hatred, then suddenly everything changed. The air around us eased, as did the rain, and for the first time, I sensed something in Val I had not seen before: sadness.

Surprised, I whispered, "You liked him."

Val looked away from me. Several moments passed before he started to speak. "I found him pretty quick." That would be understandable since Val regularly patrolled these woods. "Saw the campfire in the dark. I watched him a few nights, then one night he called, 'Come on by the fire. Sit a spell.' He took one look at me and my gun and knew what I was. Said I was nuts for joining up. Said the government messes up everything it touches. Said he protested war. I said, 'You're one of those cowards then,' and he just laughed at me." That's when Val looked at me. "Laughed."

I listened, lulled by the rain, now a soft patter, and the grieving voice of the man beside me.

"He was crazy. And he was sick. I could see that. He didn't have much meat on him, and his cough came out in rattles. I knew that cough. Heard it plenty over there in that hellhole."

Val's words melted into the rain. After a while, he continued, "He wanted me to smoke with him. I told him, nah, he needed it. But he said he could get more. Said it would put my nightmares to sleep."

"And does it?" I asked.

Val didn't answer at first, then finally admitted in a soft voice, "Yeah. Some nights."

"Good," I said.

"Man, when I saw him that morning, lying on the ground, a bullet in his chest . . ." Val paused, shook his head in disbelief. "I waited until they took him away, then I went back and got Jacques's pot. I figured he'd want me to have it. But I didn't take anything else. You saw all his stuff. I ain't no thief."

"So when you came to me that night to show me the camp you'd 'discovered,' you'd really known where it was all the time."

Val shrugged.

I don't think I could imagine two people more politically opposite than Jacques Pine and Val Miley. And yet, here, on land Evie and Larry claimed held healing powers, they'd met and become friends.

I wanted to know more about their strange relationship. "What did you talk about?" I asked.

Val stared into the rain. "He was always spoutin' about climate change, like I was gonna believe that one. And his protests, he was proud of those. One night he showed me the scar from a rubber bullet he took in some rally down south. I showed him the three I took in Afghanistan, real bullets, one still inside me." Val laughed at Jacques's response. "He said, 'Yeah, but mine really hurt.' Crazy old man."

I smiled with him and realized I was a little envious of Val's relationship with Jacques. He'd had the opportunity to talk and be with Jacques, and I had not.

The love in Val's voice was unmistakable.

"You knew what he was doing here?" I asked.

"Yeah, planting. Planting weeds. Stupid."

"You watched him."

"Hell, one night I helped him. He wasn't doin' too good that day; I could see that. So, I said, 'Here, let's get this shit done and go back to camp.' And that's what we did. He smoked some, got a buzz on, settled. I opened a can of beans for him. He didn't eat much of it, though. Didn't have much appetite."

I leaned closer to Val but didn't touch. "Thank you for looking after him," I said softly.

Embarrassed, he shifted away. I rose and dusted off the back of my jeans, ready to light out into the rain. Val stood and said, "You gonna find out who killed him?"

"Yup."

"Don't know if this'll help . . . but, a couple of times, when he was high, he talked like he knew folks around here."

That was no surprise. "He and my parents go way back."

"No, somebody else."

That stopped me. "Somebody he was afraid of?"

"Not scared exactly. Somebody he didn't get along with."

So Jacques had an enemy here. Who? I wanted to ask more questions, but from the look on Val's face I could tell he didn't know more.

I stepped down to the ground and, with a wave of my hand, said, "Keep that arsenal of yours away from your sister."

Val yelled over the rain, "You're welcome, and stop bringing all those hippies around here."

CHAPTER 22

MOTHERLESS TROLLS

THE TROLL LADY DIED, and Jorn blamed himself.

While he whined and drank beer on the patio, I considered the big question: Who gets her neat doll collection?

When I asked him, he only said, "Who cares?"

It was irrational to think Jorn had anything to do with the death of Amelie Reece, but he did carry a superstition when it came to interviewing the elderly. While in journalism school in Missouri, Jorn had been assigned a three-part series on ageism. Two of the octogenarians he featured in the series died before their stories were even published. All of natural causes, but still, it was tough on a young reporter to be dubbed Mizzou's Kiss of Death by his teasing classmates.

"It's my fault. If I hadn't written her story, she might still be alive today."

"Nonsense. Amelie had a heart attack; she was eighty-five."

"That's the problem with human-interest stories," he grumped, crossing his arms over his chest. "The humans die."

Jorn had survived years as a correspondent in hot spots all over the world without resorting to lucky charms. And yet after knowing me for only months, he carried a chipped pipestone turtle in his pocket wherever he went. The turtle totem, a symbol of good health and a souvenir from one of our adventures, had diverted a bullet heading for his heart. He said life with me was as dangerous as a mine field, surely an exaggeration.

The weather mirrored Jorn's fatalistic perspective, overcast and dark. The wind in the trees rustled, calling in another afternoon storm, and the temperature had dropped in the half hour we'd been sitting there. I pulled a blanket from the back of the wicker sofa and draped it over my bare legs and toes. Jorn, dressed in jeans and running shoes, didn't feel the change in weather. He was not one of those Minnesota men who wore shorts eleven months of the year. He also didn't "do" sandals, as he put it, no matter how hot or muggy it was.

By now, I knew the best way to pull Jorn out of a funk was to send him digging—for information. I asked about his trip to Minneapolis. "What did your friend have to say about Chris Donovan?"

Jorn dug his reporter's notebook out of the back pocket of his jeans. Flipping through the pages, he said, "Mac has an MBA and has been the business reporter at the *Strib* since forever."

"How do you know him?"

"He's an old friend of Al's." Consulting his notes, he said, "Donovan has worked at Mary Ella's for seven years, the last three as the company's sustainability officer. He's considered an up-and-comer, definitely headed for a corner office, if he doesn't screw up.

"But, according to Mac, Mary Ella isn't happy with Donovan—or the company's pollinator habitat program. It was supposed to be a big public relations boon for Mary Ella's."

"What's the problem?"

"Bad seed."

I lifted an eyebrow. "What do you mean 'bad'?"

"The program encourages its supplier farmers to create patches of land on their farms to provide food for pollinators. Mary Ella's even gives them native seed mixtures to plant alongside their fields."

I shifted to face Jorn, curling my toes into the blanket. "That sounds good to me."

Jorn nodded. "On paper, yes. But some of the seed distributed for free by programs like Mary Ella's was contaminated with the seeds of an aggressive weed."

"By accident?"

"No one really knows. Could be by accident, on purpose, or by neglect. Maybe the seed companies simply weren't watching what they were doing when they collected the seeds. The only sure thing is: This weed is a killer, takes over a field like wildfire. It can put farmers out of business."

I pondered the problem. "The farmers who are trying to help the pollinators are really bringing an enemy into their house?"

"Exactly. There have been complaints—can Mary Ella's

guarantee that it is giving the farmers good seeds?—which puts Donovan in the hot seat. He needs to fix this problem, establish more quality control over the seeds he is distributing. Or he's going to lose the farmers' trust."

"And his shot at the corner office."

My mind kept linking Donovan to Jacques Pine. Flashing back to Jacques's tent, I remembered the bags of seeds. Who knew where he got those? From what I had learned about Jacques, he would never intentionally use tainted seeds. But what if he didn't know they were tainted and what if Donovan found the environmentalist planting? What if Donovan, seeking to control the situation, confronted Jacques?

I thought about Frank Hollister and what would happen if such an awful weed made its way into his fields; already he was barely keeping his head above water. "Does Frank sell to Mary Ella's?"

"Yes, and according to my source," Jorn said, "Frank is one of the farmers who refuses to participate in the pollinator program."

That was interesting and understandable. Frank would associate any attempt to save the environment with the causes that had lured his son away from the family farm.

"Do you think Frank and Jacques had a run-in?"

"No doubt," said Jorn. "Frank wouldn't take too kindly to a guy planting weeds on his land."

The wind picked up. Soon the rain would start, and we'd have to move inside. I wiggled closer to Jorn on the sofa. He absently rubbed my leg and sighed, "No matter what we humans do, we mess it up."

He sounded so dispirited. Even though the mountain

ambush was now well in the past, Jorn still lived with the wounds from his time reporting in Afghanistan: the stiff shoulder that made him groan when he stretched into Down Dog, the scar at his temple, the hip that would never be as strong and tireless as it once was. But these physical reminders were not what kept him from returning to war reporting. No, it was a heart pain that came from seeing too much and being helpless to stop it, from writing stories that changed nothing.

I searched for a way to comfort him and redirect his thoughts. I said, "Tell me something about the Troll Lady, something juicy, something you didn't put in the story."

Jorn always gathered much more information than he ever used. He thought for a moment, then with a grin said, "She was the mistress of an 'important' man in Gabriel's Garden."

"The Troll Lady was a femme fatale?" I had trouble imagining withered Amelie—nothing much but a pile of wrinkles with a shock of orange hair—as someone's lover.

"There was a lot of history packed into that pint-sized body." He explained that Amelie Reece had ridden in buckboards, seen electricity and running water come to town, and originally told Larry, when he tried to give her a computer, that he could "just take that newfangled machine" back with him.

I laughed. When my parents moved to Gabriel's Garden, my father had dreamed of building a high-tech community and had personally delivered computers to every door in Gabriel's Garden.

"Amelie rejected the computer until she discovered she could buy trolls by the dozen with the click of a button. She was going for the troll Guinness World Record."

The world record. That's a lot of little tubby naked dolls. "And she didn't have any family?"

"She was cagey about that. Said somebody new had come into her life in the past year. They found each other through a genealogy site, and they'd been emailing."

Genealogy. So Amelie had been searching for connections, perhaps a relative to inherit her possibly world-famous doll collection.

Suddenly, we heard a shout, and Sadie came barreling out the back door. She skidded to a stop in front of us and held something out for us to see. It was an original troll, and from the looks of its vintage and care, it was from Amelie's collection. "Maya, look what Nate gave me. It's just like the ones you and Mom used to have. I'm going to name it Pine Nut."

CHAPTER 23

LIFE WITH CATERPILLARS

IT'S SAFER FOR THEM in there," Sadie told Gran. "Outside they could be eaten by birds."

"That's called the cycle of life," said Grandmother, sitting on the sofa.

Sadie and I leaned over the low table in Evie and Larry's living room, our noses nearly touching the side of the butterfly habitat. The box, about two feet high and made entirely of mesh netting, contained three caterpillars busily devouring milkweed. Sadie and Larry had found the caterpillars when they were just eggs, tiny pearls on the underside of a milkweed leaf. Now they were green with yellow and black stripes, round, and growing longer by the minute.

"They are loud and smelly," said Gran with a wrinkle of her nose.

I agreed with her about the smell, but "Loud?" I asked.

Sadie said, "Sometimes you can hear them munching."

I tilted my head and *could* hear the slightest sound of chomping as one of the caterpillars masticated, leaving a straight row of teensy bite marks along the edge of the milkweed leaf.

Ping.

"*That* is loud," said Gran. It was the sound of a tiny black ball, striking the sheet of aluminum foil Larry had placed at the bottom of the habitat.

Sadie laughed. "They're pooping, Great-Gran."

The foil was littered with caterpillar balls.

Ping.

"I can hear them in the middle of the night, dropping their waste," Gran said in disgust. My grandmother's room was on the second floor. She had the hearing of a bat.

Rearing butterflies was one of Larry's favorite science projects. I grew up watching monarchs come to adulthood in Larry's homemade butterfly houses at Whispering Spirit, and I never tired of the metamorphosis from egg to caterpillar to chrysalis (the coolest part) to butterfly.

We watched the caterpillars until Evie called Sadie to help bake cookies. As she jumped up and ran to the kitchen, I stayed with Gran. It struck me that she might know something about Mary Ella's. She was a canny, successful businesswoman who probably had those manicured fingers in many pies.

Sitting on the floor by the caterpillars, my arms draped over my knees, I looked up at my grandmother and asked, "Have you ever heard of a company called Mary Ella's?"

"Of course. I own stock in Mary Ella's," she said. "Solid business, good products, went public about ten years ago. But stock has hit a rough patch lately."

"Why?" I asked.

"Some nonsense to do with a pollinator program. In my opinion, Mary Ella's should stick with what it knows—making food products—and leave the bees and butterflies alone."

"Corporate social responsibility is important. I think it was a nice thing to do—creating more habitat for pollinators."

Ping.

"You would," said Gran, frowning at the caterpillars. "Business is business, Maya. The purpose of a business is to make money. Now, people have it all confused with saving the planet. You can't do both."

"Yes, you can. A lot of companies manage to make a profit while practicing sustainability."

Gran's gray eyebrows lifted. "Thank God you only run a small yoga studio."

I asked her if she had ever met Mary Ella. "Yes," she said, "at a shareholder meeting. She struck me as a sensible leader, someone I could trust with my money. A decision I am reconsidering given this recent publicity."

"The guy who runs Mary Ella's sustainability program lives right here in Gabriel's Garden," I told her.

"Really? Poor man. He won't have a job for long."

I had no sympathy for Chris Donovan, but Michael, Lissa, and Margot were another matter. His stress was their stress. I didn't trust Donovan, but I really had no proof except my intuition telling me that there was more to Donovan's story. I felt Donovan had the nerve to kill a troublesome environmentalist, but my heart didn't want him to be guilty. Not because he was a charming guy, but because I didn't know what his family would do without him. Could Margot hold them together if Donovan were dragged off to prison for the murder of Jacques Pine?

I heard footsteps bounding down the stairs and turned to see Larry. He dropped into a comfortable chair and nodded toward the butterfly habitat. "What do you think of this year's crop?"

"They're enthusiastic eaters," I said.

"Yeah," Larry said. He crossed his ankle over his opposite knee and jiggled his foot. "Hey, you know that Donovan guy you asked me about?" I nodded. "I have some info on him, but I don't know if it will help you. It took a bit of snooping, and there's not much—"

"Lawrence, you're not *hacking* again, are you?" Gran's voice had raised a decibel, and she said the word hacking as if she was talking about a dead mouse in her shoe.

I saw Evie's head peek out from the kitchen, then hurriedly turtle back in.

"Mother, I—"

"This is not acceptable, Lawrence. In fact, it's illegal."

Larry shot back. "We're trying to find a killer, Mother."

"And that's another thing," Gran frowned at Larry. "How can you involve your own child in this nonsense? Chasing a murderer?"

Before Larry could answer, I said, "I can take care of myself, Gran."

"Doesn't Minnesota have police for this sort of thing?" Gran asked.

I got up from the floor and sat down beside my grandmother. When I took her hand, I could feel her recoil; my grandmother was not a demonstrative person. Still, I held on. "Gran, it's okay. This is what I do sometimes."

"Do?"

"Help people."

"Like a job?"

"Like a calling. I don't know how to explain it." I looked down at our hands, mine strong and hers fragile but well maintained. I didn't want to tell my grandmother that I still needed to atone for the life I took in an alley one night, that I had betrayed the nonviolent teachings of my parents. So I told her the partial truth: I was born this way.

I started, "Larry and Evie named me after an eventful weekend in the Tulum ruins of Mexico—"

"I don't want to know the details," Gran said.

"It was the autumnal equinox," Larry piped in with a smile.

I grinned at him. "I am named after the Maya civilization, but my name is also another name for the Hindu goddess Durga."

"Pagan nonsense," Gran sniffed.

I continued, "Durga is a warrior goddess. She fights evil and demonic forces that threaten peace and prosperity."

"And you believe you're some Durga person? Oh, Maya." Gran was disappointed in me.

"No," I said, still holding her hand. "I know I'm not Durga, but I do believe, like Durga, that we all have a purpose on this earth. We all should be fighting for those who can't fight for themselves."

"That's the Lord's job."

"Maybe I'm just giving Her a hand."

This idea had not occurred to my grandmother. Gran thought for a moment. "The Lord uses us all in some way, but I doubt *He* considers you a crackerjack detective."

I laughed and released her hand. "You're probably right."

Larry cleared his throat. "As I was saying, what I could find on Chris Donovan's background is sketchy. He's from Canada, Vancouver to be exact. Youngest child of a family who emigrated from Ireland to Canada."

"Schooling?"

"He received his higher education in the United States: two business degrees from Stanford. My old stamping ground."

"If only you'd finished," Gran muttered.

Larry ignored her. "Talked to a few of his old college buddies. They describe him as buttoned-up and ambitious. Always had his eye on the prize. Only time he got distracted was when he fell hard for Margot, who also was a Stanford student at the time. She had money, was a party girl, and not at all Donovan's type, according to his friends."

"Interesting," I said. "What about family?"

"Parents are gone. He has an older brother, Charlie, and a sister, Gwen. He's the baby of the family. Sister still lives in Vancouver. A seamstress. The brother is MIA."

"What do you mean?"

"He's nowhere to be found. No records after he graduated from high school."

That was interesting. Few people could disappear to the extent that Larry couldn't pick up their cyber scent.

I stared at the butterfly habitat in thought. The Donovan

family tree had a shady side. Charlie Donovan, where are you? We need to talk.

CHAPTER 24

THE WEIGHT OF BLAME

WHEN I OPENED THE Down Dog Diary, the scent of pine needles prickled my senses. It brought to mind walking in the woods, the needles cushioning my step, and the wind flicking my hair. It felt right, safe. The entry on the page was written in a child-like scrawl with hearts drawn at the beginning and end:

The trees are listening.

Except for James Tumblethorne, I seldom thought of the contributors to the diary, those shamans of the past, the men and women who had helped others to heal. This entry made me realize, though, how human they really were. They used pots to cook with, went to jobs like everyone else, and had children who would naturally be tempted to share their wisdom in the diary—when a parent wasn't looking.

After a night of tossing and turning, an aura of heaviness hung over me. I'd come to the diary searching for something I couldn't name and found: *The trees are listening.* Not exactly the shot of inspiration I had been hoping for, but it did make me think about how trees talk to each other through their roots. Deep under the earth whole conversations were happening, warnings of danger, calls for help, discourses of a species' struggle for survival.

Conversations. I needed to sink my roots and listen, not to Spirit this time but to human conversations. And the best place to do that was Northern Lights. Hallie heard about everything that was going on in Gabriel's Garden. I entered the coffee shop through the side door, the one customers used to pick up quick orders. I peeked around the tall display case to see who was in the dining area. The only customers were three women in walking shoes, sitting at a table by the window, cups of coffee in front of them. One of them was Alice Dunkirk. The other two were familiar faces around town, although I didn't know them well: Brenda Lundgren and Sheila Glass.

As I turned back to order, I heard Jacques Pine's name and stopped.

"Brenda, you need to relax about this whole Jacques Pine thing," said Alice.

"It's been months and not one arrest," said Brenda, an unpleasant woman with a sour expression and a perm so tight it squeezed her head. Glasses dangling from a beaded strap around her neck, she squinted at Alice. "Three months. And not even a suspect. What is Watt Holmes doing over in that office of his? Pumping up his bike tires?" Brenda Lundgren ran for county commissioner two years ago on a platform to "Make Gabriel's Garden Magnificent Again." She lost. Larry had actively supported her opponent whom he described as "*not* a reincarnated drill sergeant of the Third Reich."

Sheila Glass, the youngest of the three women at the table, kept out of the discussion. Using her foot, she rocked the baby stroller beside her. Inside the stroller was a sleeping child, swimming in a too-big pink sun dress and bonnet.

"I pray every day that they find the person who killed that man," Alice said. "Ed gave me a whistle for our anniversary, said to carry it on me at all times. A whistle. I wanted a trip to Italy, and all I get is a whistle." Alice had been dreaming of touring the papal home for years. And now that two of their grown sons were working in the family insurance agency, she thought it was time for dreams, not whistles.

"A whistle? That's sweet," said Sheila.

"A whistle is no trip to the Vatican," Alice said.

Brenda snorted. "A whistle is no help when someone's trying to murder you in your bed. I've lived here all my life, and there's never been a murder before. We don't *do* murder."

Having raised enough children to field an ice hockey team, a rowdy bunch who had tackled every day as if they lived on the ice, Alice was not easily terrorized. "This is not some television show, Brenda. The case can't be solved in a snap," she said. "I feel sorry for that poor man's soul."

"He was a vagrant, a trespasser, the kind of person who never dies peacefully in his bed," said Brenda. "And did you see the ones who came to his funeral? Hippies and beatniks. Criminals probably."

"It was a memorial," Alice corrected.

The baby made a sound, and Sheila jiggled the stroller. "I saw some of them in town. They looked okay to me."

"Don't be naive, Sheila," Brenda said. "I asked Watt Holmes about them. He told me not to worry. I told him somebody's got to worry. He said, 'They're just activists, not mass murderers, Brenda.'" She leaned forward. "Activists. That's another word for troublemakers. We don't need that kind around here. And I told him so." Brenda sniffed and slipped her eyeglasses on.

Alice took a sip of coffee. "I admit it is unnerving to think there might be a murderer among us. But I refuse to let it change my routine. The person will be caught and punished. I have faith in the system."

Brenda tapped her cup with a spoon. "You know who I blame? The Skyes."

What?

Brenda continued, "They're always bringing weird ideas into Gabriel's Garden. First, those computers . . . who do you think got Amelie Reece hooked on online shopping?"

"Amelie?" asked Shelia.

"The Troll Lady," Brenda said. "Then came that yoga studio and now these crows."

"My son likes the crows," said Sheila. Seeing Brenda's frown, the young mother quickly added, "But he's only five. Any nature in mass quantities is awesome to him."

Brenda turned to Alice. "You go to yoga, don't you, Alice?"

"It's good exercise," Alice said. Alice's commitment to a healthy lifestyle was as unshakable as her faith in the Catholic church.

Sheila sighed. "Wish I could go to yoga. Dealing with two kids is so stressful."

The mother of seven raised an eyebrow but remained silent.

"You wouldn't catch me near that yoga place," Brenda said. "Reverend Miley doesn't approve of that hoodoo-voodoo stuff either." She lowered her voice. "Even though his own daughter goes to classes there."

The sleeping baby had begun to stretch and wiggle, arching her back and flinging chubby legs and arms into the air. Sheila reached over and gently rubbed one of the baby's bare feet. "Wasn't that man killed near the chapel?" she asked.

"Nearly on the chapel steps, I heard," said Brenda.

I rolled my eyes at the exaggeration. *Actually, it was in a field about a half mile from the chapel, Brenda.*

Alice looked up and saw me standing by the counter. She lowered her head and muttered something about getting back home.

The baby let out a cry. Sheila stood, continuing to rock the stroller. "Me too. This one is due to eat."

I watched the women go out the front door.

Suddenly, I was aware of the hiss of the coffee maker, the clatter of cups, and Hallie calling my name. "The usual, Maya?"

I nodded. Hallie filled the to-go cup I'd brought in with mint tea. "Are you worried that the police haven't caught Jacques Pine's killer?" I asked.

Hallie snapped the lid on the cup and handed it to me. "Everyone's a little on edge."

"Do they all blame my family?"

Not meeting my eyes, Hallie rubbed a smudge off the pastry display case with a towel. Her hands and tattooed arms were strong from kneading dough. When she finally looked at me, she said, "I don't know. I get here at four in the morning to bake, Maya. It's always been my favorite time, being here alone with the dough. But lately . . ."

I understood.

By having the gall to be murdered here, Jacques Pine had brought something dark to Gabriel's Garden, and the Skyes were guilty by association.

As I reached the door of Northern Lights, Hallie called out in a raspy voice that always made me think she should be driving a cab and smoking cigars, "It's not your fault, Maya. Or your family's."

But, of course, it was.

I drove to Julia Lune's house.

Julia Lune is a pen name. My friend insists that it sounds more romantic than her real name: Julia Danilova Dornier. But I'm not so sure about that. Julia writes romances and stars in her own love story. Born in North Carolina of Russian émigrés, she is married to Jean-Luc Dornier, a lawyer and Frenchman who can melt you with his accent. And he is madly in love with Julia, who is all softness, from her tousled Gibson bun to her wispy tunics to her kind eyes framed in round, chocolate-smudged glasses.

Julia greeted me with a hug. We sat on the deck. Behind us the house rose, a modern ship of glass and wood looking out on the Dorniers' private lake. Below us on another level of the deck was another structure with a view, Julia's crowded but cozy one-room office. The skies overhead roiled with black clouds, and I felt the silence over the lake, the pressure of waiting.

I told Julia about the conversation I'd overheard in Northern Lights. "What do you think?" I asked.

Julia leaned back and considered the lake. "My mother used to say, 'Suffering is good for the soul,' and my father would reply, 'And fear is good for the reflexes.' This was their usual response when I complained that Aunt Valeria had moved into my bed, again."

The only thing I knew about Julia's elderly aunt was that she made the rounds from one relation to another, often spending months at a time, and she carried a screwdriver in her purse.

"There was a houseful of kids. She could have chosen any of their beds, but she preferred mine," said Julia. "Because I hated peas."

"Peas?"

"Aunt Valeria would pick out all the peas in her stew and wrap them in a napkin to eat later. And later was when she was in bed."

I smiled, imagining Julia squished into a bed with an old spindly woman popping peas in her mouth in the dark.

"I can still smell those peas." Julie shuddered.

"And what does this have to do with my problem?"

"Aunt Valeria believed suffering made us stronger." Slipping into a heavy Russian accent, Julia said, "Character building. Is good."

I laughed. "Are you channeling Aunt Valeria?"

"Jean-Luc draws the line at my carrying a screwdriver," Julia said. "But really, Maya, a violent death in a community, either builds character or exposes character. It reveals the real us. Yes, people are scared. Yes, there are whispers. They want information. They want someone to blame. And you and your family are excellent candidates."

"Because we're outsiders."

"I'm afraid so. I know your family's building a history here, but . . ."

"Julia, we were raised to make a difference. That's why Larry gives away computers and plants habitat for pollinators, why Heart fights with the school board over healthy options in the cafeteria, why I opened a yoga studio."

After several moments studying the dark waters of the lake, Julia finally said, "Yes, some people in town blame your family. So what?" She lifted her hands palms up, and her next words were again thick with the spirit of Aunt Valeria. "What you going to do about it, Maya Skye?"

A fine question. This funk I was in was not productive and not like me. I was a problem solver. I needed to get back in the game, stop doubting myself. People were depending on me. My family had lost a dear friend, and we needed to know why. And the town needed peace.

Julia said, "You know, as much as people complain about the weird Skyes, your family is also the first one they turn to in times of need."

She was right. Evie and Larry donated to every charitable cause that came knocking on their door. My students looked upon me as both yoga teacher and sounding board. Even Michael Donovan and Val Miley had sought me out.

Maybe I felt stuck because I needed new ideas. "So where do I start? If you were plotting a mystery instead of a romance, what would you do to solve the crime?"

"Ooh, an interesting challenge." Julia wiggled in her seat, adjusted one of the pencils holding her bun, then jumped to her feet and rushed toward the house. "This calls for Kit Kats."

Chocolate was Julia's comfort food and inspiration; it both galvanized and soothed. Sitting on the deck, licking chocolate from her fingers, Julia said, "People are killed because of history or happenstance."

"Explain," I said, biting into my chocolate bar.

"They are either in a place where they shouldn't be. In the wrong place at the wrong time. Happenstance."

"Like alone in the woods at night."

Julia nodded. "Exactly. Or they are with someone with whom they shouldn't be. This is history. The killer and the victim know each other; there is a past between them. You need to find out who has a history with Jacques Pine. I mean, besides your parents. Someone carrying a grudge."

"That's a long list. He considered making enemies part of his job description."

Julia raised a gooey smudged finger. "Or did Jacques happen upon something he shouldn't have? Was he encroaching on someone's territory? Was he planting in the wrong garden?"

Jorn and I had already discussed this motive, but it merited further research.

I was excited again, eager to find Jorn and talk this out. I leaned over and hugged my friend. "Thank you and thank Aunt Valeria."

Julia pushed her glasses higher on her nose and dismissed my gratitude with a wave of her hand. "Is nothing."

CHAPTER 25

A QUESTIONABLE SUSPECT LIST

JULIA THE WRITER WAS accustomed to threading together the twists and turns in the fabric of a plot. She was good at that stuff—dreaming up machinations. I mulled over Julia's theories. Happenstance, being in the wrong place at the wrong time, was not out of the realm of possibility in my world view; I'd seen it happen. But there also is a part of me that believes we are cosmically always where we are supposed to be. In any case, happenstance leaves a lousy investigative trail. Now history was something I could sniff out. Between Jorn the indefatigable reporter and my father the curious hacker, I did have a "crackerjack," as Gran would say, investigative team. I was sure that Jacques had carried a long, colorful, and often-far-from-amicable history in his old backpack. He was bound to have burnt some bridges. I just had to find them.

I started with my parents.

Evie, Larry, and I convened around the dining room table Larry had built when they first moved here. It was Sunday morning, and Grandmother was at church with her crabby chauffeur, Heart. As usual, Evie looked unconcerned, while Larry's energy manifested in fingers tapping and legs jiggling. They were eager to help, to find the person who took Jacques away from this existence and sent him on to the next. My parents believed that this life was one of many, and in each iteration, they had found each other. That was a faith far different from my grandmother's, which promised she would meet up with her husband on some plane of perfection and they would spend eternity visiting celestial zoos. As for Jorn and myself, it was too soon to tell if we were ships passing in the night or destined to find each other regardless of the plane of existence. But over the past year, our relationship had evolved from reluctant investigatory partners to partners of another kind.

The big question, of course, was: Who were Jacques Pine's enemies? But I had others: Where did he come from? Why had he avoided our part of the country when some of his best friends were here? Had he come here for a purpose other than to answer Larry's call for help?

"Larry, how did you contact Jacques?" I asked.

"The usual way. Put out word in the system," he said.

"The system?"

"Activists, protestors, environmentalists. I have emails for some and know the sites where the untraceables hang out. I simply said I was interested in talking to Jacques, and one day he called me."

That was how Larry's phone number ended up in Jacques's burner phone for Sheriff Holmes to find. "Did you talk several times?" I asked.

"Yeah, we did, on that same number. Unusual. Normally, Jacques talked and tossed."

"I've been thinking about this," I said. "Maybe, with his illness, he was too tired to maintain his usual security standards. How did he seem to you in those calls?"

Thinking, Larry traced the grains in the wood table with his finger. After a few moments, he said, "He coughed a lot, but he seemed like his old self. When I invited him to come help with the butterfly farm, he seemed excited. But hesitant."

This brought a concerned expression to Evie's face. "What do you mean?"

Turning toward Evie, Larry said, "I felt that he wanted to come, and he didn't. He wanted to see us, and he didn't."

"We were his family," Evie insisted. "He knew he always had a home with us. We would have taken care of him."

"I think he was torn," Larry said in a voice thick with sadness. "He didn't want us to see how sick he was, but he also felt a need to be near us. I think he came here to say good-bye. And to be a part of one last great mission."

"The butterfly farm," I said.

Larry nodded.

I asked, "How did he get to town? Did you buy him a plane ticket or a bus ticket?"

"I sent him money. He said he was taking the bus. I planned to pick him up in Minneapolis and bring him here. But he never called to tell me when he was arriving." Larry looked at Evie. "He must have hitched."

"How did he know where to set up camp?" I wondered.

Larry sighed. "I had described the property I wanted to buy, but never dreamed he'd just go there and get to work. At the time we talked, I hadn't even signed the papers with Frank yet."

In a sorrowful voice, Evie said, "We didn't know he was here until you found him."

Not for the first time, I was struck by how alone Jacques Pine had been in this world, how many nights he had gone to sleep in his tent to the beat of one heart. It made me even more determined to give his spirit peace.

I told them that Val Miley thought Jacques knew someone else in the area, someone perhaps close to him.

Larry sat back, a look of interest on his face. "Really. I'll have to ask around about that."

"Do you think he had family here?" Evie asked Larry. "I mean, biological family?"

"I really don't know." Larry tapped a beat on the table. "I've been reaching out to the old gang. Jacques did not go to a lot of the recent demonstrations."

"He was too sick," Evie whispered.

"Yeah," Larry said. "From the way they talked, I got the feeling that he was showing up less and less on the protest lines and devoting his limited energies to smaller, more personal projects, as Angelo put it. Instead of monkey wrenching the old forests, he was planting new ones."

"When he had the strength," Evie added.

When Grandmother and Heart came through the front door, they were arguing, again.

"If the man is such an idiot, why do you keep insisting that we go to these services?" my sister demanded. "That church is hot as hell."

"Watch your language, missy," Gran said, lifting her nose as she passed the caterpillar habitat in the living room. Larry stood and pulled out a chair at the dining room table for his mother.

My sister sat in the chair beside me and continued on Gran, "You complained all the way home, like you do every Sunday, that Reverend Miley misinterprets the Bible. Doesn't that make him an ineffective leader?" This was Heart logic at its truest.

With an unusual and surprising acceptance, my grandmother said, "I have decided, in the case of the Reverend Miley, showing up is what matters."

My parents exchanged looks. It was not like my grandmother to take such a laissez-faire attitude about religion, or anything really. This turnabout made Heart throw up her hands. She looked at us and asked, "What are you three discussing? Please say it's something secular."

"We're listing enemies of Jacques Pine," I told my sister.

"You're still playing detective?" Heart pointed her finger at me. "Don't involve my daughter in any murder investigations. I do not need a Nancy Drew on my hands."

"I agree with Heart. This is not a good hobby for anyone," said Gran.

"We have to do something," I told Heart. "People in town are blaming us for the murder."

"What?" Evie was shocked.

I looked at Larry, who was suspiciously quiet, then at Heart, who had slumped into her seat as if to hide.

I explained to my mother, "They say we brought Jacques here so by extension we are responsible for him having the bad manners to be killed here."

"That's absurd," said Gran.

Evie looked at Larry; he pushed his finger across the table toward her. "It'll blow over, babe," he said. "People have to blame someone."

I turned to Heart. "Have you been getting the cold shoulder around town?"

At first, Heart didn't meet my eye. I kicked her under the table. With a glare for me, she straightened in her chair and finally admitted, "There have been a few sly digs when I drop off cupcakes at a birthday party or when I'm waiting to pick up Sadie after a play date. I didn't want to bother you with it." She lifted her chin. "I can handle it, Evie."

At that moment, I was achingly proud of my irritating, independent sister. She would break her beloved label maker in two before breaking the law. But when it came to family, all bets were off.

"What about David?" Evie asked. "And Sadie?"

"So far, Sadie hasn't mentioned it to me. And David can set people straight faster than you can say, 'Sorry, you don't seem to be on my plow list anymore.'" David's landscaping business offered the only reliable snow removal service in Gabriel's Garden. In the voice one would expect from Skyes the Limit's chief financial officer, Heart said, "We've got this, Evie. Don't worry."

Gran was eyeing Heart with new appreciation. "Ruthless. I like it. Want to come work for me?"

"I have a job, Grandmother."

"Lawrence," she said, "why can't I buy off either of your children?" When I first met my grandmother, she took one look at my yoga studio and apartment in the old fire station and offered to buy me a decent house.

"They take after their mother," Larry smiled.

My indomitable grandmother got in the last word, as usual. "Well, there's always Sadie."

Before Heart could launch into Gran, I said, "What about you, Larry? Have you been getting any blowback?"

Evie raised an eyebrow at her husband. "Larry?"

My father ducked his head. "It's nothing, Evie. Just a few emails, some crackpots commenting on our social media pages. Delete, delete, delete. There. Taken care of. Not worth answering or worrying about."

"Stop protecting me," Evie said, looking at each of us. "I have a right to know this stuff. Okay?"

Reluctantly, we all nodded.

After a moment, efficient Heart brought us back on topic. "Enough about our enemies. Let's talk about Jacques's. Who hated Jacques enough to kill him?"

"I can't imagine it being anyone local," said Evie. "They didn't know him."

"I think it was the government," said Larry.

"You would." Gran was not patient with Larry's conspiracy theories.

"Jacques did not trust the government."

"The government does not assassinate people, Lawrence."

"I say it was a corporate hit," said Heart.

"That seemed to be the consensus at the memorial," I said. "But which corporate entity? Jacques pissed off everyone. Or maybe it was someone in the movement who disagreed with Jacques. Arguments get out of hand."

"Absolutely not," said Larry, shaking his gray ponytail. "Jacques was a hero, an icon."

"But there is a new generation," I pointed out. "We saw them at the memorial. They want change now. Jacques's methods were like water wearing down stone."

Heart hated the whole culture of protest and kept her distance from most activists. "I still say it was corporate. Probably agribusiness. I'm sure he protested against pesticides. I smell money."

If anyone could sniff out a financial motive, it was Heart. I tilted my head in thought. "Agribusiness. You mean like Mary Ella's?" The company was a known supporter of using pesticides on its supplier farms.

Grandmother rapped the table for order. "I don't believe it for a second. I know Mary Ella personally, and she wouldn't tolerate this kind of shenanigans. Killing off people. Over a bunch of weeds? That's absurd."

There was a ping from the habitat. The caterpillars seemed to agree with Gran.

I returned home to meditate on what we knew about Jacques Pine's death. As I sat on my living room sofa, legs crossed, thoughts shuffled through my mind, rearranging themselves. Who would want to kill Jacques, a man who persisted in trying to save the planet even though he was dying of cancer? Someone wary of strangers like Val? Someone who hated activists like crow-shooting Frank? Someone who lied about knowing Jacques like Chris Donovan? Some anonymous corporate or government hit man who tracked Jacques here? My gaze swept the room as I thought. It landed on the coffee table, where I had last seen the old Canadian coin my parents claimed belonged to Jacques.

The coin was gone.

CHAPTER 26

THE TRAIL LEADS NORTH

SOMETIMES INTUITION JUST WON'T let go of you. It pecks at you like a mad woodpecker.

Again, I found myself thinking of Chris Donovan when I thought of Jacques Pine. Was it because of Jacques's phone calls to Canada, and Donovan being a native of Canada? Was it because Donovan had lied about knowing Jacques and yet shown up at his memorial? There was a connection, but what could it be? Maybe Chris Donovan's sister in Vancouver could tell us.

Sitting at my kitchen table, Jorn and I contacted Gwen Donovan at her business. Our excuse for the call: Jorn was writing a fictitious article about Chris Donovan and the Mary Ella's pollinator project.

Jorn's cell phone was on speaker, and we could hear Gwen's low laugh. "You're writing a story on Chris, eh? Well, you picked the right Donovan for that."

"Chris doesn't mind the press, huh?" Jorn asked.

"Heavens, no. Chris loves being the center of attention. Youngest child and all that. Always fighting for the limelight."

Jorn asked a few questions about Gwen's relationship with Chris. They laughed over childhood memories. And then Jorn slipped in, "Did Charlie and Chris get along?"

Silence on the line.

Gwen took her time answering, measuring her words, and Jorn began scribbling in the notebook on the table next to the phone. *Stalling?* He pushed the notebook in my direction so I could read it.

I took his pen and wrote: *Cautious.*

We looked at each other as Gwen's voice came on the line again. "Charlie and Chris had a different point of view about most things," she said. "Charlie was the oldest, then came me, then Chris. Charlie was never careful with his stuff. Didn't really care about clothes and toys; just wanted to be outside, tromping through the woods. By the time he was done with a pair of jeans and they were handed down to Chris, they were uglier than sin. That always killed Chris." Again the low laugh. "Mama used to say, Chris was born with the 'dapper' gene." I silently agreed, having seen Donovan's sartorial selections.

From the sound of her voice, I could tell two things about the woman on the phone: First, she had a good spirit; there was no mistaking her vibe of contentment and ease. Second, she would laugh at the prime minister himself if he got too uppity. In my travels, I had seldom met a people more helpful or able to laugh at themselves than Canadians. What can you expect from a country that calls its one-dollar and two-dollar coins, loonie and toonie? Minnesota Nice pales in comparison to Canadian amiability. I liked Gwen Donovan.

I leaned toward the phone and said, "It sounds like you grew up poor, Gwen."

"We were farmers, eh," she said as if that explained it all. "I learned to sew from Mama, thank goodness. The boys had to work in the fields with Papa, but none of us kids wanted that hard life, scratching to pay the hydro bill and fighting every crop-hungry bug and blasted wind chill that came along. No, thank you."

"And now you're a seamstress?" I asked.

"Wardrobe consultant, mind you." There was that down-to-earth chuckle again. "I work for production companies that come to Vancouver to shoot movies. I've seen a lot of famous people in their underwear."

Jorn asked, "Do you still own the family farm?"

"No, that's long gone. Like I said, Charlie loved the outdoors, but he had other ideas. And Chris hated the farm. He always said he was meant for better things. Guess, he was right."

Jorn tilted his head toward the phone and signaled: it's time. Before ringing up Canada, Jorn and I had discussed how two strangers snooping into family business should approach Gwen. He thought I was more likely to get information from Chris's sister. "You have that whole sympathy thing going," Jorn had maintained. So, I had been nominated to pose the tough inquiries.

I took a deep breath, almost frightened to hear the answer, and asked, "Gwen, did Charlie have a friend named Jacques?"

Silence.

Jorn and I exchanged looks.

Then, laughter gone from her voice, Gwen said, "I-I thought this was an article about Chris."

"It is," I reassured Gwen. "We just want to put together a well-rounded picture of Chris, his past, his beginnings."

We heard a rustling on the phone, a sniff. Gwen said quietly, "I don't remember Charlie's friends."

"Gwen, do you know where Charlie is?" I asked gently. "We'd like to talk to him too,"

Gwen's laugh was forced, a bit shaky. "You people sure are thorough."

I leaned closer to Jorn and wrote on the bottom of the notebook page: *No denial.* He nodded.

Keeping my voice soft, friendly, I followed my gut and asked, "Gwen, do *you* know a man named Jacques Pine?"

A long silence.

Then, it was as if an arctic wind swept down from Canada and slammed the door in our faces.

Suddenly, Gwen was in a hurry. "Listen, I have a fitting in ten minutes. Good luck with the article. Chris is basically a good guy, once you get past the Brooks Brothers suit."

She hung up.

Jorn and I sat back and thought.

Finally, Jorn said, "She knew Jacques."

I tapped the notebook and said, "She grew up with him."

CHAPTER 27

DETOUR INTO TROLL LAND

WHEN ROSELYN BARRIE ASKED me to drop by her house. I didn't think anything of it. It was not unusual for my students to seek me out after class. I was not just their teacher; I was their friend, their confidant, and sometimes their counselor. But the condition of Roselyn's yard immediately put me on notice that something was wrong. Roselyn's grass was ankle high and brown in a few spots, and weeds were taking over her marigolds and petunias. Being an art teacher, Roselyn was creative in her gardening, but never this sloppy.

As soon as I stepped out of the car, Roselyn, who had been standing on the porch waiting for me, swept me inside the house and sat me down on a sapphire sofa while she perched on a dainty Wedgewood blue chair.

"Thanks for coming," she said.

"Roselyn? What is it?" I asked.

Her short silver hair, tipped blue, was standing in all directions. She gave it an unconscious pull. "It's-it's Nate. Oh, Maya, I don't know if he's mad or sad or just unhappy."

For Roselyn, a single woman in her fifties, love affairs were precious things, few and far between. She once told me most men couldn't handle a woman with a strong sense of aquamarine. Now, clutching a throw pillow, she was a confused girl in the throes of heartache.

"Why do you think he's unhappy?" I asked.

Roselyn hugged the pillow closer to her chest. "I don't know. It just feels like something is off, something's bothering him. I like him, Maya; he's nice. Really nice. But lately, I can't say anything without him biting my head off."

"Has something happened?"

For a moment, I thought Roselyn wasn't going to answer, then the words burst from her, "Amelie Reece is what happened."

Puzzled, I asked, "What does Amelie have to do with this?"

Caught up in self-recrimination, Roselyn ignored the question. "I know I should be kinder," she said. "I mean he moved here to be near her."

He did?

"Imagine finding your long-lost biological mother online. On a genealogy site, no less. That's a miracle. So, of course, he took her death hard. After all, they'd just found each other."

"Long-lost mother?" I was shocked. "Amelie and Nate?"

Roselyn looked at me strangely then suddenly gasped, her hand flying to cover her mouth. "Oh no, oh, please don't tell anyone. I-I wasn't supposed to say *anything* . . . he would be so hurt. Please. I didn't mean to . . . I'm so upset I don't know what I'm saying."

I leaned toward Roselyn, calming the hand that was now plucking madly at her hair again. "How can I help?"

Her troubled eyes pleaded with me. "I just don't know what to do, Maya. I'm afraid to talk to him. What we have is so, so . . . new." Her voice trailed into a whisper. "What will I do if he leaves?"

Roselyn's insecurity pulled at my heart, and I found myself reassuring her that it was probably nothing. I joked, "Men can be so moody."

"Can they ever," Roselyn agreed in a miserable tone.

I couldn't think of any magic words for the lovelorn, so I fell back on what I always did when I was feeling lost. "Try to relax. Breathe. It will all work itself out."

Her head lifted. "You think so?"

I said, "He'd be crazy to pass up a treasure like you."

That made Roselyn laugh, then sigh. She looked down at the throw pillow in her arms.

I asked, "Would you like me to talk to Nate?"

She looked up at me, tugged at a blue-tipped tress. "Oh, I don't know. He's really private about his business."

"I'm usually pretty good at getting people to talk to me," I reassured her.

As I was leaving, Roselyn stopped me at the door. "Maya, don't say anything about . . . the mother thing. Okay?"

Many in Gabriel's Garden were surprised that Amelie Reece

left all her worldly possessions to Nate Nelson, a man who was new to town and whom she'd only known for a few months. Rumors zipped across Northern Lights like comets: Who was this guy? Was he a long-lost relative? Was he a con man who stalked the internet, preying on vulnerable old women?

Amelie had told Alice Dunkirk, one Sunday after mass, that both she and Nate were interested in finding out more about their families. That was what they had been doing all those times Nate's car, a Volvo that had seen better days, was parked outside Amelie's house: talking genealogy.

Jean-Luc Dornier, Amelie's lawyer, confirmed that Amelie had changed her will just a month before she died. When she named Nate as her beneficiary, Jean-Luc said, Amelie appeared of sound mind—and quite happy.

In general, the town consensus was that Nate was an amiable man with an amiable dog. No one knew that he carried a gun, except Jorn and I.

There were several crows parked in the trees surrounding Amelie Reece's small gray house on the day Jorn and I walked up the front steps. I nodded at them.

Although we heard noises inside, no one answered our knock. Cupping his hands around his face, Jorn peered into a window. "Man, he's wrecked the place."

"What do you mean?" I asked.

"When I was last here, it was creepy but tidy." He mimicked Amelie, "'Take your shoes off, Mr. Jorn. Sit on the plastic-covered love seat, Mr. Jorn. Don't touch the dolls, Mr. Jorn.'"

We heard more crashing from inside the house. I said, "Maybe Nate simply can't contain his grief—"

"Or maybe he's looking for something," Jorn said, banging on the door harder.

This time there was silence, then the sound of footsteps. Nate yanked open the door. He was sweaty, and there was a streak of dirt on his cheek. His curly hair was disheveled. "What?" he demanded.

"Sorry to interrupt, Nate," Jorn said in a friendly voice, "but I'm interested in doing an article about you for *The Independent.*"

"Not a good time," Nate said, starting to shut the door.

Jorn said, "C'mon, man, we don't get many treasure hunters in town. My readers will love the story." Jorn paused. "And a little publicity might help you."

This stopped Nate. "How?"

"Well, if you're looking for old stuff, many of my readers have lived here their whole lives. They'll probably have ideas where you could look. In fact, I'll even ask my uncle Al; he ran the newspaper for years, knows a lot of town history."

Nate peered at us with suspicion. The air grew heavy and unnerving. I was beginning to understand Roselyn's anxiety. Gone was the laid-back guy who rambled around with a dog and a metal detector digging up old coins and pop cans.

After several moments, he opened the door wider. "Make it quick."

I breathed a sigh of relief and sneaked a smile at Jorn. I knew he could talk us into the house. (What did you expect from a man who had hustled his way into enemy camps around the world?)

The first thing that hit me as I stepped over the threshold

of the closed-up house was the summer heat trapped with a stew of unpleasant smells. Trying to ignore the stink, I looked around me and stopped.

"Wow," I said. It was amazing.

Trolls were packed chubby cheek to chubby cheek on every surface: troll families; trolls in bikinis and tuxedos and nurse uniforms; furry hairdos in a rainbow of colors.

Many had been knocked over, and some lay on the floor. Careful not to step on one, I began righting trolls on shelves and in a village set up beside a large aloe vera whose thick, spiky leaves exploded like horticultural troll hair. Returning an aproned troll, the relative of my sister's Betty troll, to the village bakery, I cleared my throat. "Nate, what's that smell?"

He picked up a troll in a bathrobe with face cream and rollers in its pink hair, frowned at it, then tossed it on the table. "Liver and onions. Amelie's favorite. Who eats that anymore?"

I threw open a nearby window for some fresh air.

Jorn joined me, gently placing trolls back on shelves. "When I interviewed Amelie for *The Independent*, this place was neat as a pin. What happened?"

"Can't find anything in this mess." Nate's annoyed tone drew a look from Angus, who was lying under the dining room table, perhaps the safest place, given the state of destruction. Under his breath, he muttered, "I'm a professional treasure hunter, for god's sakes; finding stuff is my thing."

"What are you looking for?" Jorn asked, lining up a row of cape crusader trolls. "Treasure?

When Nate didn't answer, we both stopped and looked at him. He was watching us.

There was a stillness about Nate, a waiting quality, that put me on edge. Suddenly, he turned and plopped down on the plastic-covered love seat. "Ask your questions then leave."

Jorn and I lowered ourselves in chairs opposite Nate, the plastic on the chairs squeaking as we sat down. Jorn took his notebook and a pen from his pocket.

"How did you and Amelie meet?" asked Jorn. "Was she interested in treasure hunting too?"

"No. We met online. A genealogy site."

"Didn't know Amelie was interested in family history," Jorn said. "She never married, never had children, at least that's what she told me when I interviewed her."

A wariness crept into Nate's expression. He neither confirmed nor denied.

"Were you somehow related?" Jorn asked.

I could feel the energy change in the room.

After several moments of silence, Nate said, "She had some letters that once belonged to my family."

Jorn looked up. "Letters? Who's your family?"

Nate picked up one of the dolls from the floor. It was smaller than his hand. He regarded Jorn. When he answered, he chose his words carefully, "Old friends of Amelie's."

Suddenly, Nate flung down the tiny troll and rose from the love seat. "Have to get this place ready to sell. I sure don't want all these damn dolls." It was our invitation to leave.

His words reminded me that Nate was in mourning for a mother he never really got the chance to know. As I rose, I said, "I'm sorry about Amelie, Nate. I know you didn't know her long, but you seemed to have made friends fast."

"Yes, we did."

"Since she didn't have any family, it was good of you to take care of her, at the end. She was a nice lady."

Again, Nate did not take the chance to own up to his relationship with Amelie. Instead, he looked around the troll-crowded, chaotic room, at the dolls watching him from every corner. Softly, he said, "Yeah, she was."

I said, "These dolls must have been her family. I hope you find them a good home."

His glance, both angry and confused, swept the room again. "I never expected her to leave me all of . . . this."

Remembering my promise to Roselyn, I said, "Perhaps Roselyn could help you. She's an organized person. Why don't you ask her?"

Nate seemed surprised at the suggestion. "I might do that."

As Nate walked us to the door, I stopped and turned to him. "One last thing, we don't allow firearms on the butterfly farm."

Nate's expression hardened, and he thrust the door open. "This interview is over."

As we drove home, the pieces slowly clicked together. Nate was searching for letters. Family letters. What did they have in them? Did they reveal some family history a child born of secrets was desperate to know? If Amelie was Nate's mother, who was his father? She'd confided in Jorn that she'd been the mistress of someone important in Gabriel's Garden . . .

I said, "Could Nate Nelson be related to Gabriel Nygård—*the* Gabriel of Gabriel's Garden?"

CHAPTER 28

A HISTORY LESSON FROM AL

SITTING AT THE BREAKFAST nook in Jorn's tidy kitchen, I watched him cut into a loaf of homemade bread. This was the kitchen of a caring cook. It had a phalanx of appliances, including a new bread mixer. Motioning toward the red machine on the counter with the large shiny bowl, he said, "It's Swedish. Coulda bought an entire bakery for what that cost me, but . . . you really can't put a price on good bread."

Jorn ate for taste; I ate to keep upright. His well-appointed kitchen put mine to shame. He had more items on his spice rack than I had in my entire refrigerator. To emphasize his point about properly prepared baked goods, Jorn slid a plate of delicious-smelling French bread slices (crispy on the outside, chewy on the inside) and a bowl of perfectly seasoned butter on the table along with two beers.

I needed no invitation to begin slathering.

He sat down across from me and pulled out his phone, speed-dialing his uncle Al in Florida. While I reached for another slice of bread, an entry in the Down Dog Diary came to mind:

History hurts. We may try to outrun the pain, but too often we fail to realize that we are running a race and history is running a relay, with fresh legs waiting around every bend. How do we win? Don't compete.

Who knew how Nate's history—having a crazy Troll Lady for a mother—had screwed him up? We hoped Al Jorn could help us understand what drove Nate Nelson.

Al came on the line with the poolside sounds of splashing water and laughter in the background. As he said hello, we heard a female voice shout in greeting, "Hey, Al."

Jorn grinned. "Enjoying yourself, Al?"

Al's voice spilled sunshine and retirement from the speakerphone. "You know what they say: Any day you're not six feet under is a good day."

Jorn said, "Speaking of six feet under, Amelie Reece passed."

"I heard. A damn shame. Amelie was a weird old bird, but she was *our* weird old bird."

"Actually, that's why we're calling," Jorn said. "Maya's here with me, and we want to tap you on some Gabriel's Garden history. It has to do with Amelie. Thought you might be the man to call."

"I reported the news in GG for more than fifty years. I ought to know something. Shoot."

I raised my voice to be heard over the pool party in the background. "What can you tell us about the original Gabriel?"

"Woo, you *are* going back." More splashing. "Well, the land around GG was settled by the Amish. I don't know how many families there were in the area originally, but by the early 1900s, that community had gone extinct. Gabriel Nygård bought the land in the late twenties. He'd come into some money and scooped it up for a song. Said he felt a spiritual connection to the place."

Had Gabriel Nygård felt the power of the vortex here, just as Evie and Larry had?

Jorn asked, "Was he Amish?"

"Hell no. Gabriel was a regular in the Wabasha caves in Saint Paul back when they were filled with speakeasies, gambling, and mobsters. He drove his roadster fast and kept even faster company. But, after a few days of the high life, he always made his way home to the country, to Gabriel's Garden."

"Why?" I asked.

"Fell in love with a farmer's daughter. She didn't like the city. Refused to leave. So Gabriel built a town around her."

"A man in love." Jorn winked at me.

I flashed him a smile.

Shouts, splashing, a girl's high-pitched scream turned into giggles. Al continued, "They had one son, Gabriel Junior. He was about the same age as Amelie. Gabe Junior and Amelie grew up together in Gabriel's Garden. Were a couple in high school, but then Gabe went off to college and married a woman from back East, Audra. Unlike his father, Gabe preferred being a big fish in a small pond. He ran the town council for years. But like his daddy, he had a wild streak. He had an affair with Amelie Reece."

Gabe Nygård and Amelie Reece. This was the connection we were looking for.

"Amelie told me she had once been in love with 'an important man' in Gabriel's Garden," said Jorn. "But she refused to name him and made me swear not to put it into the story I was writing. Still, she was proud of the relationship. She wanted me to know about it."

"That sounds like Amelie," Al said. "Everybody knew about the affair, knew Gabe bought that house for her. Although she claimed she came into an inheritance."

"Tell us about her," I said.

"Amelie was a woman desperate to stand out and never quite able to. Born and died in Gabriel's Garden. I have no doubt Gabe was her one and only true love. When he and his wife died suddenly in an auto accident—that was around nineteen sixty-eight—Amelie took up with those damn trolls. That computer Larry Skye gave her nudged her from Miss Lonely Heart to bat-shit crazy."

"Hey," I said.

"I'm sure Larry meant well, Maya, but there are some personalities that should not be exposed to technology."

Remembering the house of trolls, I had to agree.

Al said, "Now that I'm thinking about it, there was a bit of mystery around Amelie."

"What kind of mystery?" asked Jorn.

"Like I said, she never left GG, except for a period in the sixties. She told everybody she was traveling on her inheritance, a trip across America. But people said that wasn't like homebody Amelie."

I said, "We think she went somewhere to have a baby."

"Baby?" I pictured the reporter in Al sitting up, bird dog alert.

"Yeah," Jorn said, "she had a child, a son, and we're betting it was Gabe Nygård's. Somehow that boy tracked down Amelie. Found her online a year ago. Struck up a friendship. Moved to Gabriel's Garden, we think, to be near her. When she died, she left everything to him."

Al was surprised. "Well, I'll be damned." Jorn and I each picked up a slice of bread. "You know," Al said, "Gabe and his wife Audra never had any kids. There was no love lost between the wife and Amelie; everybody understood that. But now I do recall that Gabe had a sister who lived somewhere back East, and she had a son."

"What are you thinking, Al?" Jorn asked. "That Gabe sent Amelie to stay with the sister until she had the baby, then gave the child to the sister to raise as her own?"

"Sounds like a soap opera, but it's entirely possible. Amelie couldn't keep the child, not in those days. And Audra would never have accepted him. By letting his sister raise the boy, Gabe could see him occasionally. What's the son's name?"

"Nate Nelson."

"You should check to see if the sister's married name is Nelson."

"I will," said Jorn.

We heard a sigh over the phone. "Poor crazy Amelie. Suppose not many came to her funeral. Most of the folks she knew are gone by now. Or in Florida."

Jorn told his uncle, "Nate arranged for a funeral mass in the Catholic church and burial in the town cemetery."

"That's what Amelie would have wanted," Al said. "A Nygård heir. That's interesting."

Jorn said, "He's a treasure hunter."

"Verrrry interesting."

The tone of Al's voice had both Jorn and me dropping our bread and leaning toward the speakerphone.

I said, "What is it, Al?"

There was a pause, and for once, the pool party fell silent. Finally, Al spoke. "Some said wild Gabriel the Senior made his money scavenging sunken ships. Rumor was he always returned to GG not just for his wife but because he kept his treasure there."

Nate Nelson the treasure hunter had Nygård blood.

It made me wonder: Why did Nate really want Amelie's old letters? Was he after family history or a clue to his grandfather's treasure?

CHAPTER 29

WAY STATION HIT

I SHOULD HAVE NOTICED THE crows circling. But as we parked by the side of the road and got out of the car, everyone was excited and talking. The last time I had visited Sadie's Papillon Farm, the rolling meadow had been in full bloom and full buzz. Feathery goldenrod, high and yellow. Giant purple thistle reaching spiky arms upward. Coneflowers, blazing star, and milkweed—plenty of milkweed for hungry caterpillars. Today I teased Sadie about giving the butterflies names, while Larry carried the butterfly habitat, which contained three butterflies flapping their wings, eager to fly. When we left the house, Grandmother had asked, "Today's the release date? Good riddance." When she spotted the shocked expression on Sadie's face, Gran added, "And God bless them."

It was a beautiful day, so bright that we had to shield our

eyes as we looked out over the field. What we saw stopped us in our tracks.

The life-giving milkweed, wildflowers, and plants had been ripped from the earth. Large ruts, deep furrows freshly made, crisscrossed the meadow. The driver of the car or truck had spun and spun, making crazy circles, tearing up the pollinator patch from one end to the other. The sanctuary that had been singing with insect life a few days ago was silent and dead.

Larry dropped the butterfly habitat. Sadie cried, "No!" and rushed into my arms. She burrowed into my chest and sobbed.

I held her tight, whispered reassurance I wasn't sure of myself, "It'll be all right."

But would it? Who would do this? I looked up and saw Larry stumble forward. He lifted his arms wide, as if to embrace all that had been lost.

I immediately pulled out my phone and called Evie. "Come to the farm," I said. "Now."

Evie arrived with Heart in a hurry; Heart must have been driving. They staggered from the car and stopped, stared.

Evie immediately ran to Larry.

"What the hell?" said Heart.

Upon seeing her mother, Sadie scrambled out of my arms and leaped for Heart, hitting her so hard Heart fell back a step. Sadie clutched her mother and cried. Over Sadie's head, Heart's eyes met mine, and I saw a fire growing. Who cares about the butterflies and bees? Somebody had broken her little girl's heart.

I nodded to her. We would fix this.

I turned to Larry and found Evie with her arm around his waist, whispering to him, his head sunk to his chest. My mother was the ultimate calm in any storm. I think this healing ability comes from the simple fact that Evie saw good in everyone. While sometimes I had to remind myself to look for that nugget of humanity, Evie automatically felt it, embraced it, appealed to it.

The person who had done this better hope Evie finds them before I do, I told Spirit.

Suddenly, I was so angry I felt my heart would explode from my chest. I automatically took deep breaths to settle myself, but they didn't help. I began to pace the field, my eyes searching—for something to salvage. When I found it, I knelt down, brought my calm back into my heart, and gently righted the plant. I stood it tall and pressed its exposed roots back into the soil, patted the dirt around it securely, touched its leaves in a blessing.

Soon the others joined me. As we fanned out, restoring what we could, the crows in the trees watched us and I wondered, *Do you know who did this?*

Jorn texted me: *How goes the big release?*

I texted back: *Help.*

Within a half hour, he was there, pulling me into his arms. Then, he stared down into my face with worry and brushed a tear from my cheek with his thumb. "You okay?" he whispered. I nodded and tried without much success to form a smile. He hugged me again and looked out over the farm.

Then he turned into the reporter. He took photo after a photo of the devastation with his phone: the ruined flowers, the tracks. He talked to Larry and took notes in his trusty notebook. I heard Jorn say, "The tracks look fresh and muddy, probably made after last night's rain."

Crouched beside a track, Larry nodded. "They're deep. Heavy vehicle. Truck or big SUV. Slid around in a few places."

"Kids having fun?" Jorn wondered aloud. "Or someone trying to wreck this place?"

Larry didn't know and didn't want to know. This type of wanton destruction, the sheer selfishness of it, was not easy for my father to understand.

Jorn snapped close-ups of the tire print. "I'll give these to Watt. He'll find the vehicle."

Larry stood. "No, I'm not filing a report."

"But—"

Larry merely shook his head and walked off, back to restoring what had been torn from the ground. Jorn watched him for a few moments, then silently began to help. I knew he was already writing the story in his head.

We did the best we could. It was far from the lush pollinator paradise it had been before. Evie probably viewed this act of vandalism as a call for help, but I thought differently. The tire tracks proclaimed: there is evil in this world, and you never know when it will find you.

My handyman father had placed blocks of wood, with holes drilled in them, on posts. With slanted roofs to keep off the rain, these pollinator hotels were places for solitary bees to make their nests. In one pass, the driver had knocked down a hotel. As Larry pushed the bee hotel back up to standing and tamped it back into the ground, he said, "At least they didn't run over Jacques's tree."

The spruce we'd planted at Jacques's memorial stood untouched in the center of the meadow. Was this significant? It made me think about the perpetrator. Was this a warning to stop snooping into the death of Jacques Pine? Or an act of revenge for bringing murder to Gabriel's Garden? Gabriel the angel was considered to be God's messenger. What was the message in this violence?

It was Heart, an expert at diverting her daughter, who said in a bright voice, "When are we going to release those butterflies?"

We all gathered around the habitat. It felt good to be back to our original mission. Larry unzipped the net door, and Sadie reached in and carefully plucked a butterfly that was clinging with its long legs to the ceiling of the habitat. She held it gently, as Larry had taught her—wings tucked together—while I placed a tiny round adhesive tag to the underside of its wing. On the tag was an identification number. Should this butterfly reach its winter home in a Mexico forest, monitors might find it and record its successful migration. Tagging the monarchs helped researchers assess the health of the butterfly population, which was in decline. In the last twenty years, herbicides and human development had wiped out much of the butterflies' habitat and more than 90 percent of North American monarchs. They were running out of places in which to live.

Sadie lifted her hand into the air, released her hold on the butterfly's wings. The monarch fluttered for a moment in her palm then raced for freedom. We watched it immediately light on a purple thistle and begin to eat, nourishment for the long trek ahead—the massive migration to Mexico.

Sadie waved and shouted, "That's Mimi. Safe travels, Mimi."

The process was repeated for the other monarchs: Manny and Boop. Sadie leaned against her mother and watched as

Manny, Boop, and Mimi flitted away, disappearing into the sky. Heart squeezed her daughter. "You did good, kid."

A look of consternation replaced the joy on Sadie's face. "But will there be enough food to attract the others, the ones coming from up north? What if they don't stop? What if the bad people come back and mow the plants down again? We were supposed to be a-a . . ."

"Way station," Larry helped her.

She turned to her grandfather. "Will they still come?"

With a determined set of his shoulders, he said, "I don't know. But I do know this will not happen again."

Evie stepped to Larry's side. "What are you planning?"

"Until the migration is over, we're going to guard Sadie's Papillon Farm," said Larry.

Evie objected. "Larry, you can't spend every hour out here."

Sadie tugged on Larry's flannel sleeve. "I'll camp out with you, Grandpa."

"No, you won't," said Heart.

Larry stroked Sadie's head. "No need, kid. We'll have help. I'm calling Angelo."

The townspeople were going to love us.

CHAPTER 30

WHEN THE BODY REFUSES TO FLY

HOW DO I DELICATELY put my feelings regarding the destruction of Sadie's Papillon Farm? I was pissed. I knew this was a phrase that Evie wished I would banish from my vocabulary, but there were times when it was needed. Times like this when I couldn't put away the rage inside me, when I couldn't forget Sadie's heartbreak or Larry's crushing dismay. I was not as forgiving as Evie. When you hurt one of mine, you did not get to walk away free of consequences.

Back in my yoga studio, and still churned up, I launched into the forms of tai chi taught to me by brawler-turned-pacifist James Tumblethorne. In tai chi, one is the tortoise, winning the challenge by going ever slower. But today my punches and kicks grew faster and more emphatic, more sloppy than mindful. I could practically hear Tum's disappointment: "Tai chi is a practice in balance, not annihilation, Maya." Sorry, Tum.

My mind was stuck on the question: Who would destroy a patch of wildflowers?

I followed the tai chi with yoga, in particular, Crow Pose. This pose, too, was an effort at regaining balance. It required calm and concentration. And I kept falling out of it, which, of course, only ratcheted up my anger. I slammed my head again and again against the unforgiving wall of Crow, until finally, defeated, I sunk back on my knees, sweat pouring from my arms.

"Try again," said a voice.

I looked up, and there was Jorn, arms crossed, leaning against the doorjamb of the studio. I waited for him to say more, but he just looked at me with a confidence I didn't feel.

Slowly, I crouched, took a deep breath, and leaned forward over my hands, which were planted on the mat. I lifted my knees and pressed them against my bent arms. I wobbled then found my center of gravity. In an instant, I felt calmer. Guru Bob always described Crow as a confidence builder. "So you fall on your face a few times," he would say in an unsympathetic tone that dared students to strengthen their resolve. "The ground is not so far away. Your nose is not so precious. The crow is the messenger; this pose sends word to your body that you can do this work—here and in life. You can soar over the obstacles in your path. Stop whining."

Jorn's voice came again as I gently set my feet down and rested my arms. "You know, I hate that pose. And not just because it hurts. It looks goofy."

I tried Crow one more time and promptly fell on my face again. I heard Jorn sigh.

"C'mon," he said. "Let's go see Chris Donovan."

Margot Donovan answered the door with an agitated air and a coffee stain on her white silk blouse. Swiping a straggle of hair from her eye, she noticed the spot on her shirt and began furiously scrubbing at it.

"Margot, how are you?" I asked.

She did not look up. "Fine." Scrub, scrub, scrub.

"May we come in?" Jorn asked.

Without answering, she kicked the door wider and turned away. As we stepped inside, the sound of trundling footsteps on the staircase caught our attention. It was Michael. I started to say hello, but he shook his head slightly at me. At the bottom of the stairs, he lifted a plate dusted with breakfast crumbs from the antique entry table, handed it to Margot, and said, "Mom, how about some iced tea for everyone?"

Hesitating, looking from her blouse to the plate, she said, "Okay," and turned toward the kitchen.

He watched her go then faced us. Lowering his voice, he said, "What are you doing here?"

"We need to talk to your dad," I said.

"He's golfing." Michael bunched his hands in the pockets of his cargo shorts.

"Where's Lissa?" Jorn asked.

"Play date. She's in popular demand now that she has a chauffeur."

I caught his eye. "Your mom seems . . ."

He looked toward the kitchen, shrugged. "She's trying. It's hard."

With the movement of his shoulders, I noticed Michael was wearing a leather cord tucked inside his T-shirt. When he shifted, I saw a glimpse of a familiar object attached to the cord.

I was about to ask him about the necklace when Margot came in with a tray, a pitcher of tea, and four glasses. She led us to the two sofas in the dead animal room. Jorn and I sidestepped the animal skins on the floor and sat down. I avoided the dark eyes of the water buffalo looming over the fireplace and looked at Margot. "We wanted to talk to your husband about his brother, Charlie."

The tray wobbled. After a pause, Margot placed the tray on the glass coffee table between the sofas, sat down, and began pouring. "Charlie?" She exchanged a glance with her son, who'd taken a seat beside her. "What-what on earth for? We haven't seen Charlie in ages."

"You've met him then?" Jorn persisted.

"Of course, I know all of Chris's family. His sister, Gwen, is delightful. She lives in Canada. She sews for the stars, you know."

Jorn asked, "Was Charlie in Minnesota this summer?"

Again, mother and son looked at each other. Michael remained silent. Margot took a sip of tea. "Oh, I-I don't think so."

I leaned forward and said quietly, "Margot, was Jacques Pine really Charlie Donovan?"

Clasping her glass tightly, Margot pretended to laugh, "That's absurd. Charlie Donovan is alive and well."

I looked at Michael, who avoided my eyes. He fiddled with the cord around his neck. "Michael," I said, "did you know? When we found him? Did you know he was your uncle?"

He stopped fidgeting.

Sounds of someone entering the back door. A look of relief passed over Margot's face. Her husband was home. Michael stared down at his sneakers.

Chris Donovan stepped into the room, took one look at us, and said, "Not again."

Donovan's entrance brought Michael and Margot to their feet. After a few moments of uncomfortable silence, Margot said, "I'll get you a glass, Chris," and hurried out of the line of fire. Chris Donovan, in a white polo shirt and tan chinos that looked fresh from the closet and not like they had just endured eighteen holes on a hot summer day, tossed his golf glove on the coffee table and sat down on the sofa, in the spot Margot had just vacated. Michael slowly joined him. Donovan silently stared at us until Margot returned with a glass, filled it with tea, and handed it to him. Although there was room on the sofa next to Donovan, she eased into a leather chair on the outskirts of the group.

"What do you want this time?" Donovan sat back, crossed one leg over the other, and pointed at Jorn. "And I'll tell you right now anything said in this room is off the record. I see one word about me and my family in your goddamn paper and I'll sue your ass into bankruptcy."

Margot stirred. "Chris—"

"Just setting the ground rules, Margot. These two are itching to poke their noses into my business."

Jorn didn't take his eyes off Donovan. "We know Jacques Pine was really Charlie Donovan, your brother."

This wasn't exactly true, but all Jorn's information and my intuition were leading to this conclusion. Jorn wanted to rattle Donovan's cage and get confirmation.

Donovan's expression didn't even flicker. He took a casual sip of tea. "You're full of shit."

Jorn relaxed into his chair, appearing as calm as Donovan. He said, "I always wondered why you never walked down to the crime scene. You stayed up by the road with your son. It would have been a natural thing for a parent to do—investigate exactly what kind of mess his child had gotten into. Weren't you even curious about the dead man your son had found? Weren't you even concerned about what he had seen?"

Silence.

"You know what?" Jorn said. "I think you already suspected that Charlie or Jacques had come to a bad end."

Michael looked at his father, questioning. Donovan remained stubbornly silent, his eyes boring into Jorn.

Jorn kept at him. "You stayed by the cars, chewing your son out for stupid stuff. Did you even notice that he was upset? Did you ask if he was all right? What kind of man is more concerned about a few scratches on a car than the feelings of his own son?"

The muscles in Donovan's chiseled jaw began to work.

"Why didn't you check it out? A man was murdered, and your son found the body," Jorn demanded. "It couldn't have been the blood. I mean, the big white hunter surely has seen his share of gore." Jorn's voice grew louder. "Did you care about your brother at all?"

Margot gasped.

Then Jorn gave the final shove. "Or did you already know

who was lying in that field because you killed your own brother?"

CHAPTER 31

TOO MANY FAMILY SECRETS

MICHAEL LOOKED AT JORN with horror. *Too far, Jorn, too far,* my mind whispered. It was a monstrous thing to say of a father in front of his child. In the dead animal room, a verbal shot had been fired, and for a moment afterward, there was that eerie silence when the world has been shaken and those in that world realize it will never be the same.

Donovan slammed his glass down. A fissure streaked across the glass tabletop. Margot jerked as if stung. Michael went rigid. The dead room became deadlier. Suddenly, Donovan exploded from the sofa and reached for Jorn. But Michael was faster. He grabbed his father's arm. Michael was as tall as his father now, not as muscular, but still strong. He had grown up in more ways than one.

"Dad," he said, tightening his grip, "why don't you just tell them? They just want to find out who killed him."

For a moment, we were frozen like trophies: Donovan about to hurl his son aside, Jorn jumping up to defend himself. I looked at Margot, who was shrinking back into her chair. I stayed seated, sending calm vibes into the hot energies that swirled around us, sucking reason from the room.

Then Michael tugged at his father to sit, and I grasped the fist at Jorn's side. Tension oozed off him, but he remained silent for once. Finally, Jorn looked at me, then Donovan, then slowly sat down. Donovan resisted his son for a few seconds longer, then with a scowl relented as well.

Margot muttered, "God, I need a drink."

When I felt the vibrations in the room begin to settle, I plucked the pitcher of tea from the tray, refreshed Margot's glass, and handed it to her. Michael's eyes were on his father. I refilled Donovan's heavy glass, which had fared better than the table, and offered it to him. It took a heartbeat or two, but eventually Donovan reached for the glass.

I felt a rush of sympathy for the Donovan family, who had felt the need to hide their grief. Placing the pitcher back on the tray, I said, "I know this stinks, and we hate it too. My family loved Jacques. We want to find justice for him as much as you do—and we'll do better if we work together."

Donovan stared out the window. Outside, in the living world, the birds carried on as usual, their voices drifting through the open window. Someone fired up a lawn mower and began mowing.

Breaking the silence, I turned to Michael, whom I could hardly believe had evolved from juvenile delinquent to the voice of reason. "When did you learn that the man we found was your uncle?" I asked.

He glanced at his father, who was a storm cloud, then looked down. He rubbed his hands on his baggy shorts. "I heard Mom and Dad talking one night after we found the body. Talking about Jacques Pine. About him being Dad's brother, Charlie . . . my uncle." Donovan stirred. "I was blown away." Michael's voice rose. "I mean I never met the guy until . . . until that night. And he was my uncle. And now he was dead. All I could think about was what he looked like there on the ground."

Margot made a sound, her eyes intent on her son.

Michael cleared his throat. "I read the stories about Jacques in *The Independent*. Searched for some more online. It was all different, you know, knowing we were related. He wasn't just a . . . dead guy anymore. He did all this stuff. He stood for something. And he was *my* uncle."

Michael looked at his father. "It made me proud."

I asked, "Is that why you stole the coin?"

Michael pulled the necklace from its hiding place, and for a second, I heard the old arrogant Michael in his voice. "Well, it *was* my family's."

I frowned at him, annoyed and disappointed that irritating Snowboard Boy had made a reappearance.

"I saw it when Lissa and I were at your house. Recognized it. It was just like the one Dad wears. So, I took it." He looked at the coin. "I, like, wanted a part of my uncle Charlie." There was a plaintive note in Michael's voice.

Sitting beside his son, Donovan turned to Michael in surprise. He pulled out his own necklace from inside his polo shirt. While Michael's was threaded on a leather cord and

Donovan's glinted on a silver chain, the coins were identical. Donovan rubbed his coin between two fingers. He leaned toward his son, and in a low voice, memory wrapped the two. "My mother bought these for us when we were kids on vacation, in some cheap souvenir shop. We thought we were so cool." Father and son shared a smile.

Then Donovan leaned back and said, "It was one of the few things we agreed on."

I said, "Please tell us about Charlie."

Donovan studied the coin in his fingers for several moments. When he looked up, he said, "The environment was everything to my brother. Even when we were kids, he'd disappear into the woods around our farm for hours. I complained to Dad that Charlie was lazy, skipping out on chores." He paused. "But I think sometimes he really did just get lost in time, poking around in rotting logs, playing with bugs, climbing trees. He'd bring stupid stuff home: turtle shells, leaves, pinecones. They were gold to him." Donovan shook his head. "He was the oldest—by six years. He was supposed to shoulder the chores, not me."

Past slights were never buried deep enough, when it came to family. There were things I can't remember about growing up that my sister, Heart, held on to with a tight fist. I said, "We've spoken with Gwen."

Donovan gave a small laugh. "She always made excuses for Charlie. It used to drive me crazy." He fingered the coin. "When he took on the Jacques persona, he kind of drifted out of our lives. I was glad. I was building a career, developing a résumé; I didn't need his antics shadowing me. But Gwen, she really missed him. It pissed me off the way he treated her."

"Persona? So you knew he had become Jacques Pine," I said.

"Yeah, what a dorky thing to do." He looked up to the ceiling as if asking for patience. "As Jacques Pine grew more radical, Charlie distanced himself from Gwen and me even more. He was drawing attention, getting a record. Said he didn't want his deeds to mess things up for us. He bought a fake ID. And Charlie Donovan disappeared."

Knowing Jacques's dislike of authority, I said, "He also didn't want law enforcement to trace him through you."

"That too. Charlie knew I didn't approve of what he did. We had a big fight about his stunt at the White House, didn't talk to each other for a year."

"The White House?" Jorn asked.

"My crazy brother tried to climb the fence of the White House to give the president a piece of his mind about opening national parks to oil drilling. The Secret Service plucked him off the fence and charged him with trying to enter a restricted building. He was back a month later attempting to hang a white sheet on the fence. He'd spray painted 'No Oil. No Spoil.' on it."

"Catchy," I said.

"By that time, he was on a first-name basis with the Secret Service guys." Donovan shook his head in disbelief. "Gwen the peacemaker got us back together, but we had an unspoken agreement after that: I stayed out of Charlie's business and he stayed away from mine. Especially my family."

The energy in the room was charged with memory. I asked Margot, "Charlie never came here?"

She jumped, a rabbit suddenly discovered. Sliding her gaze

toward her husband, she said, "No. The few times I met him were before we moved to Gabriel's Garden."

Donovan said, "Charlie always thought Margot was too good for me. The jerk." A smile passed between the couple, the first exchange of intimacy I'd seen between them.

Jorn asked, "Were you surprised when Jacques appeared in this neck of the woods?"

Donovan turned from his wife to Jorn. "I knew Charlie was here. He called me and told me he was coming to help a friend." Donovan looked at me. "Your dad."

I nodded.

"He asked me to meet him at his camp." Donovan paused. He raked a hand through his near perfect hair, dislodging strands. "He looked terrible. Told me he had cancer. Man, I couldn't believe it. He was only fifty-one years old." Donovan looked at his hands.

No words could bridge the silence.

After a while, Donovan said, "I wanted to take him to a hospital, right then; I had contacts at the Mayo Clinic. But he was stubborn, as usual. 'Don't want to die in a sterile box, Chris,' he said. 'I'm gonna die out here with the trees and the wind and the birds.' He had some crazy plan to live out his days in that old tent. Wanted to pay somebody to help him. Like he had the money. We argued. Blew up at each other, again."

I bet Jacques already had a caretaker lined up: Val Miley.

"But in the end, you gave him money," I said, now sure where the cash in Jacques's backpack had come from.

"Yes."

"You've kept his identity a secret for years," I said.

Donovan nodded. No one spoke. Finally, he looked at the dead animals hovering over us. "You know, Charlie would have hated this room."

Michael watched his father with an inscrutable expression.

"Chris," I said, "what can you tell us that'll help us find Jacques's killer? Who do *you* think did it?"

With a jab at Jorn, Donovan said, "Well, it wasn't me. I went out there to buy off Charlie."

Beside me, Jorn moved. "Buy him off?"

"I thought he was messing with my pollinator program."

I said, "Jacques would never intentionally harm the farmers."

Donovan looked at me. "I know. But I couldn't be sure he had uncontaminated seeds, and neither could he. I just wanted him to stay away from our supplier farms. We're trying like hell to control those areas."

"Why?" asked Jorn, automatically searching his pockets for his reporter's notebook.

With a hard look for Jorn, Donovan said, "I told you: nothing leaves this room. You still want my help?"

Jorn took his time, sizing up his opponent. The notebook stayed in his pocket.

"If this gets out . . ." Donovan rubbed his face and sighed. Finally, he explained, "There's a crazy killer weed out there called Palmer amaranth."

"I've heard of it," said Jorn.

"Then you know it shoots up seven feet high with stems so thick and roots so deep you can't kill it by hand. Herbicides are useless against it."

Jorn nodded.

"It multiplies like mad. Ruins once-productive farmland in

a matter of years." Donovan gulped his tea and looked at it as if he wished it were something stronger. "Palmer amaranth is scary stuff. It puts farmers out of business. The bad news for us, for Mary Ella's pollinator program, is that Palmer amaranth seeds have been found in seed mixes going into some pollinator programs."

Donovan was quick to add, "Not ours. So far, none of our supplier farmers have spotted Palmer amaranth in their fields. But it's made them jumpy. The tags on the seeds claim they're 100 percent safe, but the farmers don't trust them. And frankly, I don't blame them."

"What a mess," Jorn said.

The sustainability officer for Mary Ella's nodded. "Yeah, it's made for some real pleasant meetings at work."

"What do the seed providers say?" asked Jorn.

"Not much. Dozens of companies sell seed mixes used in pollinator programs sponsored by corporations, nonprofits, and the US Department of Agriculture."

"Doesn't the USDA license the seed companies?"

Donovan shook his head. "No. The USDA only inspects the seed tags on the bags. The tags are supposed to accurately represent the varieties and ratios of seeds in the mix and the presence or absence of harmful weeds."

"But unmonitored, any company can cut corners for profit," Jorn observed.

"We hope it's just been a few accidental cases," Donovan said.

"How far has this Palmer amaranth spread?" Jorn asked.

"It started in the South and has marched north. It's here, man. In the Midwest."

This made me incredibly sad. "This is terrible," I said. "The pollinator program is such a good thing."

"I have to stay on top of this," Donovan said. "So far none of Mary Ella's pollinator areas have been infested but—I'm just one frantic farmer call from losing my job and from Mary Ella's shareholders taking a hit."

Margot reached out as if to comfort her husband then let her hand sink back to her lap.

"Some farmers have begun misusing herbicides to control resistant weeds like Palmer amaranth."

"How do you misuse herbicide?" asked Michael.

"Some eradication products can only be used under certain conditions," Donovan explained. "The problem comes when they move off target by the way of drift."

"What's drift?"

"Used in the wrong way and at the wrong time, the spray can drift and cause damage to nearby farms, killing good crops along with the weeds. One farmer actually shot and killed his neighbor in an argument over spray drift damage."

Michael's eyes widened.

Donovan hung his head. "I wish my brother had never gotten involved in this mess."

I cleared my throat. "How many times did you visit Jacques?"

Donovan shrugged. "I checked up on him. Took him food a couple of times. He liked Hallie's muffins."

"You never told me," Margot said. "We could have invited him to dinner."

Donovan glanced at his wife. "Both Charlie and I knew we couldn't be seen together."

Jorn leaned forward, his arms resting on his knees. "What

do *you* think happened to Jacques? Your brother wasn't a popular guy in some circles. Could it have been a corporate assassination? Oil industry, loggers, food distributors?"

Donovan sat up straighter. "Whoa there. Mary Ella's would never sanction that. No way." He stopped. "But someone was after him. One time when I visited, he looked like someone had beat him up. I asked him what happened. He shrugged me off. I wanted to take him to a doctor, but he refused."

"He was assaulted *before* he was shot?" Jorn frowned.

"His cheek was bruised, and he was moving gingerly. Hurt ribs, maybe."

"The same assailant or two different ones?"

"Who knows? My brother led a dangerous life. I wanted to keep that away from my family." He looked at Margot and Michael. "Charlie was fearless. He'd step up and get into the face of anyone: cop, angry logger, even the president. He'd lay down in front of bulldozers and snapping dogs."

There was a wistful pride in Donovan's voice, as if he almost admired his brother's daring and commitment to something greater. As swiftly as I had heard it, it was gone. "My brother was crazy," Donovan said.

I took out my phone and found the photo Jacques had carried. I showed the image of the three kids smiling into the camera to Donovan.

"This is you, Gwen, and Charlie, isn't it?"

Donovan gasped as if punched. "Where did you—"

"It was among Jacques's belongings. He'd carried it everywhere, from one protest line to the next, from one end of the country to the other, year after year. He never let it go. He never let you go."

Donovan stared at the photo then rubbed his eyes.

"Did you pay for Jacques Pine's cremation?" I asked.

Michael watched his father intently.

Donovan said softly, "Yeah, I'm the anonymous donor. Maybe someday, when this is over, I'll claim those ashes."

But he wouldn't do it today and make public his connection to a murdered man. That was still a step too far for Chris Donovan.

A quiet Michael walked us to our car. By the hunch of his shoulders and the troubled expression on his face, I could tell he had something on his mind. At the gate, he said, "I wish I had stayed with Uncle Charlie. You know, that night."

"His spirit was long gone, Michael."

Head down, he said, "But it would have been the right thing to do."

"The right thing?" I said. It was an odd concern coming from Michael.

Michael looked back at the house then at me. "About a year ago, I started going to these meetings," he said in a low voice. "Just a bunch of kids. We talk about stuff. About living with parents who drink."

"That's cool."

"Mostly I listen. Don't want to look like a jerk; I know I don't have it as bad as some."

I nodded.

"We talk about the Three C's—I did not cause it, I cannot control it, and I cannot cure it." He kicked at the white picket fence. "I change the things I can, you know?"

"The Serenity Prayer," I said.

Michael gave the fence another rap. "Look, I know I'm not why my mom drinks. But I can't *not* help her, you know? And I can't *not* wish I had been able to do something for Uncle Charlie."

"Your uncle believed he could change things."

Michael stopped going at the fence and looked at me. "Yeah."

This former kitten tormentor was breaking my heart. I playfully bumped him with my hip. "Look at you, Snowboard Boy. Making changes. Getting all responsible."

Michael fought back a smile. "Don't let that get around."

I was still holding my phone. He motioned for me to give it to him. He swiped and found the image of the Donovan siblings and sent a copy to his phone. I heard the ping in his pocket.

Then he tossed my phone to me and swaggered toward the house. Halfway there, he turned but kept walking backwards. "You find the guy."

CHAPTER 32

CONTEMPT WITH YOUR CROISSANT?

HALF THE TOWN DROVE pickup trucks, SUVs, or roll bar-equipped four-wheel drives—vehicles that took to mud like automotive swine. I'd been keeping an eye out for any ride decorated up to its headlights in the remains of Sadie's Papillon Farm. A wildflower caught in a grille would send my investigative juices racing. But so far, there were no real suspects.

Jorn's article on the attack on the pollinator sanctuary had the town talking, though. I stepped into Northern Lights, and before the bell over the door had stopped jingling, Merlin Huus called me over to his table.

A regular in my Thursday class, Merlin was a retired Danish carpenter. As usual, his arthritic fingers were bandaged up from hours of cabinetmaking, and even in summer he wore a red scarf around his neck. He was having coffee with two men: an older gentleman whom I did not know but who nodded to me in greeting, and Frank Hollister, who ignored me.

"Hey, have they caught who tore up your wildflowers?" Merlin asked. The idea that the Skyes were farming weeds was either the butt of jokes or the source of curiosity in the town.

I shook my head. "The culprit's still on the loose. Better watch your gardens."

Eyes averted, Frank snorted. I knew Frank's opinion on wasting good farmland on weeds.

The third man, a bald fellow encased in a fishing vest with a million pockets, said, "Probably kids. Pullin' those wheelies." I couldn't take my eyes off his massive mustache, which harbored enough crumbs to feed a nation of mice.

Merlin agreed, "Vandals. Don't understand why kids have such a destructive streak."

"Kids," muttered Frank.

"Always had to keep my eye out on my construction sites," Merlin went on. "They'd turn over paint cans, toss supplies around, spray-paint the plywood with nasty words and pictures. Complained to their parents, and all I got was 'They're just kids.' Bull."

The coffee machine let out a low rumble, and Mustache Man raised his voice. "They all need wholesome hobbies. Nothing like catching a nice walleye to change your perspective."

The others grunted in agreement. Talk of juvenile delinquents made me think of Michael and his friends. Maybe he knew of some kids racing their hot rods through the goldenrod. I would have to talk to him about it.

Suddenly Merlin said to Frank, "When's Fritz gettin' in?"

"Fritz is coming home?" I asked.

"Yeah, guess the whales and polar bears can do without him for a week," grumped Frank, slumped over his coffee.

I smiled. "Well, tell him hello and have him stop by for a class while he's in town."

"Yeah, I'll do that," said Frank in a tone that promised to do anything but.

I placed my order with Hallie and scanned the rest of the shop. The walkers were at a table: Alice Dunkirk, Brenda Lundgren, and Sheila Glass, the young mother rocking a stroller with her foot. Brenda and I exchanged hard looks.

From her station behind the counter, Hallie handed me a muffin and tea. As I reached for my order, she saw me studying the table of walkers and said, "Don't want any trouble, Maya."

Tossing my change into the tip jar and turning toward the walkers' table, I said, "Wouldn't think of it."

Hallie just shook her head.

Now, in my logical mind, I doubted Brenda had taken a joyride amid the coneflowers in her monster SUV that required a stepladder to get in to, but that didn't keep me from ambling over to the walkers' table. Noting it was a "good morning for a chocolate muffin," I sat down, uninvited. The women eyed me.

Taking a bite of muffin, I asked, "Alice, are you coming to class today?"

Brenda turned a condemning eye on Alice, but Alice believed raising a boatload of children (none divorced or in prison yet, she was quick to add) had earned her dispensation from judgment, especially from someone like Brenda whose daughter, everyone knew, had run off and now dealt blackjack in Reno. Alice simply said, "Does Minnesota have mosquitoes?"

Like my grandmother, Brenda Lundgren didn't believe in the nondenominational side of yoga. "You're a Catholic, Alice, for goodness sake." Alice, whose devotion ran to two masses a week, lifted an eyebrow. But Brenda carried on, "Plus, you have to walk past all those awful birds to go to class. I don't know how you can stand it."

Alice said, "Brenda, I heard even the pope practices yoga occasionally."

I hid a grin behind a sip of tea. "Actually," I said, "I wanted to talk to you all about the problem we had at the pollinator sanctuary. Have you heard anything? Any rumors about who did it?"

Trim Alice, who had passed on the pastries for a good cup of fair-trade coffee, no cream, no sugar, said, "Everybody's saying it was kids."

"I think it was terrible," said Sheila, tearing off a part of her croissant and popping it into her mouth.

"It was just a field," Brenda huffed. "Nobody was hurt."

"I disagree," I said. I nodded at the baby sleeping in the stroller. "It would be tragic if she grew up in a world without butterflies and bees."

Brenda, waving her hard biscotti in the air, said, "The world isn't ending because a few weeds got run over. I think all this climate change stuff is a hoax."

"Our food supply depends on those bees and butterflies," I said. "If they disappear, so do we."

Sheila frowned, pulled the stroller closer to her chair, and smoothed the sleeping baby's onesie.

With a tip of her head toward the young mother, Alice said, "Stop scaring the child, Maya."

Brenda leaned toward me. "You all brought this on yourselves."

"How do you figure that?" My tone drew a quick glance from Alice, who had years of experience refereeing disputes in the Dunkirk household.

"This used to be a nice, quiet town, Maya Skye," Brenda said. "Now we have murder and vandalism and birds. Filthy birds. Causing a public nuisance and a menace. I had to wash my car *twice* this week already. Sheila's afraid to leave her baby in the yard because who knows what might swoop down and grab it. And Alice has to carry a whistle on her walks for safety."

"The whistle was my husband's idea," Alice said. "He's too cheap to take me to Rome."

"There's a murderer running around out there somewhere!" Brenda's voice rose, drawing a worried look from Hallie.

Sheila gulped.

I turned to her. "The crows won't harm your child, Sheila. I can't say the same for ridiculous rumors and fear mongering."

"Fear mongering?" Brenda shook her biscotti in my face. "Your family brought that man here. What was he doing out in those woods? Living like a vagrant? He was probably crazy."

"He was an environmentalist," I said through gritted teeth. "And a darn good one too."

Brenda's eyeglasses, dangling from a beaded chain on the chest of her sweaty T-shirt, bounced with her indignant breath. "He was a troublemaker. All of you people are. You and your radical friends. You come to town with money and think you can change things. You think we're not good enough."

Brenda's face had begun to turn an unattractive purple shade.

"We come in peace, Brenda."

Brenda threw down her biscotti, which bounced across the table and into Alice's lap. "Don't give me that Zen crap. You come here with your computers and your money and your yoga. I bet you don't even know how to make a hot dish."

Sheila gulped down her coffee and made a sudden excuse to go. She bundled the rest of her croissant in a paper napkin, tucked it beside the sleeping baby in the stroller, and wheeled out of the café.

Unperturbed, Alice calmly lifted the biscotti from her lap and handed it to Brenda, then took a sip of coffee. "Don't be so dramatic, Brenda."

Brenda ignored Alice. "And now those weird people are back. Hippies. Criminals probably." She glared at me. "Camping out on your land again. I can't believe it. Your own militia."

I was glad Brenda lost last year's town council election, ending what some people called her twelve-year reign of terror. "Bite me, Brenda," I said.

Brenda gasped. When she recovered, she said, "How do we know those people aren't killers?"

"They're nonviolent." I looked right at her. "But I'm not."

Brenda's eyebrows nearly shot off her face. She sputtered, "I'd like to know what Watt Holmes has to say about all of this."

Actually, the sheriff wasn't happy with my family either. Watt's exact words had been: "We don't need more nuts in this hot dish, Maya."

CHAPTER 33

THE CAVALRY ARRIVES

THE FIRST TIME I met Angelo was at a protest in Seattle. There were seagulls careening through the skies and protestors juggling signs and chanting. Evie had given me a loaf of homemade bread to occupy me, while she, Larry, and about fifty others occupied the entrance to a logging company. I was four and intent on lining up bread chunks in a row on the curb. The game drove the seagulls wild. They plucked the bread from the curb in screaming dives, stealing as fast as I could tear off a chunk and lay it down. At one point, Angelo crouched beside me, his dreadlocks brushing my cheek, his smile movie star bright and perfect back then. "Be careful," he'd told me, "or they'll follow you home, Maya Girl."

"Really?" I'd said, hopeful.

With a laugh that drew glances, Angelo picked up his sign and rejoined the others.

The Angelo who walked beside Evie and me around Lake Michael had streaks of silver in his massive ponytail and a missing front tooth, but he still was the hero of my memory, my guardian angel. He, along with a few others, had arrived with their camping gear to guard Sadie's Papillion Farm. My parents' friends came in all shapes and sizes, all levels of intent and resilience. But Angelo was my anchor. He unfailingly answered the call of the Skye family.

"Thank you for coming," I said.

"Was there any doubt?" He shook his head at my lack of faith.

I bumped his shoulder with mine. "No."

With a smile for Evie, he said, "Larry and Evie don't put their bodies on the line much anymore, but they back our causes. They're just protesting in a different way." He stretched his back. "I don't blame them. Sleeping bags aren't as comfortable as they once were."

"I can send some cots and mattresses out to the campsite," Evie offered.

Angelo shook his head. "No. The younger ones need to learn how to rough it. Activism is not for the weak."

Evie nodded.

A crow lit on the path and, bobbing its head, began to walk in front of us as if leading a parade. Lately, the crow or one of its brothers had been following me whenever I left the house. This creeped out Jorn, but I didn't mind. Sometimes, when I was alone, I took a page out of James Tumblethorne's book and turned to the crows for guidance. The crows, for their part, seemed to listen as I asked the questions I used to ask Tum: "What should I do? What is right?"

For the record, the crows never answered.

I heard steps on the path behind us, steps that never stroll. Stamping the earth with a sureness of personality and purpose was Alice Dunkirk. As she passed us, pumping her arms and legs, she said, "Exercising the militia?"

I replied, "Unarmed and ready is our motto."

She cracked a smile then plowed down the trail, startling the crow into the air.

"Militia?" Angelo asked.

"The locals think we are amassing an army for world domination. They blame us for Jacques, the crows, you name it. If their socks fell down for no reason, it would be the Skyes' fault."

Angelo's laugh echoed through the trees.

We walked on in no hurry. "Everyone seems to think the attack on the farm was just a childish stunt," I said.

Angelo considered the idea, keeping his pace slow for Evie. "It's possible. Kids hear their parents talk at the dinner table. 'Those stupid Skyes did this or that.' The kids start thinking: Wouldn't it be cool to take those stupid Skyes down a peg or two?"

Evie agreed, "So many of our beliefs are formed early and over tuna casserole."

"But I have a feeling," I said, "that there's something more behind it."

"Follow your gut, Maya Girl. You always did sense things before the rest of us."

"It feels like a message," I said.

"But if it was a message, what is someone trying to tell us?" Evie asked.

Angelo thought for a moment. "Who says it's a message for you? Maybe it's simply a cry for help."

I hadn't thought of that. None of us want to believe our neighbors are capable of this kind of violence—until somebody finds human body parts in the freezer with last year's deer steaks.

Could tearing up our wildflowers be someone trying to get our attention? Or could they just be frustrated with what's happening here in Gabriel's Garden?

We came to the trailhead on Elm Street, a half block from Breathe, my studio. Roselyn, Nate, and Angus were just getting out of a mud-splattered Jeep. Angus rushed to me, tongue hanging and tail wagging. I rubbed his head and said hello to Roselyn. Nate nodded at us then whistled for Angus. As they headed down the path from which we had just come, Angelo said, "I know that guy."

"That's Nate Nelson, Roselyn's boyfriend. He's a treasure hunter."

Angelo kept his eyes on the trio until they disappeared around the bend in the trail. "Treasure hunter?" He shook his head. "Ran into him a few years back. In Florida. At a protest. Remember him, Evie? You and Larry were there. So was Jacques."

Evie froze, then recognition dawned on her face. "That's why he seems so familiar."

"Was he one of the protestors?" I asked.

Angelo and Evie both looked back at the path where Nate had disappeared. "No," they said.

We turned toward my house. As we neared the fire station, the clop-clop of Angelo's big boots on the sidewalk was replaced by the noise of the birds in the trees in my front yard. As we stepped into the yard, he nodded at them. "They know."

"Know what?"

"We're killing this planet."

Sitting on the patio with Evie and me, Angelo ran his big hands through the shinys in the basket on the table. Nodding at the basket, I explained, "Gifts from my friends."

He smiled. "You can never have too many friends."

Evie had been quiet on the walk to my house. She had that look when she is sorting through drawers of information in her brain, looking for something. "We were protesting about ocean pollution in Florida. The dead zones, right, Angelo?"

I pulled my legs up and rested my arms on my knees as I searched my memory for what I knew about dead zones. "Dead zones are areas in oceans and lakes where there isn't enough oxygen for plants and animals to live."

Angelo settled back into the cushions. He was a big man and took up a fair share of the love seat. "Yeah, blooms of algae deplete underwater oxygen levels. Fish die or leave. Find someplace where they can breathe."

Evie said, "I remember. Jacques organized the protest."

Angelo grinned at Evie. "Man, he was hot when he learned what that company was dumping into the ocean."

"What company?" I asked.

"I can't remember the name, but it was a chemical producer," said Evie. "Chemical nutrients in the water was causing the excessive algae."

"Like chemicals used in agriculture?"

Evie nodded. "One of the biggest dead zones in the world is in the Gulf of Mexico. That's why we targeted the company in Florida."

"But what does this have to do with Nate Nelson?"

Angelo turned to me, his braids rattling. "We were pushing for more regulation on polluting companies. And Nate decided to push back."

I hugged my legs tighter to my body. "What happened?"

Evie said, "It was terrible. The chemical company seeded the crowd with instigators. Thugs."

I dropped my chin on my updrawn knees, afraid to hear the rest.

"People were hurt. Seriously hurt, Maya," Evie said, lifting her arm. "I got a sprained wrist; Larry was knocked unconscious. And we were the lucky ones."

"How did I not know about this?" I asked. Suddenly a thought occurred to me, and I looked at my mother. "Did this happen on your Florida vacation a few years ago?"

Evie looked guilty. "Yes."

"Evie, why didn't you tell us—"

She waved my concern aside. "It was one of the worst protests we'd ever been in, Maya."

Angelo reached out to Evie. She grasped his hand. "Yeah, it was fucking bloody," he said. "People kicked and clubbed. Saw three guys beat the shit out of Jacques. I couldn't get to him. He was obviously the target."

"He was our voice, and they silenced him," Evie said. "I sat by his side at the hospital. Three days, before he woke up.

His first words were 'Get me out of here.' And we did. Larry and I made plans for him to recuperate with some friends who owned a farm in Kansas."

Evie continued, "But refused to leave until he had his say. He held a press conference right at his bedside. He told it like it was: the dead zones, the company's involvement in destroying the environment, the protest turning bloody. 'That company hired people to kill us,' he said. The media jumped on the story."

"It was a stupid move. The thugs," Angelo said. "Company denied everything, of course. But eventually, after the bad PR died down, they quietly closed the plant."

Angelo looked at me.

"Nate Nelson was the manager at that chemical plant," he said. "It was his decision to crush the protest."

CHAPTER 34

KEEP BREATHING

NATE NELSON HAD KNOWN Jacques Pine. As soon as Angelo and Evie left, I called Jorn. When there was no answer, I rushed to his house. Because I was sure now. I had no proof, but my intuition sang like a bird on a wire. I knew.

Nate was our killer.

When I pulled up to the curb, Jorn was sitting on his front porch step with Randy, his often-confused and seldom-sober neighbor. When Jorn traveled, Randy was the official caretaker for Jorn's only plant—a petite zebra cactus, which Randy had named Armadillo.

Randy lived with his mother and was still trying to pick a major in his fourth year of junior college. Recently, he'd bought a tiny cactus like Jorn's because, as Randy said, "I felt it was time to take on more responsibility in my life."

"Hey, *namaste*," Randy greeted me with a sloppy grin. I could smell the dope on him from steps away. Skinny enough to slip through a keyhole, he peered at me through his wire-rim glasses and stroked his unsuccessful goatee. "Heard about what happened at the butterfly place, Maya. That's so not cool. If you need any help . . ."

It was a sweet, and unexpected, offer.

"Thanks, Randy," I said, "I'll keep that in mind. But right now, I just need to talk to Jorn."

Randy took the hint, slapped his bony thighs, and got up to leave. As he passed me on the sidewalk, he gave me a fist bump and said, "Stay calm and eat more brownies."

I took Randy's seat on the step. There was a plastic bag of brownies next to Jorn. "A gift from Randy?" I asked.

He said, "I wouldn't try them if you want to do anything else today."

I told Jorn about the Florida protest and Nate Nelson's involvement.

"And get this," I said, "Jacques organized the demonstration. The thugs targeted him."

Jorn's eyes widened. He jumped up and went into the house, returned with his laptop, and began researching the Florida protest. While yellow finches and chickadees fluttered and fought at the birdfeeder, we flitted from story to story. I read over his shoulder. Each report confirmed my feelings: Nate had a reason to hate Jacques Pine. In the press conference Jacques held from his hospital bed, he blamed Nate for the violence at the rally.

Motioning to the laptop and the articles we'd found, Jorn

said, "Nate's no fan of environmentalists, especially Jacques. They cost him his job. A nice job with a nice fat pension."

"It all makes sense," I said. "Revenge. He had a motive for murder."

"We know Nate's been snooping around with his metal detector." Jorn shifted. "He could have run into Jacques. He had opportunity."

"And we saw the gun in his backpack. He had the means to kill Jacques."

Jorn drummed his fingers on the laptop then started putting together a timeline. "Nate Nelson heads a chemical company targeted by protestors. He hires some guys to break up the protest. People get hurt. Bad publicity forces the company to shut down Nelson's plant. Nelson gets his walking papers. He turns up in Gabriel's Garden looking for his birth mother and Gabriel Nygård's treasure. Encounters Jacques while he is treasure hunting. Blames Jacques for ruining his life. Jacques winds up dead."

I picked up the story. "But Nate can't afford to leave town because he still hasn't found the treasure. He continues to romance Roselyn and connect with the Troll Lady, allegedly his mother. He believes Gabriel Nygård's letters will give him a clue to the treasure's location. But then Amelie dies."

"Before he can get control of the letters," Jorn pointed out. "As Al said, Amelie was desperate for attention. She might show them to Nate, but I bet she wouldn't just hand them over to him."

"Because the letters kept Nate coming back to her." I leaned back against the step in thought and watched the birds squabble at the feeder. "But how did he even know about the letters, the treasure, and Amelie?"

"Maybe his father told him."

"He was just a kid when Gabe Junior died."

"If Gabe gave Nate to his sister to raise, he did it to keep the boy near so he could see him, talk to him."

"Keep him close. Pass on the Nygård legacy to him. Tell him about his adventurer grandfather who supposedly had hidden treasure."

Jorn ran a hand through his hair. "But this is all supposition. We have no proof."

"We need a confession," I said.

"How good are you with a rubber hose?"

"Um, yoga teacher here." Spotting the time on Jorn's watch, I started to get up. "A late yoga teacher. I have a noon class."

"I'll make some calls," he said. "See if I can find out more about Nate and the Florida protest. Research torture methods."

I hoped he was kidding.

The noon class was small: a few regulars including Alice Dunkirk and Merlin Huus and a visiting student, Fritz Hollister. Tanned and loose-limbed, he looked healthy and happy. Saving the planet obviously agreed with him. As I handed Fritz a mat, Evie walked in with my grandmother. I cast a questioning glance at Evie, who only shrugged and said, "Sylvia wants to take your class."

Surprised, I said, "Gran, welcome to yoga."

Gran was wearing one of her usual summer suits, including a hat. I couldn't even imagine my grandmother in yoga pants.

Evie said, "Let's set up Sylvia with a chair at the back of the studio."

Good idea. Evie unrolled her mat near Gran and began to do some stretches. As I settled my creaky grandmother into a chair, I whispered, "What are you up to?"

"Thought it was time to see what you do here."

I didn't trust my grandmother, so I laid down a few house rules, "No talk of pagans. Don't try to convert my students. And don't break yourself. I'll give you alternative poses that you can do in a chair."

Back straight, jaw stiff, she centered her handbag on her lap and settled her hat securely on her head. "Don't bother. I'm just spectating."

To still my own nerves, I began the class with a longer-than-usual meditation to focus the breath. For some reason, it mattered to me that my grandmother was observing me and the class. *Why did I need her approval?* I wondered. I knew she would never be a yoga advocate, but maybe this experience would broaden her perspective and help her recognize yoga as something other than the devil's handiwork.

I always try to customize the class to the students. I knew Evie loved flows, sequencing several postures together. Fritz, young and energetic, probably was eager for more challenging work. Merlin appreciated a gentler pace, while Alice would set her jaw and try anything. So, I mixed it up, always coming back to the breath. And soon I sensed a happy hum in the spirit of the class.

As I bowed my head in a final *namaste* to the class and

the students responded in like manner, I snuck a peek at my grandmother. She was watching me. I couldn't read her.

While the others packed up, I sat down next to Evie on her mat. Looking up at my grandmother who was still in her chair, I asked, "What did you think of the class, Gran?"

She took her time answering. I prepared myself for her usual sharp assessment, but all she said was, "You breathe a lot."

Evie laughed.

Fritz joined us, gracefully folding into lotus on the floor, and I introduced him to Gran.

"Mom told me about the crows, Maya." Fritz shook his head. "I can't imagine what got into Dad."

I said, "It was your birthday," as if that explained it all.

Fritz tried to make a joke of it. "Yeah, great gift for a pacifist. Killing birds."

I thought about what Angelo had said about the destruction of the butterfly sanctuary. A cry for help. Maybe killing the crows had been just that.

Gran had been watching this exchange with interest. I said, "Gran, Fritz is working for Greenpeace."

With a lift of her eyebrow, she asked, "What do you do?"

Fritz tucked his wavy, red hair behind an ear and said with a grin, "Mainly pick up plastic bottles in the ocean."

"Important work," I said. "As the saying goes, there is no second nature."

Fritz's expression sobered. "When I'm out there in the war against plastic, I feel like I'm doing something big."

"Bigger than a farm in Minnesota?" I asked.

Fritz looked at me. "You've been talking to Dad."

"The farm's all he has, Fritz," I said. "I can understand that he would want you to farm it with him. He's keeping it for you."

Fritz nodded. "I know. I've tried to tell him—I'm not going to be with Greenpeace forever. But he just won't listen."

My grandmother, a quick study even in her eighties, knew business and how tough it was to keep one going, no matter the field. She also was familiar with having a son determined to go his own way. Looking over the top of her glasses at Fritz, she said, "Suppose he can't hold on until you sow your wild oats, young man?"

Fritz ducked his head. "I just hope he can, ma'am."

"Hope is a slippery fish to hold on to when you're old," said Gran in a kinder voice. "Remember that when you're out plucking bottles from the deep blue."

I shared a smile with Fritz.

"I will, ma'am," he said.

Suddenly, Fritz's cell phone buzzed. He checked the caller ID, apologized, and answered it. "Mom? Calm down. What? Okay, okay, I'll be right there." He punched the off button and leapt to his feet.

"What's wrong?" I asked, rising just as quickly.

"Mom can't find Dad. He came in, madder than a hornet, grabbed his gun, and took off."

I hoped Frank wasn't shooting crows again. I turned desperate eyes toward Evie. "Go," she said. "And, Maya, be careful."

There was no time to run upstairs and retrieve my phone or satchel. "Call Jorn."

Evie nodded.

As I was about to follow Fritz, Gran seized my wrist and stopped me. "Take this," she said and pulled her tiny bottle of holy oil from her handbag. I looked into her calm warrior eyes, saw the stubborn set of her lips, and reached for the bottle.

As I headed out the door, my fist closed tightly around the bottle, I heard my grandmother say, "Evangeline, take me home. I have some powerful praying to do."

CHAPTER 35

IT'S MINE

FRANK HOLLISTER'S PICKUP WAS held together by rust and dust. The shocks were gone, and Fritz had to battle with the stubborn steering wheel and sticky gear shift. He pressed the accelerator to the floor, but the truck refused to go above forty-five. As we bumped and crept out of Gabriel's Garden toward the Hollister farm, a sense of urgency rose in me. *Can't we go any faster?* I wanted to scream.

As if he read my mind, Fritz cast a hapless look in my direction and said, "Nothing is easy with Dad."

I didn't know if he meant the old pickup that Frank refused to put down, or the fight over Fritz's future, or Frank's recent inexplicable behavior.

I kept silent.

At the Hollister farm, Fritz slammed on the brakes and was

out of the truck before I could open my door. Louisa came running from the house.

"He's in one of his moods," Louisa warned.

"Where did he go?"

Louisa threw her hands up in exasperation. "Took the ATV and hightailed it out to the fields." She reached for her son. "Oh, Fritz, what if he turns that dang thing over on himself? And what does he need a gun for?"

"We'll find him," I reassured Louisa.

The Hollister farm was home to acres of crops—corn and soybeans—as far as the eye could see. I peered out at the wall of tall corn edging up to the yard. Where to look for Frank? What would have drawn him out to the fields in such a state?

Then I saw them. Crows.

I pointed to the birds circling the air, ten or more of them. "He's there."

Fritz shielded his eyes from the sun as he scanned the skies. "Are you sure?"

"Positive."

Louisa wanted to come with us, but Fritz said, "Stay here. I'll bring Dad back."

I had a bad feeling about this. As Fritz and I piled into the truck and pulled a U-turn, I shouted to Louisa, "Call the sheriff."

Then Fritz was pushing the truck as fast as it could go in the direction of the birds. I clutched the car door with one hand and the bottle of holy oil with the other. I was wearing yoga pants and had no pockets. So, I tucked the tiny bottle of oil down my bra.

When we were about even with the birds over the field,

Fritz steered the truck off the road, and we bounced down a ditch and back up to the edge of the cornfield.

I spotted Frank's ATV parked near a row of corn and yelled, "Stop." We scrambled out of the truck and sprinted into the corn. Fritz and I dashed through the close rows of cornstalks, dodging the sharp blades. There wasn't a breath of air between the rows, just the heat of the sun and the cries of the birds. Calling me. I kept glancing to the sky, using the crows as my compass.

And then we were upon them.

Frank Hollister and Nate Nelson.

In a standoff.

The birds wheeled in the sky, occasionally dipping down to strafe the head of one man or the other. They remembered Frank from the crow-killing rampage. And it was obvious, they didn't like Nate either.

Nate had been digging. Cornstalks were trampled, and his metal detector lay on the ground next to a pile of black dirt and a hole.

Our appearance, bursting through the curtain of cornstalks, startled both men. Nate whipped a gun from behind his back and pointed it at us. Fritz and I froze. In a second, Frank's rifle was up and aimed at Nate's chest.

"Whoa!" I shouted, hands stretched out as if to separate the two men. "Stop! Everyone just stop!"

Nate and Frank eyed each other.

"Let's all take a breath," I pleaded.

Fritz's voice shook. "Dad!"

Frank didn't look at his son. "Fritz, go on back to the house."

"Not without you, Dad."

"I'm not going anywhere until this thief gets off my land."

"Thief?" Fritz asked.

"Look." Frank nodded to the earth at Nate's feet. "That hole's full of gold coins."

"My gold," Nate said.

Frank shook his head. "My land. My gold."

Nate exploded, "My grandfather buried that gold! It's my inheritance!"

"Your grandfather," said Frank as calmly as if he were commenting on the weather. "Bull."

Something grim took over Nate Nelson in that moment, transforming the charming beach scavenger into a forbidding and frightening man. Nate's tone turned deadly. "I'm taking that gold, Frank."

Lifting his gun higher, Frank said, "You'll die tryin'."

Suddenly a large black bird swept in, plucked a coin from the dirt by Nate's foot, and flew off.

"Hey, that's mine!" Nate yelled.

Nate's outburst startled both Fritz and me. Fritz took a step toward Nate, but I halted him with a hand on his arm.

"Fucking birds," Nate fumed. He was coming apart. His eyes darted from Frank to me and Fritz and back. He moved his head, a slight tic he repeated every once in a while, to release the tension in his neck. His gun hand was steady, but I didn't know how long that would last. He was wrapped in stress.

If ever there was a time to get a confession out of him . . .

I asked Spirit for help then took a chance. "Nate, before you shoot us all, why don't you tell us why you killed Jacques Pine?"

The cornfield rang with silence. Nate's head whipped in my direction, and his eyes narrowed on me. How much did I know?

"Maya, what in tarnation are you talkin' about?" asked Frank, not taking his eyes off Nate or lowering his rifle.

I had Nate's full attention. The gun was aimed at me now. Waiting.

I forced my body to relax, took a breath. Returning Nate's look with a calm I didn't feel, I said, "Nate used to dump chemicals into the ocean in his former life."

"You bastard," Fritz said. Fearing Fritz was going to launch himself at Nate, I tightened my grip on Fritz's arm.

Nate remained silent, but I sensed something was shifting. I could get to Nate, but this was a dangerous game I was playing.

"Careful, Fritz, Nate hates environmentalists. Don't you, Nate?" I taunted. "In fact, you never wanted to see another activist for the rest of your life, after the events in Florida. Then you met Jacques Pine, here, in Gabriel's Garden."

"You're full of shit," said Nate.

I shook my head. "You ran into Jacques while you were metal detecting and recognized him. And he recognized you."

The more I talked the clearer it all became to me. After a pause, I went for the jugular. "Jacques brought you and your rotten polluting company down. He knew who you really were. A polluter, a cheat, a coward who hires other people to do your dirty work. Related to Gabriel Nygård? I don't believe it. You're just a failure."

Frank said, "You don't have any claim on this gold."

Nate's restraint snapped. "I *am* a Nygård!"

"Prove it," I said.

Nate straightened, his expression stubborn. "I don't have to prove anything to you."

The only thing I could think to do was keep Nate talking until Watt Holmes found us. Ready to push Fritz to the side if bullets began to fly, I needled Nate, "You come here and romance Roselyn. You take advantage of poor Amelie and her desperate desire for family. You're a liar. A con man."

Nate's eyes darted between me with the wild accusations and Frank with the gun. "Amelie *was* my mother, and Gabe Nygård *was* my father," he said. "But he sent her away."

Jorn's uncle had been right. Poor Amelie had been an unwed mother in a small town in an unforgiving time.

"Away? Where?" I asked.

"To my dad's sister. She and her husband raised me because Amelie couldn't. Their name was Nelson." He sneered. "But I never felt like I belonged with them. They were boring people. I came from adventurers, treasure hunters. My father told me so. I was a Nygård, not a Nelson."

"You still don't have any proof," I said.

"Amelie had letters from my dad and my grandfather. They prove that I'm his son and that my grandfather Gabriel had treasure. This treasure is mine."

"Amelie Reese was half crazy," said Frank.

"She was not! She was my mother, and she had letters to prove it. I saw them. I read them. I *am* Gabe Nygård's son." His voice trailed off, and he grew distracted. "But I couldn't find them after Amelie died."

Suddenly, Nate's eyes searched the ground around him.

Was he looking for Angus the dog? The missing dog seemed to bother Nate.

"Where's Angus, Nate?" I asked.

"Didn't come today."

"Why?"

"Damn birds spook him. Always watching us."

Had the crows been following Nate as they had been following me? Slowly, more pieces of this tenuous puzzle began to slide together in my head: Nate dropping a coin for Sadie to find; the crows retrieving the coin, which turned out to belong to Jacques, and presenting it to me. Did the crows see Nate kill Jacques?

The crows had gone quiet. They watched us from a windbreak of trees in the distance. Crows and coins. Could I really trap Nate into a confession with a coin?

Behind Nate, I saw something move. It was Watt's skinny form sliding between the cornstalks. And then I saw another movement to his right. A face peeked out. It was Jorn. He made a rolling motion with his hands; he wanted me to keep Nate talking. Of course, facing desperate men with guns was easy for Jorn to do; he had experience in that. But I was terrified. I looked at Watt. His face was calm, confident. He slowly nodded at me to keep it together.

I took a deep breath and flicked my head toward the sky. "No wonder those birds hate you, Nate. They saw you kill Jacques."

"Bullshit."

"Really?" I said. "The crows brought me a gift." Nate eyed me with suspicion. "The coin you dropped from your pocket for Sadie to find with the metal detector. Pretty stupid to accidentally lose Jacques's coin."

I had his attention. "You're lying," he said.

I smiled at him, said nothing.

"I dropped a plain old American quarter for Sadie to find," he insisted.

"No. It was Canadian, and it belonged to Jacques. You pulled it out of your pocket by accident. How did you get Jacques's coin, Nate? Did you rip it from his neck after you killed him?"

Frank was shocked. "You really killed that old man?"

Nate shot Frank a look. "Of course not."

"He was a nuisance," Frank went on, "but he didn't deserve to die."

I said, "No, he didn't, Frank."

"You can't prove anything," Nate said.

"But I can, Nate," I said. "You left your fingerprints on Jacques's coin." I didn't tell Nate that so many people—and birds—had handled that coin, which now was in the possession of Michael Donovan, that it probably wasn't evidence anymore.

Nate's gaze flickered and he nervously cracked his neck, but the gun didn't waver.

"Were you afraid Jacques would find the gold? He *was* digging everywhere, planting. What if he found it first?" I raised my voice. "Or, was it just an act of revenge? Jacques had taken you down once, and if he found the gold first, he would defeat you again. It must have driven you crazy, thinking of Jacques with all that gold. What would he do with it? Probably donate it to every environmental group he could think of. He'd give your money to the people you despise. Once again, Jacques would take everything away from you."

Although Nate's eyes looked at me with hatred, I pulled my calm around me, the way I'd seen Guru Bob do, and Guru Bob was one hell of a poker player. I continued to bait him, "Who will take care of Angus when you're in jail, Nate?"

Suddenly, the tense energy in Nate exploded and hit me like a wave. "You couldn't mind your own business, could you?" he gritted. "You're just like Jacques."

"You flatter me."

"He ruined everything in Florida and then I come and find him here. In my way. Digging all over the place, planting shit. I warned him once."

"You beat up Jacques."

Nate didn't deny it. "He laughed at me. Said *my kind* would never win. He threatened to tell his friend Larry Skye who I was."

"Why would that matter to you?" I asked.

"'Cause Amelie told me the treasure was on Hollister land. She said it was mine. She wanted me to have it. I needed Larry to let me keep looking."

"Because the butterfly farm used to be Hollister land," I said, remembering that, at one time, the Hollister farm had spread across both sides of the county road. Now Sadie's Papillon Farm was on one side, and Frank's cornfields were on the other.

With the gun still steady, Nate tugged at his earring, cracked his neck. "And all this time I was searching on the wrong side of the road. But in the end, I won. I got Jacques and the gold. Kinda evens things out."

Watt and Jorn had heard enough. The cornstalks rustled,

and they slowly stepped out. Startled, Nate swung the gun from us to them and back to us.

"Put down the guns. Everyone," Watt ordered, aiming his weapon at Nate.

I dared not look at Jorn. I kept my eyes on Nate, who was trying to back away from us all.

Frank froze.

Watt raised his voice. "Put down the gun, Nate. Frank, you too."

Frank didn't lower his rifle. He said, "This here's my gold. It's on my property, Sheriff."

"It's mine!" Nate yelled. "I'm a Nygård!"

Nate's gun swung wildly, finally stopping on me. Suddenly, I felt a flutter of air by my head, black crow wings brushing past me, going directly at Nate. He shrieked and fired the gun.

Fritz slammed into me.

I hit the ground hard.

"Maya!" screamed Jorn.

When I lifted my head, I saw Fritz lying beside me, eyes closed, face covered with blood.

"Fritz!" Frank cried out.

Guns exploded again. Nate dropped to the ground.

Frank threw down his rifle and ran to Fritz. Collapsing to his knees, he pulled Fritz into his arms. "No, no, no."

Watt kicked Nate's gun aside and knelt by him.

Jorn rushed to me, but I was turning to Fritz and Frank with one thought in my mind: I needed to get Gran's healing oil on Fritz. I had no idea if it would help, but it certainly couldn't hurt. This was faith in a foxhole. Snatching the bottle from my bra, I whispered, "Frank, Frank. This will help."

He looked up at me, terrified.

"It's a head wound. Let me wash it for you. Please, Frank," I begged.

After a moment, he unwound his arms enough for me to pour the oil over the wound at Fritz's temple. I emptied the bottle over the wound. The blood flowed away, revealing Fritz's pale face, then started to flow again. Jorn pushed a handkerchief into my hand, and I pressed it against the wound. I felt reiki heat, the pull of energy that was both the body's cry for help and its reassurance—we were not too late.

As Watt called for an ambulance, and energy streamed through my hand, I prayed, "Keep breathing, Fritz."

CHAPTER 36

WAITING

THE CROWS WERE GONE. Angelo and the activists were gone. And there were still no monarchs.

When I look out at the empty trees in my yard, I believe that the crows accomplished their mission: They brought balance back to Gabriel's Garden and, maybe, even took us a step closer to transcendence. In my mind, it was never a bad thing to be reminded of our oneness, even if the reminder was nature screaming from the trees.

Jorn found this theory about the crows ludicrous. "They moved on to bother some other town," he said.

It had been two weeks since blood was shed in Frank Hollister's cornfield. Fritz was mending. Nate Nelson turned out to be a lousy shot, or maybe the crow saved us. Fritz's wound was a graze that bled like there was no end but was not fatal.

However, Louisa, the commandant of his care, insisted that he stay home until the headaches went away. Between sips of Louisa's chicken noodle soup, Fritz had begun to discuss sustainable agriculture with his father, who rolled his eyes but let his son keep talking.

Unfortunately for Nate, Frank Hollister was not a lousy shot. Or maybe it was Watson Holmes. Both of their guns were fired that day. Nate was still in the hospital and would be there for some time recovering from abdominal wounds that nearly killed him. According to Watt, Nate will stand trial for the murder of Jacques Pine and for the shooting of Fritz Hollister. Angus the dog was now living with Roselyn, whose broken heart will take some time and many blue projects to mend.

What will happen to Frank is a bit of a mystery. The police are being mum about whose bullet—Frank's or Watt's—took down Nate. If the police discovered it was Frank's, a case could be made for self-defense. Jorn said Watt and the prosecutor have been doing a lot of talking lately behind closed doors and avoiding his questions. As for now, the prosecutor doesn't seem to be in any hurry to press charges against Frank. And if he does, Frank will have plenty of money to defend himself. All that gold under his corn, Gabriel's treasure, now belonged to the Hollisters. "Of course, Fritz will want to donate it to the polar bears," Frank groused, but without his former edge.

My seldom-locked front door opened. It was Jorn. I knew his step. From the bottom of the spiral staircase, he shouted up, "C'mon, sleepyhead. Are we going out there or what?"

He had risen earlier, fumbling in the dark for his clothes,

as I pretended to be asleep. It was kind of sweet when he tried not to wake me. But I knew where he was going—to sit in Northern Lights with his laptop and a cup of something stronger than my mint tea. He thought he was fooling me, but I smelled the coffee on his breath when he returned.

We drove to Sadie's Papillon Farm as we have every day to look for the monarchs. With Jorn carrying a blanket and me carrying hope, we walked in silence past Jacques's spruce tree. A few days ago, we saw Michael Donovan and his father emptying ashes at the bottom of the tree. When Michael looked up and spotted us, he nodded. Jacques had finally come to rest.

As we made our way through the tall grass and flowers, Jorn said, "I found out who tried to destroy this place."

I stopped. "It was Nate, right?"

"Nope."

Disappointed, I whined, "Don't tell me it was Michael." I didn't want to admit it, but I had actually begun to like that kid.

"Wrong again."

"Then who?"

"It was Frank."

"You have to be kidding."

Jorn shook his head. "I matched the photos of the tire tracks with Frank's worn truck tires."

"But why?"

"Frank claims it was a temporary fit of insanity. And he may be right. Kept saying something about 'those goldarn crows driving him crazy' and the absurdity of growing weeds on good farmland. Louisa made him promise to apologize to Larry. He wants to buy back the land now."

I laughed. Fat chance of that happening. Sadie's Papillon Farm was here to stay.

As was my grandmother. She had begun looking at house plans because, of course, nothing currently for sale in Gabriel's Garden was up to Sylvia Skye standards. Evie, who designed her own octagonal home to bring balance and integration into her life, tried discussing sacred geometry with her mother-in-law, to no avail. Gran straightened her Chanel summer jacket and declared she was not interested in Evie's odd ideas on architecture. "Four walls are enough for me. I'm a simple person."

It was an incredible late-August day, the kind that filled my spirit. The air carried a sense of life. I could feel it in the warmth of the sun, the playfulness of the breeze, the hum of the insects and frogs. The field was active with various species, but no monarchs. Jorn stopped, flung the blanket into the air, and it fluttered to the ground. We sat.

He looked out over the field. "All the monarch reports say the numbers are down again this year."

I'd heard the same news. "We'll turn it around," I said. "We'll try again next year."

Silent, Jorn kept his doubts to himself and let me have my dreams.

I leaned back in Jorn's arms, my face tilted to the sun, and sighed, "This is *santosha*. This is contentment."

Jorn groaned. He hated when I threw "yoga words" at him. I grinned.

We sat there for a long time, in the quiet embrace of the summer day, waiting. One hour lazily moved into another. We were about to leave when . . . I spotted something. A movement. A dream.

I squinted into the sun. Riding the summer air currents, the image grew more distinct as it came closer. Brilliant orange and deep black, with large majestic wings. It made a delicate, perfect landing on the head of a purple flower about ten feet away. Then it began to eat, its wings lazily working the air.

A monarch butterfly.

I smiled at Jorn.

He kissed me, and I smelled coffee.

ACKNOWLEDGMENTS

THE CROW IS A SYMBOL OF TRANSFORMATION, and *Crow Calling* is a story of people who believe they can transform both themselves and their world. Even as we face an environmental crisis of epic proportions, I believe we have the power to transform the situation. It is why I work to save the monarch butterfly, whose population is in free fall because of pesticide use, loss of habitat due to development and greed, and climate change. Humankind is squeezing out pollinators and other creatures that bring balance to this planet and make it liveable for them, us, our children, and our grandchildren. We are allowing whole species to disappear. This must change; we must change. As the Skye family says, "You only get one world," and I might add, "So don't blow it."

Stories also transform us. They help us make sense of our existence and remind us of our humanity. They make us feel less alone. I am eternally grateful to my readers, for those who love stories and words as much as I do. You make me feel less alone.

I also would like to thank these "Darling Girls": Marlys

Dooley, Lois West Duffy, Miriam Karmel, Janet Hanafin, Jean Housh, Ann Woodbeck, and the truly amazing and generous Faith Sullivan. You are my compass, keeping me heading in the right direction with your wisdom and friendship. I am so fortunate to have all of you.

Thank you as well to others who have answered questions, read early drafts, and helped me see more clearly the path I needed to take: Gini Ewers, Dan Koopmans, Elisa Korentayer, Heather McLean, Jessica Mork, Patricia Morris, Timya Owen, Gari Plehal, Geanette Poole, and Tamara Robinson.

I owe my stunning cover to Kathey Amaral, Cathleen Tarawhiti, and Monique Wanner. Thank you.

To Sarah Roberts Delacueva, I am so grateful to have you in my life. Few editors are as talented as you are. You make me a better writer. Your observations, questions, and suggestions thrill me. And your love always warms me.

To Suzanne Roberts Claseman, thank you for your eternal support. You have always been my butterfly, full of light and love. I adore every moment that we share.

Finally, and most importantly, thank you to Tony Roberts. From the day we met in a college newspaper office, you have been my guide and my friend. I am a better me because of you and your love. You inspire me to reach higher, go longer, and never give up—may we never stop dreaming together.

ABOUT THE AUTHOR

SHERRY ROBERTS is the author of award-winning mysteries and fiction. *Down Dog Diary, Warrior's Revenge,* and *Crow Calling* are part of the Maya Skye novels (Minnesota mysteries with spirit). *Down Dog Diary* is a Midwest Book Award finalist and a *Library Journal* SELF-e Select title. In *Book of Mercy,* also a Midwest Book Award finalist and a *Library Journal* SELF-e Select title, a dyslexic woman fights a North Carolina town banning books. *Maud's House* is the story of a Vermont artist who loses and finds her creativity.

Sherry has contributed essays and short stories to national publications such as *USA Today* and anthologies including *Saint Paul Almanac* and *Dark Side of the Loon.* She lives in Apple Valley, Minnesota. Visit Sherry's author website at sherry-roberts.com. Her essays can found at The Hearth: hearth.sherry-roberts.com.

WHAT'S NEXT?

SIGN UP FOR SHERRY'S EMAIL LIST (sherry-roberts.com) for updates on future writing—plus get free books, short stories, or other offers available only to fans! Your email will never be shared, you can unsubscribe at any time, and Sherry promises not to paper your inbox with emails.

Also follow Sherry Roberts Author on Facebook to get the latest on her books and writing in general.

LEAVE A REVIEW. If you enjoyed this book, please consider leaving a brief review online at your favorite retailer site. Readers spreading the word to other readers is incredibly important to authors and their work. If you're shy, just drop me a line on the contact page of sherry-roberts.com. Your support and ideas are important to me. I promise I'll write back.

CHECK OUT MY OTHER BOOKS. In Maya Skye's first adventure, *Down Dog Diary,* she goes up against killers to protect a mysterious diary. In book two, *Warrior's Revenge,* mysterious messages hurl Maya down a trail of betrayal, revenge, and grief. In *Book of Mercy,* a dyslexic woman takes on a town banning books. In *Maud's House,* an artist loses her creativity but finds love. All of my books are available in paperback and eBook at sherry-roberts.com, Amazon, and other retail outlets. If you can't find my books in your local bookstore, ask for them. Also please ask your local library to carry my books. Thank you.